The Sword of Souls

A FORGOTTEN RELICS NOVEL

Ellie Di Julio

ELLE BELLE MEDIA

The Sword of Souls

A Forgotten Relics Novel

First Edition

Content © 2014 Ellie Di Julio

Cover image © 2014 Desiree Kern

ISBN-13: 978-0-9936290-4-4

Published by Elle Belle Media

for lino –

we are not who we once were

PROLOGUE

The music with too much bass, the dazzling LED lights, the scent of sweat and lust: He'd have never found the warehouse without them leaking into the streets. The address he'd scrawled on the back of a bar napkin washed away in the late autumn downpour, leaving him to guess whether he'd be axe murdered or have the time of his life if he ever arrived. The red-faced chick at last night's rave certainly insisted it'd be the latter.

Standing at the rusted door, bones rattling in time to the muffled beat, he knocks a precise pattern, silently praying someone hears him. The ecstasy he dropped on the last block is kicking in, and a rain-slicked wharf is no place to start rolling.

A high peephole opens with a metallic hiss, making him jump, and a bloodshot eye appears, roving up and down, calculating some arcane bouncer algebra. He pulls out his particularly expensive fake ID and hopes it's enough. The peephole slams shut but the door doesn't open. Shit.

He's four steps in the other direction when a muddy voice calls out behind him. Eyeball's holding the massive steel door open a crack and making annoyed gestures for him to come in. As he slips out of the rain and into the viscous air of the flash club, X creeping up his temples, he absently wonders how it'd feel to rub his cheek against the bouncer's shaved head.

And then he's inside.

Rose and emerald lights dance over the cavernous space, illuminating the crowd. No decorations, no pretense—just a sea of bodies churning against itself to the throbbing music. He half closes his eyes and lets the human electricity wash over him. The hair on his arms stands up, and he can't stop his grin from showing his gums.

He dives in. Arms, legs, hips—everything moving of its own volition, flailing against sweat-slick strangers and galvanizing every nerve ending. Velvet and sandpaper. Sugar and vinegar. The spinning rise and fall of stepped-up electronica pulses through his veins at cocaine speeds, producing a craving for a higher high. Thunder from the storm outside double-times the beat, urging the dancers faster, harder. No space to think or breathe. For eons, he's not human. He's pure motion, pure energy.

But when the bass drops, the world tips dangerously underfoot, and suddenly bringing Molly along wasn't such a great idea. He staggers out of rhythm, the beautiful lights now too harsh, the press of hot, filthy flesh too close. Dagger glares chase him off the dance floor, and he trips toward a folding table at the back to steady himself.

"Water," he croaks, leaning heavily against a column by the makeshift bar.

The bartender, a kid of maybe eighteen with a teardrop tattoo, snorts and digs in a red cooler and holds out a plastic bottle. "Ten bucks."

"Are you fucking kidding me?" he shouts.

He digs in his greasy jeans and shoves a crumpled bill into the kid's waiting hand. He snatches the wet bottle and guzzles it in one deliciously painful drag. His dehydrated brain immediately begins to re-expand, shooting fresh waves of X through his blood. A contented sigh.

The music pounds in his bones, no longer an enemy, tempting him back into the pit. As he starts to bounce on his toes and rev his engine to dive back in, a hand on his shoulder pulls him up short. He wheels around, fist raised for the fight he's been both dreading and wanting, but his assailant easily swats the punch away. Anger-fueled and terrified, he glares up into the face of the most beautiful boy he's ever seen.

Bass pounds in the space between them. Pretty Boy blinks slowly as rose light slides across his angular face and sets fires in his eyes.

He waits. Pretty Boy waits.

The bass drops. The moment breaks.

Pretty Boy tugs him gently away from the glare of the bartender to a cooler, darker space near the back exit. Then he pulls him close. He can practically taste the subtle flowery musk of Pretty Boy's pale skin over the grimy scent of the dancers. Their chests touch. He doesn't resist.

"I saw you out there. Rolling pretty hard," Pretty Boy says, leaning in. Perfect lips brush his ear. "I've got something else you might like."

Without breaking their embrace, Pretty Boy reaches long fingers into a smooth leather jacket and produces what looks like a quarter. He smiles reassuringly. The cool invitation of the expression encourages him to scoot closer. Maybe whatever Pretty Boy's got in mind matches what his lower half is thinking.

"Open up," Pretty Boy instructs.

He does.

Rather than the metallic tang he expects, thought, the disk Pretty Boy lays gently on his tongue is warm, almost hot. The taste of sun-ripened raspberries and the scent of fresh air over cut grass slam down on him like a hammer on an anvil. His knees buckle dramatically, but strong arms keep him upright. The music and lights of the club swim in and out of his senses, now far away, now too close.

Pretty Boy's face looking down at him starts to flicker. Or is he the one that's flickering? A picturesque meadow intercuts the darkness of the warehouse. Too bright, too dark, too bright, too dark. The confusion of parallax is too much for his hopped-up brain, and his body protests by retching.

He looks up to Pretty Boy for help. But the sweet

smile he'd hoped to see in his apartment tomorrow morning has hardened into a scornful line of laughter. Panic spikes his animal instincts, and he squirms against the iron-strong hands in an attempt to escape, but none of his limbs are responding.

Pretty Boy presses his cool forehead to his cheek. "Shhh, it'll be over before you know it. You just have to believe."

Flicker, flicker, swirl, swirl, collapse.

The last thing he sees in the club is Pretty Boy standing over him with triumph in his glassy eyes.

The first thing he sees in the meadow is the hem of a shimmering gold dress covering pointed black shoes.

Reflexes previously on pinpoint alert from drugs and fear are curiously dull as he rolls over in the grass to get to his knees. Sunshine burns his eyes as they adjust from the gloom of the warehouse. He rubs them, hoping to wipe away the hallucination. But when he takes his hands down, the meadow, the dress, and the sunshine are still there. He briefly wonders if he's having an acid flashback to when he saw mermaids in the yard.

"Welcome, young man," says an alabaster voice above him.

Indignation and confusion rise up, and he slurs out, "Where'm I? Who the fuck're you?" Aching hands reach for her dress to help him to his feet.

She takes a dainty step out of his grasp, then there's a rush of hot wind as her foot shoots out, connecting neatly with his shoulder, spilling him to the ground. The air bursts with the cloying scent of apples as he tries to catch his breath.

The woman leans forward so he can see every millimeter of her huge, whiteless black eyes. A cruel grin turns up one corner of her perfect mouth.

"I am your Mistress," she says. "Welcome to Faerie."

PART I
SHE'S THE MAN

ONE

"You've got to be shitting me."

"I shit you not, Riley. I shit you not."

I shake my head with a chuckle. "You know, ever since I got to DC, my mind's been blown so often I'm surprised I've got any brains left, but this takes the cake. Never imagined my first real assignment would be a *Night at the Museum* remake."

The leather in the standard black SUV creaks as I shift my weight, trying to get comfortable. The freshly-issued Supernatural Cases Division credentials that label me as Agent 6 are tucked into my starched black suit jacket and press against my sidearm. Both badge and gun seem heavier than they are. I haven't decided which makes me more nervous.

In the driver's seat, Agent 21 laughs right back at me. "You ain't seen nothin' yet, rookie," she says.

I roll my eyes extra sarcastically, and she grins,

flashing pointed canines that are hyper-white against her perpetual tan. I relax a bit.

I've been shadowing Sofi Strella for a month, and it's taking a bit of adjustment from the strict discipline of FBI basic at Quantico to this loose, buddy-cop style. If I'd so much as thought about being snarky with my instructors, there'd be hell to pay. With Sofi, it's mandatory. She's nearly a decade younger than I am, but man, has that girl got a mouth on her. Which is fine by me. Makes me think maybe I'm not totally insane to think we're friends, something past co-workers. Hard to tell, though. Those particular skills are rusty after fifteen years. Small town like mine, high school friends are for life—not a lot of opportunity to practice making new ones. But I'm taking it as a good sign that Sofi and I have been reprimanded four times for giggling during briefings. Turns out, we're a damn good team, too. Between her year of SCD experience and bountiful street-smarts and my weird affinity for paperwork and mental mythological encyclopedia, we've already gotten positive nods from brass.

I'm off to a running start in this new life, much to my competitive, perfectionist delight.

Although....

I'll admit I sort of hoped I'd be assigned to Jack Alexander—excuse me, Agent 97—for SCD training, seeing as he's the one who dragged me here in the first place. And is the one other person on the planet who shares my powers.

That seems to have been a silly, romantic pipe

dream, though. They attached me to Sofi the day I graduated Quantico, citing compatible psych evals; I haven't seen or heard from Jack since July. Not an email, not a phone call, not a damn memo to make good on his promise of sidestepper training. Zilch. For all I know, he's gone back to being another boring old suit, a weird, skinny man tucked away in a dark office, shuffling papers and not giving a shit about anyone else.

Not that I've been great about trying to contact him, either, if I'm being fair. A friendly text or two, a couple unanswered calls. But I got the message: He's either forgotten about me or doesn't think I'm worth his time. I let myself be furious for a while, maybe even a little ashamed for wanting to see what, if anything, is between us. Then I sunk any leftover feelings into twenty weeks of grueling FBI training and got over it.

Or at least I thought I did.

I sigh to clear my tightening chest.

"Aw, sugarbean, it ain't that bad," Sofi chides, nudging my leg for emphasis. "It'll be over soon."

Ow, my feelings.

I know she meant the case, but the juxtaposition hurts. She doesn't know about Jack—whatever our status, I've kept him under my shirt. So to speak. And there's something about talking guys with your boss that seems wrong. There's nothing to talk about, anyway.

I run a hand through my chin-length copper hair, letting the squeak of the windshield wipers carry away my internal pity party along with the puffy snowflakes.

"Sorry. Was a million miles away," I say, giving her an apologetic smile and turning my attention back to the case. "Not every day you're called in to investigate a real live folk hero." Pause. "Or is he technically still dead?"

"Both, I think. Fortunately, we don't have to make that call. All we have to do is find the guy, clean up the magical mess as best we can, and bring him in for processing." She takes her dark brown eyes off the icy road for a moment. "You okay, Riley? Seriously, I'm asking," she says.

Her concerned look generates warm fuzzies more intimate than our short acquaintance probably warrants. Mamma bear powers are awesome that way. The feeling tugs on homesickness I've buried along with the memory of Jack's touch. But I nod and brush it aside, trying to stay focused on the present.

"Yeah, I'm good," I say. "I mean, I'm one more hard right from throwing up my breakfast, but I'm pretty sure that's your driving."

Sofi makes a face at the dig, then nods knowingly, her blond ponytail bobbing. "Can't blame you for being wound up. You've been stuck inside filling out forms and reading textbooks and shooting at paper targets while I'm out there cracking heads and taking names. You've got to be itching for some play."

"It's not that," I object, faster than I mean to. "I'm fine with studying and research. It's what I'm good at. But I'm the new guy. I don't want to screw this up, you know?"

Sofi shrugs. "I wouldn't worry about it. Everyone's first case is a shit show. Get it out of the way. Move on."

I groan. That is not what I need to hear right now. I slump against the seat, looking angstily up at the ceiling. "Please tell me yours wasn't that bad."

"Oh my god, yeah it was," Sofi says emphatically. "My first case, I had to detain a selkie that'd come up in the tidal basin and left his skin draped over the feet of the Jefferson Memorial. Kids were poking the thing with a stick and asking their parents awkward questions. Agent 50 was my mentor, and he sent me in by myself. Got sort of a 'sink or swim' approach to rookies. I did okay, didn't upset any of the mundanes, but I seriously couldn't stop staring at the guy's crotch while I questioned him." She laughs. "Selkie dudes are hung."

The bizarre pornographic image sears my mental retinas. "Sofi!" I squeal.

"What? It's true! Don't lose your sense of humor because you're The Man now, Riley. It'll keep you sane."

I shake my head and chuckle, turning my attention out the window. The thin morning light of December gives the National Mall a haunted feel. When I first got here, it was summer, and the lawn was thronged with joggers, picnickers, tourists, and protesters. Winter's turned the place into a lonely expanse of snow bordered by empty buildings.

My school never took the field trip to the Capitol

that bigger towns offer graduating seniors, so I'm discovering the city for the first time outside a textbook. I hate to say it, but I may love it more than New York. This place combines the charm of my home town with the energy of my dream town. There's something about the history of Washington, underpinned with an abundance of culture and art, laced with an odd small-town vibe for such a busy metropolis. Its spirit creeps into the soles of my feet as I walk my neighborhood, around headquarters, through museums, along the subway.

Sofi cranks the SUV down Constitution, bringing the stone edifice of the Smithsonian Natural History Museum into view. She shimmies through the side lot and into the back without a glance from security, carefully inching the vehicle's massive rear end up to the loading dock. Kind of a weird place to park. I raise an eyebrow as Sofi pulls the keys from the ignition.

"Never know what shape he'll be in," she explains. "We might have to shovel the dude into the trunk."

I want to ask but stop myself. There's no way this can be worse than the crime scene photos from last week's wendigo case. I didn't know people bent that way.

Sofi hops out of the car, shoving the keys into her pocket with one hand and straightening her jacket with the other. I pause for a moment to relish the sensation of being alone. The non-stop people and action since I left home is taking its toll on my introverted, country-girl psyche, but there's no sign of it letting up anytime soon. The SCD's overrun with fresh incidents—even the old hands are raising eyebrows—and practically everyone's in the field, from the top to the bottom. I have to take my peace where I can get it.

A knock on the rear window shatters the precious silence, and Sofi says something I can't make out. I'm not sure if it's the safety glass or if my hearing's going; it hasn't been the same since Azrael bloodied my eardrums in the underworld. I wave Sofi off and scoot out the door.

I land with both feet right in a puddle of disgusting brown slush. I swear loudly as my uniform-mandated black pumps soak clean through. You see those lady detectives on TV and think there's no way they'll make you wear such stupid shoes in real life, but they do. I make a note to see how long I can get away with combat boots starting tomorrow.

"Watch out for that puddle, Riley," Sofi says.

"Gee, thanks. Why couldn't they have paired me with a psychic?"

She grins as I pick my way around other treacherous puddles to meet her at the stairs leading up to the museum's employee entrance. "Sorry, spookybutt," she says, pulling out a pair of shades and sliding them on. "You're stuck with Mama Bear."

"Fine," I sigh, reaching for my own shades. "As long as you don't give me a spit bath, I guess I can live with that."

"Only if you ask real nice."

"Only if you buy me dinner first."

Sofi grins and takes a step back to inspect me. We're about the same build—short and solid—but she carries herself with such absolute physical confidence that I feel tiny in comparison. I let her brush a speck of lint off my suit jacket, then she purses her lips thoughtfully with a Project Runway sort of pout. I play along and mime a model turn with my arms out and nose in the air.

"I'm ready for my close-up, Miss Strella."

Sofi snorts. "Alright, I guess you are," she says. "Radar up?"

The smile melts off my face faster than the ice in my shoes. I was so wrapped up in thinking about Jack and Sofi and the case and the city that I totally forgot why I'm out here in the first place.

As a sidestepper, it's my job to check for doorways between the mortal world and the Otherworld to ensure that our "person of interest" didn't arrive or doesn't escape that way. The uptick in missing persons reports has both the FBI and SCD extra concerned about accidental interworld travel, including the possibility that someone or something is tearing new, unstable portals in the Gauntlet. Background magic levels have nearly doubled since last year, and it's got to be coming from somewhere. Thus, my field debut two months before the average SCD rookie would see action.

Which is what's got me nervous about my first real case. Not the early promotion—the mundane stuff is easy. Top of my class in procedure and forensics, thank you very much. It's that no one else knows why it's so supernaturally crazy right now, despite glaring signs that the balance between worlds is horribly off. No one knows about Eris.

As much as I want to, I haven't breathed a word to anyone about what I know, not even to Sofi. Jack promised to take the information to the top and start things moving. But as far as I can tell, he hasn't done shit.

That's not the worst thing, though, here in this moment. No, the worst thing is that between the insanity of FBI boot camp and the supernatural world losing its shit, I haven't tried to tap my energy in months, much less raise a sensor circle. Haven't had time. And even if I did, I'm not trained—Jack's ghost act biting me in the ass yet again. I've got no idea what'll happen when I use my powers in the real world as opposed to the already-magical underworld. There are endless stories of heroes losing their gifts after returning to mundane life, after they've healed themselves and completed their quest, that I'm not sure my powers will work now.

I must be screwing up my face something awful because Sofi peers meaningfully at me over the top of her shades, the look of a parent anticipating an epic tantrum in the cereal aisle.

"Everything okay?" she asks.

I exhale sharply to force out the poisonous self-doubt, smiling in what I hope is a convincing way. Shooting for "nervous, untested rookie" instead of "paranoid about the end of the world and not sure if my powers work."

"Yeah, it's fine. Been a while since I had to use magic instead of a pen or a gun, that's all."

There's a continued question in Sofi's eyes, but I ignore it. I draw in a lungful of the heavy, freezing air to ground myself, then shut my eyes. As I try to concentrate, an evil thought burbles up, drawing on my fears.

You're nothing without his help.

The condemnation is met with a rush of anger that burns through my mind, making way for a flood of electric blue power. The familiar tingle shoots from my scalp to my frozen toes and back in a long, invigorating circuit that extinguishes both the fear and the anger, centering itself into a peaceful ball under my ribcage.

Relieved I'm still magical, but worried about killing the charge by trying too hard, I gingerly inch the power out from my body. First a few feet, then a few yards, stretching out and erecting the interworld doorway radar in one fluid movement. The edge of the completed circle hangs like an invisible hoop skirt around my midsection. The whole thing takes less than a minute, and the integrity is perfect. A far cry from the nuclear blast of my first attempt behind the doorfield.

Ha. Take that, I say to the nasty, doubting voice. *I don't need his help.*

I wait a beat or two while my consciousness travels the perimeter of the circle, looking for Otherworld passages. Something erratic or glowing or sucking or overcharged. But nothing pings. If there are any doors, permanent or accidental, they're not within a block radius of us.

I open my eyes one at a time, taking care to leave enough focus channeled into the sensor circle to hold it up in the background. Sofi's watching me patiently.

"Nothing," I report with a shrug. "If this guy is up and walking around, he's on this side."

"Roger that." Sofi pushes her glasses back up her nose, tightens her ponytail, and knocks sharply on the rear entrance. To me, she says, "Ready for your big debut, rookie?"

Approaching footsteps inside the building say I don't have a choice. I nod with a lopsided grin. "Ready as I'll ever be."

"That's my girl," she says, replacing her smile with the stone-neutral mask of an SCD agent.

As the wet metal door creaks open and we step inside, I find myself wishing her words had come from someone else's lips.

TWO

The curator of the Smithsonian's natural history branch called in the incident this morning, starting with the Metropolitan Police Department who called the FBI who transferred it to the SCD who'd already sent a car by the time the call hit the switchboard. One of the first things they teach you in secret agent school is that the phone tree is mostly for show. It makes the mundanes more comfortable when there's a system to follow. Having magical men in black show up at precisely the moment you need them can be unsettling, to say the least.

Sofi and I are escorted to the roped off and empty second floor by a volunteer who deposits us at the Egyptian section and hurries away before we can thank him. I want to grab him by the collar to ask some pointed questions about his shifty behavior, but Sofi nudges me in the ribs. Not sure if she's disciplining me or if she was thinking the same thing and stopped herself, too. I let the guy go with minor annoyance and turn my attention to the room.

There, in a sky-blue nook of preserved ibises and felines, sits the display case that until four o'clock this morning held history's most famous mummy. Shattered glass sparkles under display lighting that highlights the emptiness of the massive gold sarcophagus, its lid upended on the floor. There's an eerie hush over the scene, as if the museum specimens are watching, holding their dusty breath for thousands of years in anticipation of this moment. The air rings with the weight of it.

Sofi breaks the solemn quiet by using the toe of her shoe to turn over a brass plaque in the tinkling wreckage. It reads *Tutankhamen, 8th Dynasty, New Kingdom* with picture of the ubiquitous mask.

Even in my podunk hometown, every kid knew his name. The boy god-king. The pharaoh of pharaohs. Movies, books, TV, academia, internet memes. He was famous in his own time, then became a paragon—the SCD term for folk heroes— in ours. I'd have thought the length and sheer quantity of belief in Tut's legend would've never let him die in the first place. Other guys like Johnny Appleseed never went away; if Tut's been down this long, why wake up now?

I'm about to ask, but the sound of voices coming our way cuts me off. I lift a questioning eyebrow at Sofi who gives an annoyed sigh.

"Guess we're not the first ones on the scene," she says, turning to greet our company.

A pair of identical suits round the corner, flanking a harassed-looking woman must be the ruined exhibit's docent. I recognize them both. With exactly a hundred agents in the entire organization, and those divided between five field offices, you get to know your coworkers pretty quick.

The young guy on the left is Scott Kim, Agent 19, built like a sagging brick shithouse with heavy black glasses and greasy hair. Word is that he's the only deadspeaker on this coast. The older guy's Russell Sharpe, Agent 41, a seasoned operator in way better shape. Not entirely sure what he does, but it's his name and unsmiling picture on the SCD interrogation manual. I've never seen these two together, so I'm guessing it's their first assignment as partners. The insane supernatural workload sure is making for strange bedfellows.

"And you have no idea where he went," Russell's saying. "You have cameras everywhere—how did you lose him?"

The docent fusses with a lace handkerchief. "I have no idea. That's why we called you. By the time the guard made it up here to see what the noise was, the mummy was gone. Officer Cook went straight to the security room to check the tapes, but there's no break-in, no robbers, nothing." She honks her nose into the hankie. "It's like the damned thing turned invisible and walked away all by itself."

Sofi and I exchange a look over the top of our shades. Definitely our kind of case.

The three of them reach us by the ruined display, and I can see the panic and confusion written across the docent's face like poorly-planned graffiti. Like maybe she wants to believe it was magic but can't because that's silly kid stuff. Seems a natural reaction to an exceptionally dead guy disappearing in the middle of the night. The tears in her eyes tug at my heartstrings. What I wouldn't have given a year ago to be that emotional about anything, much less my job.

Russell doesn't see it, though. He's about to go in for another round of questions when Sofi slides into the conversation.

"Could you bring that guard here so we can speak with him, please?" she says to the traumatized woman.

The docent does a quick reassessment of the situation, weighing the agent who's badgered her against the one asking nicely for someone else to harass. She wipes at her eyes, then nods and scuttles off.

The remaining four of us wait until the door clicks shut behind her. Then Sofi leaps to speak first, cutting off the invective Russell's gearing up.

"Nice to see you, Russell," she chirps with sarcastic friendliness, her professional tone set aside now we don't need to show off for mundanes. "Even if I thought this was a two-man job." She nods toward his stout companion. "Good choice bringing Scott along. He could stand to get some practical experience under his belt."

Scott blushes. I hear he's been on desk duty

since signing on, and not by choice. The rumor mill says he's got an explosively violent temper. Keeps blowing up at the wrong people, hence the low agent number despite five years behind the badge. From where I'm standing, though, he seems pretty meek. He's tugging at the hem of his jacket, eyes glued to the empty sarcophagus.

"Figured he'd be useful," Russell says. I can feel him eyeballing me behind the dark glasses. Not in a creeper-type way, but in a what-the-hell-are-you-doing-here way. Ugh. "Guess there was a mix-up at dispatch," he continues. "Don't know why you two'd be needed on this one."

Sofi bristles. I can practically see her hair poof up. But she reins it in, managing to keep her tone light.

"Riley's here because somebody up the chain wanted her out on the street ASAP. I didn't ask questions. You get a memo from the Nineties, you do what you're told." She sneers. "I'm here because I'm damn good at my job and can tear a phonebook in half."

He says something back, but I don't hear it. My heartbeat's drowning out the conversation like an adrenaline-fueled jackhammer.

A memo from the Nineties? Did Jack sign those orders?

The slamming of the stairwell door mercifully keeps me from thinking too hard about it. The docent returns, accompanied by a security guard who towers over her in his bulletproof vest. He's pointedly unimpressed by the four government agents waiting for him.

Scott and I stand to the side to observe while our superiors question Officer Cook. Scott's scribbling furiously in a pocket notebook, but I didn't think that far ahead, so I'm basically eavesdropping. Between Russell and Sofi's questions, it doesn't take long to find out the guy doesn't know anything. Which is fairly typical for these situations—humans are great at ignoring the magically obvious—but procedure dictates that you ask. You never know.

"Thank you for your time, sir," Sofi says in her flat, official voice. "We'll be in touch if we require anything else."

The security guard grunts his acknowledgment, then strides out of the Egyptian exhibit heading toward the butterfly pavilion. All attention turns back to the soggy-faced docent and her wadded hankie.

"Ma'am," Russell says as he steps to her side. "My colleagues will need unrestricted and undisturbed access to this area for the next hour. I will accompany you back to your office for further debriefing." He half-turns and says to Sofi, "Keep me informed of further developments," then nods to the docent who leads him toward the administration offices.

Before I can open my mouth to ask what he's doing, Scott's telling me.

"Memory manipulator," he says. "We have to fuzz up her recollection of the event so that once it's over she doesn't freak out and make trouble."

"Isn't that, I don't know, immoral?" I look to Sofi

for help. "I get that mundanes can go nuts after too many hits on their perception of reality, but damn."

Sofi shrugs noncommittally. "It's a balancing act, like I said. The more people see of the supernatural world, the more they believe in it, the stronger supers get. But then we run the risk of them doing awful shit because they can. They get cocky and start thinking about mundanes as toys. Or worse, livestock." She smirks at the shocked look on my face. "You should know that better than anybody, Riley. Mythology isn't exactly filled with supernals who see humans as precious beings."

A word in the last sentence trips me up. My brow creases in confusion, and I wave my hands for a time out.

"Hang on a sec. Maybe I don't have a handle on the SCD jargon yet. I get mundanes, metahumans, and paragons, but what the hell's a supernal?"

She shrugs. "Another category of supernatural. You know, gods and goddesses. Actual deities as opposed to folk heroes or generic magical beings like vampires or unicorns."

The image of an all-powerful Eris playing with world leaders like action figures leaps up at me, spiking my pulse. I want to blurt out everything I know about her and her plot to overthrow the human world, but I bite it back. This isn't the time or the place.

"Got it," I say instead, looking to the stairwell where Russell and the docent disappeared. "Still seems messed up to brainwash people, though. Even if it is just a bit and for their own good. You'd think the SCD'd have a way to make it easier for supers and mundanes to live together."

Sofi's face darkens. "Yeah, you'd think," she mutters. There's an odd note in her voice that gets my attention. Regret? Sadness? But she clears her throat and it's gone.

"Scott, you're on tracker duty," she says, pointing at him. "See if anybody else is awake in the museum and if they saw where this guy went." Then she turns and nods to me. "Cora, double check that there aren't any open doors he could've stumbled through. We've got about twenty minutes while Russell does his thing before he comes back and tries to take over again. Let's show him you don't have to be a Thirty Plus to do good field work."

We both nod and head off in different directions. Scott for the dinosaur exhibit, me for a quiet corner. I can hear him starting to whisper in that creepy-ass language that marks his powers. Feels like watery sandpaper in my ear canal. It gives me the willies, and I put my fingers in my ears to block him out. Even with my radar already up in the background, it takes concentration to actively use it, and Scott's deadspeak isn't helping.

I train my eyes on the wall, taking the opportunity to try something new since I've swept the place once already. I need to be able to use my powers with my eyes open. Way less likely I'll get eaten by a griffin or demon. It's harder, and at first I'm not sure it's working, it takes so much longer. The craving for sidestepper training pops up immediately. I assuage it—and prevent another depressing thought about Jack—by promising myself I'll check the SCD library again soon.

Eventually, I build up enough energy with my eyes open to circumnavigate the sensor circle. Nothing's pinging, which is bittersweet. On one hand, it's a successful experiment and there's no illegal doorways, but on the other, it means Tut's walking around in the real, which could be a disaster if we don't catch him right away. Great.

I sigh and let the circle drop, then head back to rejoin Sofi.

I find her bent over Tut's display case, her face screwed up in thought as she examines the wreckage. This kind of delicate business isn't something I associate with her bear strength, but it's a good reminder. When you have super powers, it's easy to forget that solid police work is the foundation of the job. And forgetting is dangerous. The SCD's lost a lot of agents who used magic to solve their problems instead of common sense.

Right now, though, Sofi looks more constipated than insightful.

"Anything good?" I ask, suppressing a smile.

She straightens and brushes glass dust off her latex-gloved hands. "DCPD probably won't find anything, but there's some things of note for us. Why don't you give it a shot, Riley?" She smirks. "Show off that big ol' brain of yours."

I make a snarky face. "Yeah, alright. Whatever you say, boss."

Sofi takes a step back to give me space. I start by circling around the case, taking in as many details as I can compile. FBI training has dovetailed nicely with the way Dad taught me to see what's really there instead of what I assume should be. With a bit of practical knowledge to balance out the fairytales, I'm not ashamed to say I'm becoming a damn good investigator. Watching every episode of *CSI* hasn't hurt, either.

Here's what I notice: No footprints going to the case and light partials leading away. The glass was broken from the inside with no evidence of tools. Deep gouges on the underside of the lid. The other displays are intact.

I relay all of this to Sofi, who nods encouragingly.

"What else?" she says.

I crease up my forehead as I think it through. "I don't get the tech stuff," I admit. "Staff said there's nothing on the cameras, and no alarms sounded. He's not a ghost, demon, or projection. Shouldn't he have left some sort of recorded trace if he's in the real?"

"Good job, Riley. Indeed he should have. Being a magical folk hero doesn't mean he's immune to natural laws." A pause. "Well, generally speaking. There's exceptions here and there, but not for this guy."

"So...?"

She shrugs. "No idea. We'll take the evidence back with us and hope there's something under the mundane bandwidth. But as far as I know, this is the first time a corporeal super's avoided detection efforts."

I take another long look over the scene, hoping something new will pop out.

"Okay," I say after a while, "I don't get it. What would make him so eager to wake up now? Tut-mania's been on before, and his belief levels have been higher in the past."

Sofi's brow furrows. "Yeah, good point."

What I want to say is, "Do you think these inconsistencies have anything to do with Eris' evil plans to overthrow the mundane world?" But I keep it to myself. Again.

Instead, I say, "Maybe there's an imbalance somewhere? Like, more than we're being told. Between the tech issues and the sudden wake-up call, I can't help feeling something's way more messed up than we think."

Sofi considers it for a second, flexing her hands as if she could punch the problem into clarity. "Maybe," she says thoughtfully. "That'd explain the spike in cases, for sure." She shrugs again, visibly shifting lean muscles under her suit jacket. "But it's definitely above my pay grade. Mooks like me don't get to know shit like that. Our job is to take the cases and lock up the bad guys."

Frustration threatens to get the best of me. That she can pretend this doesn't bother her is driving me up the wall. But I count to three and let it slide. For now, anyway. No good fighting about it here.

"Fair enough, I suppose," I say, peeking at my phone for the time. It's been nearly twenty minutes since the other agents took off, but no one's reported back. "We better find Scott. If he hasn't figured out where our mummy went by now, he's probably lost. Pretty sure Russell won't care, but I'm the one that'll have to go after him, and you're the one that'll have to explain to Ninety-Nine how an agent evaporated in the Smithsonian."

Sofi nods distractedly and heads out of the Egyptian wing with her eyebrows beetled up in thought. I give her a couple paces, then follow behind, wondering for the eighty bazillionth time if I'm doing the right thing by keeping quiet about the attempted apocalypse brewing on the other side of the Gauntlet.

Surprisingly, we don't have to look far to find Scott. I duck my head into the Hope Diamond exhibit, and there they are: a stocky Korean guy in a sharp suit sitting on a bench with a leathery, linen-wrapped ruler of a bygone empire. And the conversation appears to be getting heated.

Scott's gesturing wildly, getting red in the face, while the mummy's ancient jaw works madly in hacked-off syllables. I give silent thanks to any small gods of crowd control that the curator closed the museum when the "robbery" happened. Russell would've had a hard time memory-adjusting the hundreds of people that might've seen Scott and Tut's chat.

"What's his problem?" Sofi asks as she strides in.

The debate stops as she approaches, and I hide a smirk at their reaction. Few people that small can command a room the way Sofi does.

The first words out of Scott's mouth are in the wrong language, and he clears his throat hard, pounding his sternum to readjust. "Basically, he's mad because I told him what year it is. He refuses to accept he's pushing four thousand."

"Wait 'til you show him the magic light box in your pocket that contains the knowledge of the universe," I say from the doorway.

But Sofi doesn't see anything funny in the situation. "Did you find out what he knows about how he woke up?" she says, all business.

"Yeah. He says he was sunning himself on Ra's boat, enjoying a foot massage from a sexy handmaiden when he was overcome with...." He turns to Tut and asks a short question in deadspeak, then continues, "The feeling that he had to pee? Which was weird because nobody in his afterlife does that. When he stood up to go deal with it, he was here, standing in the wrecked glass box."

"That's it?"

"As far as he knows, yeah. I found him wandering through the geology section, staring at fossils. Said they made him sad."

A crawling sensation prickles my skin as I listen, and I whip around to see Russell standing inches from my back. I keep from squawking out of stubborn refusal to look like a weenie. I shift to let him by, rubbing down the raised hairs on my neck.

"I'll take it from here, Agent 21," he says, waving Sofi aside.

She cedes the floor with minor hesitation. I don't

need to see her eyes to know daggers are shooting out of them, and I have a momentary flash of worry for Russell's safety. Pushing aside and dismissing a woman with the supernatural strength and instincts of a mother bear isn't the smartest idea. This guy either needs a sensitivity course or his ass kicked by a girl. I'm pretty sure I could make that last one happen, no problem.

Russell starts in on Scott, asking the same questions Sofi did but in a deeper register. It's ridiculous and a huge waste of time, but he's the ranking officer, and that means he's in charge.

I step into the room to join Sofi, who's got her arms crossed over her chest and is propped heavily against the far wall. I lean in conspiratorially. "What an asshole," I whisper, barely audible, knowing her heightened senses pick up what most humans can't.

"Right?" Sofi whispers back. She sighs with resignation and slips her sunglasses into an interior pocket. "One of these days, I'll figure out how the damned agent numbering system works and outrank that jerk." She grins evilly. "Or maybe I'll turn his four by four into a compact."

I chuckle quietly and take off my own shades in solidarity. We stand there for a moment, listening to Scott stammer through Russell's interrogation. There's a tangible relaxation between us instead of the awkward silence I've come to associate with other agents on the job. Maybe I'm not as shitty at making friends as I thought.

"Hey," I say after a minute or two, "once we're

done here, you want to head to the Fifth? I get the feeling we could both use a beer after this."

"God, yes," Sofi breathes. "Between a cranky pharaoh, Scott the Creepy, and Captain Misogyny? Yes, all the beer."

THREE

Beer has to wait, though. Turns out that SCD procedure for processing a paragon is more arcane than the individuals themselves. Every facet of their supernatural life has to be documented, every psychological deficiency noted, every potential threat accounted for. Tutankhamen more than achieved folk hero status over the last couple thousand years, but he's never been booked, and the paperwork going back that far is tedious. Fortunately, being a mummy makes you pretty damned patient.

The same could not be said for me.

"Look, your majesty," I huff, clipboard in hand, "I don't give a good goddamn about your joint pain and ashy skin. What I need to know is...," I glance at the list of Terrorist Threat questions and read the latest one for the third time, "...whether or not you intend to rebuild your dynasty within the continental United States."

In my peripheral vision, I see Scott raise his thick eyebrows at my tone. We're crammed into an icy interrogation room outfitted with steel chairs and tables, no windows, and little heat except for the residual warmth from the desktop computer. It's been three hours since we unpacked Tut from the back of Sofi's SUV, and we're barely halfway through processing his information. I can think of at least seven other places I'd rather be and two other people I'd rather be with.

I sigh, pinching the bridge of my nose and exhaling sharply to relieve the pressure building in my skull. "Sorry. Don't translate that," I say to Scott. "Ask him the official question again, would you?"

"You sure you don't want me to do this? It's probably easier without me having to parse everything for you."

"I wish. But Sofi said I have to learn the system, so I get to be the bad cop. Let's just hurry this up."

Scott pinkens, a hint of his rumored temper, but nods. "If it's any consolation, he'll pick up a regular language. They always do. All he needs is some time."

"Not soon enough for me. Now, come on and ask him. We're thirty questions from the end, and it's not looking good for Mister I Used to Rule the Universe."

I know I'm being bitchy, but I can't help it. As much as I enjoy filling out paperwork—tax time is actually fun for me—having to rely on Tut's broken memories and shit language skills to finish sixteen questionnaires is pushing it. Patience isn't a skill I picked up at the academy.

But I do feel a pang of contrition as we continue to fill out Tut's registration. It's the most time I've spent with another agent outside of shadowing Sofi, and I'm not making a good impression on Scott. With whatever storm is brewing in the Otherworld, it seems like a good idea to be friends with as many metas as possible if—when—shit goes down. I should try harder to be nice.

Another hour passes before the forms are ready to submit. Tut's snoring with a sound like underwater chainsaws, head back and jaw hanging loose, propped upright in his chair while Scott checks the translations. We swap papers back and forth for signatures and pack them into carefully labeled manila envelopes, then I turn my attention to finalizing the digital records.

"Done," Scott says with satisfaction as he plops the last envelope onto the stack.

"Awesome," I mutter, eyes glued to the screen. It's all I can say for several minutes. This dual record system probably makes sense to someone, but it's not me. I remind myself to file an official complaint.

Soon there's nothing left to click, and I send the report winging off to Agent 100's inbox, the final resting place for digital records. I stand a bit creakily and stretch my arms and legs, willing the blood to start flowing again. Even with my back turned, I know Scott's eyes are all over me, which gives me the willies, but I don't say anything. Much as I hate to be That Girl, the attention feels good. With Jack being such a spook, it's sort of reassuring to know I didn't magically turn into a troglodyte.

Scott twists in his chair to crack his back. "What do we do with this guy?" he says, jerking his thumb at the snoring mummy. "We won't get his final assignment until tomorrow at the earliest."

My knowledge of SCD operations isn't fully cemented yet, though another week or two of studying should fix that. I dig into the bottom desk drawer to pull out the agency's procedures manual. I ignore Scott's chuckling at my bookwormishness and find the right subsection.

"Handbook says any subject not yet assigned goes into holding. And there's a special area for non-criminal cases."

He nods as if he'd forgotten. Maybe he did, maybe he was testing me. Hard to tell in these early days on the job. Seems like everything's a test.

"Right," he says. "The facility off Ohio."

"Yeah. You want to take him?"

"Can't. Cid and I are going to the casino tonight, and I'm already late."

"Oh, come on," I huff, tossing the manual onto the desk. It lands with a loud thud that makes Tut snort and shift. Scott and I both hold our breath, but he doesn't wake. I turn back and whisper, "I'm supposed to go to the Fifth with Sofi. Do me a favor? I'll owe you one."

Scott smirks. "No chance, rookie," he says, matching my low tone. "Lady Luck is calling my name, and I outrank you." He stands and ambles to the door, letting in too-bright light as he pulls it open. "Have fun, Riley," he says with a wink. "I'd suggest you watch your six. This one likes the ladies."

I give him the finger and a sneer as he disappears. So much for being nice.

After the door eases shut on its hydraulics, I turn to look at my charge, arms crossed over my chest. Tut's slipping down slowly in his chair, his non-existent butt nearly on the floor and his crumbling wrappings hitching up to show bone. One of his fingers has fallen off. I can't help laughing, but it's followed by a small sigh of compassion. As frustrating as it's been wrangling him, I can't imagine what the day's been like on his end. Poor guy's obviously wiped out. Between the trauma of his wake-up call, the realization that he's four thousand years and half a world away from home, and the scary white girl yelling at him, who can blame him? I certainly can empathize with being thrust into a world where nothing makes sense.

It's pushing 1800 according to my phone, which makes me thirty minutes late for my date with Sofi. I shoot her a quick text update on Tut's status and mine.

I get a string of emoji in return: a thumbs up, a winky face, a beer mug, an octopus. It takes me a minute to decode the rebus: *Sounds good. I'm already drinking. Octopus.*

Okay, maybe I'm not that great at Sofi-speak yet.

Pocketing my phone, I gently shake the sleeping pharaoh by the shoulder. There's an alarming creak from the joint, and I snatch my hand back. Last thing I need is him literally falling apart on me.

"Hey. Your Majesty," I say quietly. "Time to wake up. I need to take you to holding for the night."

The mummy stirs, then his papery eyelids slide back to reveal perfectly normal, healthy brown eyes. I take a step back as a measure of respect as he scoots up in the chair. His unfocused gaze trawls around the room for a moment before falling on me. Without speaking, I offer him my hand, but he waves it away, hoisting himself up to standing with minimal difficulty. Which is impressive, considering how broken and weak state he was when he arrived. His body's reconstructing itself, drawing from the background magic of the area and the massive levels of belief that woke him in the first place. He turns to face me once he's steady.

"Are you ready to go, sir?" I ask.

He says nothing for a long moment, then says, "Yesss," with a sound like sandpaper over icicles.

I smile. Guess Scott was right.

The Roosevelt Center for Curious Cases, the SCD's magical holding facility, is hands-down my favorite place in the city. So far, anyway. I haven't been to the Spy Museum.

I trundle the borrowed SUV across the restricted service road, stopping behind the center wall of the Franklin D. Roosevelt Memorial, then hop out and open Tut's door for him. He fumbles with the seatbelt but manages to not plummet to the ground once it releases. He panics a little when his feet hit the snow, doing a wiggly dance in the unfamiliar wet, cold stuff. I suppress a giggle and hold out my arm to steady him before we start walking. His touch is lighter than a child's although he's fully my height, belying the enchantment I requisitioned for him before we left.

Although it's been dark for hours, I insisted that public relations drop a glamour over Tut before we headed out. They reassured me he'll "fill in" by this time tomorrow, taking on a human form shaped by the flavor of humanity's belief in him. I'm curious to see how he'll turn out. Sort of like watching a cake rise. But I couldn't take him into public as he is, a rickety mass of rotten, mobile bandages. Not that he's much less ugly now. The disguise they gave him is that of an obnoxiously white bread tourist, complete with Hawaiian shirt under a massive parka and a camera around his neck.

We shuffle through the closed park down the shoveled path toward the centerpiece of the installation. Frank, the werewolf park ranger from our own security force, minds the perimeter for any looky-loos as I open the gate.

Which is the best part.

Standing to the side of the life-size bronze statues of the late president and his dog, I tug the glove off my right hand and press my palm onto Fala's nose. The metal stings with the promise of frostbite. I hold it long enough for the biometric reader to recognize my credentials, then yank it back to my pocket. The dog's nose is bright with the oil from thousands of other hands that've touched here, but you can't open the door unless you're a SCD agent with special clearance. Which, today, is me.

There's a vapor hiss as the titanic cement platform supporting the statues disengages from its mooring and swings gracefully outward, revealing a shallow cellar containing a short staircase and a pair of elevator doors.

Tut's goggling, mouth agape.

"After you, your Pharaohness," I say, gesturing at the hole with a courtly half-bow.

He stares at the plume of my breath hanging in the frigid air, a sparkle of curiosity in his new eyes. Then he focuses on me.

"Why?" he asks in a voice now smooth as glass.

The question takes me aback. It's the first one he's asked. The rest of the time, he's readily gone along with what we've said. I rebound quickly, but the answer I should give—the SCD official line about further information and securing his safety—isn't what comes out of my mouth.

"To make sure you don't run off and cause havoc in the mortal world until we're sure you're not a threat."

Tut looks shocked, and I wince. I bombed my withholding information classes in training. Obviously. But then he brightens. "I like you," he says. "You do not lie when you should."

His attempt at smiling looks more like a stroke, but it's endearing, and I can't help smiling back.

I nod toward the stairs, and he gamely goes down ahead of me. The panel next to the elevator scans my handprint a second time, then does a full-face scan of Tut, registering his energy signature and case number. A green light flashes to indicate we're good to go, then the scrape of concrete echoes overhead as the hidden entrance seals behind us. We step into the oversized metal box, and I punch B2 on the panel.

Down we go.

I shouldn't be surprised that Tut loves his room, with its slablike cot and dim lighting. All the open space he's suffered since waking up is probably super uncomfortable after millennia in a coffin. When I unlocked the six-by-six overnight cell, he practically fell on his face and started kissing the ground. Now he's dug in like a tick, the glamour melting away as he investigates the tiny space.

I stand in the hallway as he gets situated, pretending to pay attention while listening to the ambient sounds of the facility. This is the minimum security area, reserved for low-risk supers and brief stays that don't require special constraints. The doors are biometrically locked from the outside, but there are decent windows cut into them for airflow that allow the residents to chat. Seems like a stupid idea to me—what if they start cooking up some crime?—but it's not my call. From Tut's room at the end of the hallway, I catch bits of conversation between a gremlin that yanked out kids' teeth while impersonating a tooth fairy and a chain-smoking talking swan in the tank for harassing mundanes at the park. The place echoes, which helps me keep tabs on their conversation. Mostly, they're talking about reality shows and how shitty the food is, but then they drop to a conspiratorial whisper, which gets my attention. Whatever it is, they don't want me to hear. Guess what I'm going to ask them on my way out.

I clear my throat and make my excuses to Tut. "I'm heading back up top, but someone will be down in the morning to let you know the verdict on your placement. If you need anything overnight, buzz for Cynthia, and she'll come take care of you."

He swivels his unsteady head toward me, brow lowering with thought. Slowly, he says, "What will happen to me?"

"Honestly, I have no idea. You're the first new arrival I've had to process." That doesn't seem to assuage him. "Can't imagine they'll leave you in here, though. You're too big of a deal to let you rot in prison for no reason."

The awakened king nods gravely and gestures me away. I bristle at the servant's treatment but say nothing. He's been fairly pleasant otherwise. Besides, I've got something else on my mind.

After sealing Tut inside his room, I pace down to the fake tooth fairy's cell in the middle of the hall and tap on the metal door. He must've heard me coming because he's pretending to be asleep. Covers up over his head and everything.

"I know you're awake, Lanshar. Get out here—I

need to talk to you."

There's a grumble from the blankets, then a pair of sickly yellow eyes in a too-small head peek out. "Lanshar not here. Wrong room."

I roll my eyes. "Fine. *Sprinkle Princess*."

At the mention of his preferred name, the gremlin gives a happy squeal, then rolls out of bed and sprints to the window, up on tiptoes in his garishly pink sequined dress. "How can Sprinkle Princess help Agent 6?" he grins. His smile has too many teeth in it, not all of them his own.

I gag but hold it together. "What were you whispering about with Honk?"

Gremlins aren't good liars. The randomly roving eyes, slack jaw, and shifting posture would give it away to a blind cyclops, but he fills those awkward seconds with, "Uh... Sparkle Princess doesn't know what you're talking about."

I'm about to light into him when someone further up the hall interrupts.

"Ignore him. He's gossiping about something I said under the influence."

Lanshar sticks his tongue out and makes a nasty hand gesture with his claws, then darts back under his blankets, tutu poking out behind him as he pouts. I shake my head and head to the end of the hall.

The rooms before the exit are reserved for longer stays for more manageable cases. Only the one on the left is occupied. From what I know of the records, it's been home to the same paragon for a classified amount of time, locked up for refusing to maintain human form.

I peek into the small window and smell musty air. I also notice that the entire floor has gone totally silent. A prickle of déjà vu tickles my neck hairs as I remember the last time I talked to someone in prison.

"You want to tell me what you're talking about, Arachne?" I say into the darkened room.

There's a chitinous scuttling noise followed by an annoyed sigh. "Not really. Do you ever want to talk about stupid shit you said when you were drunk?"

Point. But still. "Maybe if you tell me what the hell's going on, I'll forget to tell the warden you smuggled alcohol down here. I'd hate to revoke Anansi's visitation rights because you guys broke the rules. Again."

"Fine." A huff. "Gods, you guys are pushy."

A woman's face appears at the window out of the darkness. She's quite beautiful with her green eyes and glossy black hair and pissy pouted lips. It's where she turns into a black, hairy spider at the ribcage that gives me the willies. I keep my eyes respectfully trained on her eyebrows.

"What happened?" I ask.

She rolls her eyes and says in a sing-song voice, "Anansi may or may not have slipped me a fifth of gin on his last visit, and I may or may not have drank it all in one night on an empty stomach, and I may or may not have started drunk-weaving."

"Drunk-weaving? That's a thing?"

"Duh," she scoffs.

"Wait a second. You don't have a loom anymore. As far as the records show, you haven't woven anything in years."

No response.

"What'd you make that's got Lanshar and Honk riled up?"

A shadow of uncertainty passes over her face and is gone so fast I'm positive I imagined it. But then her eyes narrow, and she says, "Promise you'll get my original loom out of storage, and I'll show you."

Of course. A bargain. Everything's a deal with supers. This one's an easy fix, though. The artifact warehouse is on the fifth level of the facility, and as far as I know the loom itself isn't magical. Shouldn't be a problem.

"Deal," I nod.

Arachne gives a curt nod, then retreats into the darkness. There's a lot of shuffling and scraping of furniture. I'm about to ask if everything's okay when the overhead light comes on, and the syllables fall useless out of my open mouth.

The tapestry fills the entire floor of her room, which is otherwise totally barren of cloth. Her bed sits on its side against the wall, the dresser drawers piled empty on top of it. Every stitch of blankets, sheets, towels, and T-shirts are woven into the design. Which is crude and obviously done in a rush, but something about it worries me.

It shows a throng of stick people held inside a wobbly-lined golden circle, packed so tight they're almost a solid field of black. The crowd is presided over by a single enormous person on the opposite side of the picture, waving a silver sword and wearing a crown. A purple line separates the two sides and seems to radiate or shine, casting a reflection of the sword-wielding figure across both the purple and gold boundaries. A dozen nameless and faceless individuals float near the figure like flies around a carcass. The entire panorama resembles a child's crayon drawing of how to rule the world.

There's a too-familiar stir of anxiety in my gut, like barfing weasels fighting to get out. This smacks of prophecy.

Goddammit.

"What does it mean?" I ask.

"I don't know," the spider woman groans as she surveys her handiwork. "I don't remember doing it. I woke up with a pounding headache and bloody fingers and nothing to wear." She chews her bottom lip thoughtfully, all traces of defiance gone. "It doesn't even look like mine."

"Have you shown this to anyone else?"

She shakes her head. That's something at least. If what I'm feeling is intuition and not paranoia, then this needs to stay quiet.

She looks at me with genuine concern. "Is it bad?"

I pull out my phone to snap a series of high-res pictures, then ask, "How fast can you dismantle it?"

"An hour? Maybe two?"

"Good. Do it."

I turn to leave, brain already churning away, when she calls me back.

"Agent, am I in trouble?" she stammers. "Will I be okay?"

There's real fear in her voice. A warble that deepens my dread—if she's scared, it's because she doesn't know what's happened to her, which means something is seriously wrong. Paragons aren't as in control of their existence as supernals, but they're damn close. If she's been compromised, I need to worry about more than jailhouse contraband.

"You'll be fine," I say, hoping my own uncertainty doesn't come across. "I'll take care of it. Just make sure you shred that thing ASAP."

She nods, and I shut off the light. The sharp sound of ripping cloth begins to punctuate the troubled air.

I can't run back to my car fast enough.

PART II
FRACTURED
FAIRYTALES

FOUR

Two pairs of dark brown eyes lock over stacks of neatly-arranged papers. Brows are furrowed. Jaws are clenched. Wills are clashed.

"This is completely unreasonable," Jack Alexander is saying from the visitor's side of the polished desk. "Sir," he adds with a hint of disdain. "You're jeopardizing the entire nation—potentially the entire world—by refusing to investigate these claims."

He's been in this same office, having this same dead-end conversation, five times in as many months. Hel's prophecy is all he can think about since he returned from the underworld. Every assignment has been tainted with the knowledge that this crime could be related to Eris' plan to destroy the Gauntlet and invade the mortal world. It's consumed him, waking and sleeping, leaving room for little else.

If he could deal with it himself, he would. God

knows he's done more reckless things and taken on more hopeless causes before. However, this threat is far bigger than one man, even if he is the much-lauded Agent 97. He needs approval to use agency resources to investigate; he can't budge forward without it. But the person in charge of those resources seems determined not to see the disaster looming over his own backyard, despite Jack pointing right at it.

The man on the other side of the desk blinks first. Agent 99, the owner of the office, rubs his eyes under bushy white brows made more striking by his russet skin.

Samir Patel is the longest-sitting 99, since before Jack's time, and he looks it. Most agents in the SCD are under fifty and promotion isn't based on seniority; someone pushing seventy holding the penultimate seat of power is highly unusual. Where Jack's tenure as Agent 97 has generated its own legends, Patel's reign has turned up twice as many, most revolving around the "old man on the mountain" trope. Under him, the agency has flourished, transforming it from the laughable pipe dream of a classified president—believed to be Fillmore—into a vital cog of the government machine. His leadership has built bridges between the supernatural and the mundane, creating interworld peace essentially from scratch. Everything about him has been long-sighted, careful, and tidy.

Which is why Jack is restraining himself from punching the old man square in the nose for being so goddamned obstinate.

Patel sighs as the staring contest ends. "I want to believe you, my friend," he says, steepling his fingers. "But as I've said each time you've come to me with this, you have no concrete evidence to support these claims of Otherworld sedition. These are serious charges to lay against anyone, regardless of their criminal past. All you've brought me is one supernal's word against another's." He gives Jack a look that borders on pity. "I'm afraid it's not sufficient, Ninety-Seven."

Jack digs long, frustrated fingers into his thighs, the bones under his thin flesh grimly reassuring. Flying off the handle at superiors isn't an aspect of his old self he's eager to invite back.

"It's not just Hel's word against Eris'," he says with measured patience. "Don't overlook the incidentals. There's been a two hundred and twelve percent increase in supernatural activity this year, levels we haven't seen since the Sixties. Hundreds of those cases are coming from previously inactive areas, and dozens feature sightings of rare beings and spontaneous generation of power. Mundanes are coming across seventy-six percent more Otherworld doorways by accident, and we're stretched too thin to assemble statistics for how many are unnaturally opened." He stabs a finger at 99's computer for emphasis. "How can you ignore those facts?"

"I'm aware of all of that. Why do you think we're calling every available agent into the field?" Patel gives a short laugh. "Did you see the look on Sixty-

Three's face when he got that chimera assignment? I actually called Doc Sandow, I was so certain he'd drop dead of a heart attack."

Jack ignores this, keeping a stony silence. Any other time, he might humor his boss with a chuckle, but this is too important. He's running out of time to change the course of the storm that's coming. What is it going to take for him to understand?

The senior agent realizes he's laughing alone, and his face shifts abruptly from mirth back to patient annoyance. "You must remember your magical history and interworld ecology," Patel says. "This isn't the first time any of these things have happened, and I'm certain it won't be the last. The baby mote boom during the Salem Witch trials, for example. The explosion of minor revenge and magic spirits that nearly wiped out the Eastern seaboard? Any time Perat has seen upheaval, the Otherworld moves, and vice versa." Jack flinches at the supernal term for the mundane world, but Patel carries on. "Even if things are changing," he says, "it's not necessarily for the worst. It seems rash to assume that a spike in background magic and half a prophecy will mean anything this time next year."

"If it takes that long for everything to go to shit."

Patel sighs. "Jack, we've known each other for what, ten years? I'm the one who hand-picked you for SCD assignment. You're meticulously dedicated, and your instincts have never led us astray, at least in the last five years. I do want to believe you, but you've got nothing except hearsay. If you can provide a single scrap of verifiable evidence, anything real to go on, I'll give you whatever help I can." He spreads his hands on the desktop in a gesture of helplessness. "Until then, there's no reason to expend government resources on a potentially dangerous recon mission when we need attention on home soil."

"Dangerous for whom, exactly?"

"For everyone. Mundanes and metas, supernals and paragons alike. Trespassing into the Otherworld or even on known outposts on this side, asking uncomfortable questions—it's going to stir unrest in what you've accurately described as a volatile atmosphere."

"Isn't it better to know than to guess? If you would—"

Patel holds up a hand for silence. "This conversation is over, Jack. I've given you my lynchpin terms."

Jack lets his anger leak into his expression, knowing it'll startle the senior agent to see any emotion there at all. Patel gives a satisfying eyebrow-raise and lowers his hand, so Jack continues, leaning forward.

"This is the last time I'll ask for your help, Samir," he says. "If you wave me off again, I'll have no choice but to take it to One Hundred, and she'll sort it out without you."

He stares into his superior's face, willing there to be a sign of acquiescence. This man has been his mentor, his lifeline when he was adrift as a rookie and again after the werewolf attack that nearly killed him. To find himself on the wrong end of his trust and unable to convince him of the truth is demoralizing.

Then he notices a faint warmth seeping into his mind, wrapping around it, softening its edges ever so slightly, reaching for something. His eyes flutter with the effort of staying awake, although he was nowhere near tired a second ago.

A sharp thought hacks through the haze: He's doing it again.

Jack bolts up to standing, the chair toppling over behind him. "You're not allowed," he hisses through clenched teeth. "Section Eleven, Subsection E: 'Agents are not permitted to use their abilities on other agents without express written consent.'"

Patel shakes his head as his eyes refocus. "I'm sorry, Jack," he says. The apology is flat, and his face is neutral; Jack isn't sure if he's sorry for using his empathic abilities against him, for his refusal to support the investigation of Eris, or for getting caught. Regardless, it's completely disingenuous.

"If that's how it's going to be...," Jack says, letting the sentence hang for an explanation.

There is none. A wounded silence grows between them instead. It's quickly too much for Jack to stand, and he makes a disgusted noise and goes to leave.

"One moment, Agent 97."

Jack doesn't turn around, his hand on the doorknob. "What."

There's a soft thud from the desk and a rustle of paper. Jack looks to see a fat manila envelope sitting in the center of the desk.

"Your barging into my office and throwing this tantrum has actually saved Twenty-Four a bit of time." He taps the paperwork. "Your next assignment."

Despite his fury at being dismissed, patronized, and mentally violated, the part of Jack that values duty first is operating at full capacity. It generates a familiar excited buzz at the prospect of a fresh case. He walks back to the desk and takes the envelope Patel pushes toward him.

The label reads: *Missing persons/Narcotics/ Interworld*.

"Interworld? Which one?"

"Faerie."

It's a simple word, a common one in this job, but it lands in Jack's psyche with the impact of a neutron bomb. His breath seizes in his chest, piercing his heart with adrenaline icicles. His thoughts move in slow motion as long-repressed memories rattle the bars of their cages.

I can't go back. Not now. Not ever.

He almost hurls the dossier back across the desk, eyes wide and accusing. "Are you fucking with me, Samir?" he spits.

Agent 99 shakes his head. "It came to our attention through the Bureau after the total victims reached twenty—each recovered and accounted for without any police involvement. Preliminary intel is sketchy due to the nature of the problem, requiring further investigation, but it seems that Mab is involved." The barest hint of a smile. "And since you're our primary expert on Faerie after Kerowyn disappeared, it falls to you. You're also currently unassigned, I believe."

Both true. Both unwillingly, but true nonetheless.

He gropes for an excuse, anything to keep him out of this case and throws out the one card he's holding. "I'm classified as Underage Specialist. This isn't my area," he insists. "Besides, if the intel isn't complete, it should go to a lower-ranking field team before it's assigned to a top agent."

Patel's grin widens lopsidedly. "As you correctly pointed out earlier, Agent 97, the recent rise in supernatural activity has forced us to adjust protocol somewhat. Agent 100 and I have agreed to dissolve the archaic specialization system in favor of a more straightforward one. More similar to our parent agency and less like an encyclopedia of magical mishaps." He motions at the case file gripped in Jack's fingers. "Your assignment to this case represents the first step in that direction. Congratulations."

Jack opens his mouth to retort, then shuts it again, hard. Patel's got something up his sleeve, but the combination of Faerie shock and the rising red mist of anger is short-circuiting his ability to discern what it might be. He needs to get his head clear before he tries to tackle the unorthodox situation.

"Thank you, sir," he says, every syllable audibly clipped.

He turns on his heel and stalks out of 99's office, down the sterile white hallway toward his own. As he shuts the door behind him, before he has a chance to switch on the lights, a voice speaks inside his mind like sand blowing over a dune.

Your next trial is swiftly coming. It will ready you for the full extent of your promised service to me.

The memory rises up: A ceremony filled with dead warriors swearing their eternal allegiance to the gods that watched over them in battle as they pass into the afterlife. It's followed by the click of recognition and a burning curiosity. He hasn't heard from her since he left the underworld. Why now?

What do you want with me, Lady Ishtar? he thinks back.

But there's no answer.

Jack sighs and leans heavily against the inside of his office door for a long moment. It's been years since anything could be said to truly unnerve him, but the combination of Patel's severity, the fear of returning to Faerie, and the sudden intrusion of his accidental patron goddess is doing the trick.

His eyes rove around the room as he breathes through the rising anxiety, landing on the solitary picture frame on his desk. He doesn't have to see the photo for it to trigger memories and the soft, hot emotion that accompanies them. The phone in his jacket pocket is suddenly heavy with insistence to be used.

He slams his eyes shut and holds his breath, willing it all away. He's gone these long months without contact, leaving her to start her new life without his interference. Breaking that silence now would do neither of them any good.

With a sharp exhale, Jack crosses to his desk and drops into the leather chair, where he begins to devour the case dossier as if it could somehow save him from the world spinning out of control.

FIVE

The Fifth Amendment straddles the corner of East and 10th, half a block from historic Ford's Theater and within stumbling distance of the Hoover Building itself. Outside, it's two stories of sandblasted marble with art deco windows holding up a further six floors of executive apartments with zero indication of what's behind the polished walnut doors. Inside is a throwback to English private clubs of the 1900s—buttery gaslight, sturdy wood fixtures, deep leather chairs, and obscure yet tasteful artwork. Hundreds of mundanes a day pass the tinted, mirrored windows completely unaware that they're inches away from America's oldest exclusively supernatural bar. The clientele is exclusive, access granted via an application that includes two background checks and special SCD clearance. Magical beings of every description come to drink and socialize here—or "take the Fifth"—because it's one of the rare places they can be truly themselves. Plus it's funny to watch the gross stuff people do when they think they're looking in a mirror.

Sofi's ensconced at the second bend of the U-shaped bar with her back to the door. It's after seven—1900, she corrects herself—and no sign of Cora. She has a pang of guilt for letting the newbie go alone, especially for a high-profile case, but she swallows it down with another swig of beer. Judging by the increasingly alarmist memos hitting her desk, the job's going to get worse before it gets better. Better to throw Cora into the deep end and hope she floats. If she's learned anything from being a meta, it's that protecting people from reality makes them more susceptible to it.

Like what happened to Zara.

The bitterness of the thought outmatches the hoppy IPA on her tongue. She drains the bottle in one long gulp, then pushes it away. It clinks into five others lined up in front of her, and the delicate noise summons the bartender.

"Another round, Mama Bear?" asks Darynda as she surveys the graveyard of empties. "Or are you done for the night?"

Sofi raises her eyes morosely and lets out the breath she'd been holding. She's spent a lot of time in the Fifth since coming to DC, which means Darynda's gotten to know her pretty well. Not that Sofi can find more than a buzz at the bottom of a glass since getting her powers, but she likes the company.

"One more," she says with a wry smile. "Maybe

seven really is a magic number."

There's a pause as Darynda narrows her eyes at the agent across the bar, then she lays a warm brown hand on Sofi's arm with concern. "What's going on, Mama Bear?" she says with an encouraging smile. "You know I'm always here for you. Tell me?"

She wants to. In this moment, torn between past hurt and present anxiety, Sofi would love nothing more than to unburden herself on this woman she likes to pretend is her friend. But the words pile up behind the rock wall surrounding her heart. Some things are too personal.

Sofi shakes her head. "I'm good, D," she says with a thin smile. "You know how it is. Same shit, different day."

The bartender raises an eyebrow but doesn't press the issue. Instead, she gives Sofi's arm a quick squeeze and a pat, then heads to the beer fridge for her drink.

It's scary how quickly Sofi's mind leaps from the cliff it'd been balanced on once Darynda walks away. Ghostly memories run fingernails down her psyche like a chalkboard, making her clench her teeth against the sob building in her throat. The grief of failing her best friend threatens to break her down right here with the terrible weight of its secrecy, but Sofi refuses to give in. Breaching that wall means she'll be forever tied to the person she tells, and all that can lead to is more devastation.

A fresh bottle appears in front of her. Not an IPA this time—something fruity and smooth. The perfect thing to sweeten and lift her mood. Darynda always knows exactly what you need to drink and when. Sofi wonders if there's more in the bartender's veins than Navajo blood and the rumored talent for empathy.

"Geez, I can't be that late," says a nearby voice.

Cora slides onto the stool next to Sofi, lightly jingling the now six empties on the bar as she waves at Darynda. Sofi laughs and shrugs, grateful for the distraction.

"Hey, when I said five-thirty, I meant it, missy," she says. "Not my fault you went AWOL on me."

She meant it as a joke, but the way Cora colors tells her she touched a nerve. She waits until the rookie has a drink in front of her—something pink with an umbrella in it—before she asks about the job.

"Did everything go okay with Tut?"

Cora munches the booze-soaked fruit skewer for a moment, her eyebrows drawing together into one red line. When she finally says something, it's with the unmistakable warble of doubt.

"Yeah, it went fine. He's a decent guy for being dead." She chews another piece of pineapple. "Had trouble with Lanshar and Arachne, though."

Sofi's eyebrow goes up. "Like?"

But she doesn't elaborate, just stares into space and chews a grape. Sofi gives her a full ten seconds before she gets tired of waiting and prods the rookie in the knee. Cora shakes herself and comes back to reality, if a bit resentfully.

"Arachne had some kind of vision," she says

distantly. "Made a messed-up tapestry out of her clothes." Then her brain seems to come back online, her eyes lighting up. "Hey, do you think I can get in to talk to the Lorekeeper?"

Sofi squints at Cora. While she's decent at reading people, she has trouble sussing out this abrupt change of subject. She's forced to ask, knowing she probably won't get a straight answer.

"Why?"

Cora's eyes dart to one side and back. "I'm trying to figure out how to use my sidestepping powers, but I can only do so much by myself. I figured he'd be able to point me in the right direction, at least."

The Lorekeeper, as far as Sofi's aware, is the SCD's chief librarian, archivist, history buff, and part-time oracle rolled into one. Rumor mill says he's holed up in the artifacts section of the Roosevelt and is at least four thousand years old. Top agents consult with him on tough cases or when truly bad shit is going down. She's pretty sure he doesn't give audiences to newbies looking for Magic 101 classes.

"Don't think so, Riley," she says with an apologetic smile. "You have to be at least a Seventy to get through that red tape."

Cora's face falls in darkly funny contrast with the sticky pink cocktail in her hand. Sofi has a stab of sympathy. Her own powers are basically an extension of her natural abilities, but sidestepping goes way beyond that. While she may not have needed a teacher to get comfortable in her new reality, Cora obviously does.

Sofi reaches over and pats her trainee reassuringly. "Hey, it's not a total loss. I mean, it's not as if there's no one who can help you. Maybe you can apply to shadow Ninety-Seven after our term is up. He should be able to teach you what you need to know, right?"

About halfway through the question, she realizes Cora isn't listening. She follows her wide-eyed gaze back over her own shoulder.

Well, speak of the devil.

Agent 97 is standing in the doorway of the bar, still in full uniform way after hours, his head on a swivel as he scans the room. He towers a full foot over everyone else but doesn't seem to notice how badly he stands out. One by one, the patrons notice him and fall silent. Even Darynda stops filling drinks to stare, he's in here so rarely.

Sofi rolls her eyes at the melodrama; it's hard to be impressed by a guy you once knocked unconscious with a stop sign and left for dead on the side of the road. But she can practically taste the tension burning the air as he locks eyes with Cora. Sofi's about to heckle him to unfreeze the crowd, but he beats her to the punch.

He points to each of them in turn. "Strella. Riley. I need to see you in my office. Now," he says. Then he walks out of the bar without a glance backwards.

There's a beat, and the crowd returns to normal, as if he'd never been there.

Sofi turns to see Cora completely dumbstruck. "You look like you saw a ghost," she chides her.

Cora blushes hard, her cheeks matching her hair.

"Sorry. Not every day a Ninety calls your name, you know?"

Sofi smirks. She recognizes a massive crush when she sees one. It's adorable and exciting to think there's something juicy to gossip about after a long, dry spell of nothing besides SCD procedures to talk about. Also kind of weird and sad that anyone might be crushing on that freak machine. But she tucks it away for later. Don't want to keep the boss waiting.

"C'mon, we better get moving," she says, hopping down from the bar stool. "If he came all the way down here to look for us, it's important."

Cora drains the rest of her drink in one long swallow, then pops up to join her as she heads out the door.

"Don't stress, Riley," Sofi says as they cross the street toward headquarters. "He has to get special permission if he wants to bite you."

The sputtering noise the rookie makes is more than enough to chase away the last of her blues.

A place for everything and everything in its place. Looking around the room, it seems like the saying was invented just for Agent 97.

Too bad he isn't running the show anymore.

Since his nervous breakdown and recovery last year, Jack's office has shifted along with his personality. The machine he used to be couldn't function without the clean comfort of Spartan living. These days, the place is too tidy for cleaning staff to visit, though he often can't find his keys in the existing mess. Folders, envelopes, and loose papers are heaped along the baseboards, a necessary strategy after the filing cabinet started buckling. The blackout shades are gone, allowing natural light to illuminate the room and nourish a cactus perched in the sill. He even took down the framed awards and replaced them with pictures; they came with the frames, but it's a start. At least he's going home nights.

But there's power in clichés: The one about old habits dying hard is proving especially true right now. He should be reviewing the case file as he waits for the summoned agents to arrive, but all he seems able to do is stare at the silver frame tucked next to his computer monitor. The frame that used to hold a hierarchy chart of the SCD and now holds an actual photograph. The intensity of his gaze might disturb an observer, his heavy brows furrowed and his chin resting lightly on clasped hands, deep in conflicted thought.

I didn't keep my promises. Does anyone know? Should I have tried to make contact? The risk factor is too high. I've done too much damage. Do not pursue.

A sharp rap on his glass door jams a stick in the hamster wheel, and he shakes his head. It dispels the phantoms, but it doesn't clear his monotone voice when he tells them to come in.

Then there she is.

What Jack wants to do is vault the desk, gather her in his arms and press her tiny body against him, feeling her warmth and inhaling her cotton and leather scent, telling her how much he's thought of her over the last five months, why he's kept his distance, his failed efforts to deliver on his promises. He wants to kiss her smooth forehead, her rough hands, her pink lips. He doesn't care that Strella's standing right there.

What he does do is to stand politely as they stop in front of his desk and nod his acknowledgment to each of them.

"Riley. Strella. I've called you here because we need a small team to finish the recon work from this dossier." He holds up the folder Agent 99 gave him. "You'll be traveling to New York City to investigate a potential supernatural drug ring. We'd go ahead and pursue current suspects, but we need a least one confirmed user to provide testimony and a sample of the material to ensure we're rounding up the right people.

"The good news is that we already have a handful of leads, and you've got two days to do the work. You also won't be going it alone. Agent 42 from the New York office will be your point of contact and lead agent. He's a native New Yorker, he's aggressively friendly, and he knows the meta underground like no one else. Between the three of you, I'm confident you'll find this a quick and easy assignment."

There's a sliver of a moment of silence before both agents start talking at once. Strella's insisting they aren't ready for an out-of-state assignment, that there are plenty of other unassigned agents who could go, that their skills aren't right for that kind of job. Cora's mostly agreeing with her mentor, but she throws out a couple of rookie questions and won't look directly at him.

The jumble of insubordination presses the red button on his patience with lightning speed.

"Enough!" he shouts, slamming his open hand onto the desktop with a sound like a felled redwood.

The junior agents gasp and sputter into silence, effectively terrorized. Cora in particular seems taken aback, and he instantly regrets the outburst. He clears his throat and straightens, softening his posture to remove any traces of threat without losing his air of authority.

"I understand your concerns, agents," he assures them, "but these are your orders. Keep arguing, and you'll see disciplinary action. Is that clear?"

A duet of "Yes, sir."

"Good," he says, then turns his attention to Sofi. "Agent 21, as Six's mentor, you're needed to oversee her. And while your physical abilities may not be needed, your high closing rate is encouraging. It's an important assignment, and if you see this through properly, it could mean a Thirty-Plus promotion for you."

There's a gleam in Strella's eyes that tells him he hit the right note. She may hate him, but they're more alike in their ambition than either of them would admit.

Jack takes a surreptitious grounding breath as he turns to look into Cora's gray eyes. It's been so long since he's seen them up close that he'd nearly forgotten how like storm clouds they are when she's upset; he can hear the thunder rolling now. A somersault in his chest pushes a tiny, apologetic smile onto his face, but her expression stays neutral. She lifts her chin respectfully as he addresses her in his most professional voice.

"Agent 6, given your rare abilities and the potential for Otherworld involvement in this case, your inclusion is practically mandatory. You'll be looking for accidental and forced rips in the Gauntlet that the traffickers could be using, as well as documenting any mythological data that may have been missed in the initial reports."

Cora gives a sharp nod but doesn't offer anything more. He knows he doesn't deserve more but it wounds him nonetheless.

Sofi starts to say something, another protest, he's sure, but he cuts her off.

"That's it, agents," he says with finality. "Be on the runway at DCA for oh-six-hundred. Complete assignment dossiers will be on board when you arrive, and Agent 42 will meet you at JFK. Dismissed."

There's an icy moment where no one moves. The three of them stand locked in complicated lines of conflict. Then Cora turns on her heel and stalks out, sweeping Sofi along in her wake as she goes, the door easing itself shut behind them.

Jack waits until the sound of footsteps down the hallway have disappeared before he folds himself back into his expensive desk chair. He sighs heavily as his stiff muscles unbind. Having both Strella and Cora standing in front of him, he couldn't help being torn between strange, fatherly pride in their promising careers and paralyzing guilt at how both women came to the agency in the first place. His world is getting unmistakably smaller as it fills with people whose stories are tied too intimately with his own.

SIX

New York City hasn't changed. But she has.

The first time Cora set foot here, it was the dead of summer and she was young, naive, hopeful, and searching for anything that'd point her in the direction of her destiny. She'd thought coming to New York would make everything make sense. It hadn't. All she learned was how sheltered and unprepared for the real world she was at twenty-five. And how much coffee costs in the big city. The press of people, the never-ending noise, the *rushrushrush*—she couldn't take it. She'd come home defeated after two laborious weeks, compromised her dream of being somebody, and settled in for a rural Missouri life of boredom.

Six years, a moment of courage, and a trip through the underworld later, though, and she's back, standing in the heart of Manhattan as a supernatural powerhouse. A new life created by the second chance she earned and the specialness she'd craved. Now, looking around the neighborhood where she gave up on her dreams, things feel oddly disjointed. The snow dusting the windowsills and the crispness of the air give the city the feel of a fresh promise. It's as if she could reach back in time and give scared, depressed Cora a hug and tell her things would turn out okay. Mostly.

"Hey, Riley. You in there?"

Someone's snapping their fingers in front of her face. She blinks hard to focus on Sofi, who looks both concerned and amused under her black parka hood.

"Yeah, I'm fine. Feeling a bit nostalgic," Cora mutters, her breath coming out in a hot cloud. She glances up at the Art Deco edifice of the New Yorker Hotel with the fondness of whitewashed memories. "This is the same place I stayed when I visited before. Hard to forget."

Sofi nods. "Yeah, city life sticks with you. Especially these big, dirty, crowded ones. They're the best." She inhales deeply, with every sign of enjoyment.

Cora wrinkles her nose in disgusted disbelief; all she smells is rancid trash and exhaust as a garbage truck rumbles past.

Her mentor grins. "Poor country girl," she says. "Maybe we can duck down to Central Park and bottle some fresh air for you to huff in case of emergency."

"Don't think I haven't thought about it." She chuckles and checks her phone. "Ugh. Where are they? It's nearly lunchtime."

They've been standing in the slush for an hour, waiting on Agent 42, Immanuel "Call Me Manny" Boxer. He'd picked them up from the airport in a black sedan stocked with sugar-shiny donuts and a gallon of coffee, then brought them downtown amid a flurry of conversation, none of it about the case. Cora stopped trying to keep up after mile five and cup three, doing her best not to giggle from the back seat as Sofi answered unending questions about their powers, SDC politics, Mexican food, and poker. She also ate all the donuts because, hey, they weren't going to eat themselves. When they'd pulled up at the hotel, he'd said he'd be right back with their contact, but now Cora's starting to wonder if he's actually an agent or a random NYC weirdo.

To her relief, it's the former.

"Here he comes," says Sofi, nodding toward the corner.

Both agents straighten up and try to look official as a tan man in a black suit and parka approaches with a sketchy guy in tow. Even though they met this morning, Cora can already identify Manny by his walk. He takes long, loping strides that bounce when his foot hits the pavement—more hippie than authority figure. The way Jack talked about him, she'd expected a grim, older guy with a stick up his ass. Manny couldn't be less that person. She can't help liking him.

"Agent 6. Agent 21," Manny says when he stops in front of them. He indicates the twitching, sniffing urchin in greasy jeans and ratty Cosby sweater that he's brought with him. "This is Devin. He's graciously agreed to take us on a tour. Says he knows where we can find the witnesses we need." He peeks over the top of his sunglasses. "And all it'll cost us is a couple tabs of ecstasy."

"I said four," Devin snaps. But his defiance withers under the combined glare of the three agents.

"We'll work out the fine details after you've held up your end of the deal, my shaky friend," Manny says cheerfully. He pats the junkie's shoulder, and the guy flinches as if it's a punch. To Cora's surprise, Manny looks apologetic, though he doesn't say anything.

Instead, Sofi pipes up. "Thank you for your cooperation, Devin." She holds out a hand in invitation. "Please lead the way."

Devin doesn't need to be told twice. He power-walks down the block at a clip barely short of a sprint. The agents have to jog to keep up at first, then fall back to a respectful distance. It's like walking a dog without a leash—they know he won't ditch them as long as he doesn't get spooked or distracted.

As they cross from the touristy part of the borough into a more disreputable area, Cora notices the prickle of watching eyes on her back. Which isn't too surprising. Three matching, impeccable black suits stand out down here. She'd argued with Sofi about wearing street clothes to keep a lower profile, but there wasn't anything to be done for it, even if she did agree. SCD policy forbids alternate clothing while on duty and that's that. But strolling down the streets of New York trailing a drug addict, Cora can't help feeling like she's wearing a red shirt in an episode of *Star Trek*. It's only a matter of time before something awful happens.

Cora catches up with Sofi. "You trust this crackhead?" she says. "He could be leading us anywhere."

"The dossier said Devin's the guy to talk to. He's got connections everywhere in town, and he's managed to not get killed for all the times he's helped out the authorities with narco busts."

"That's because he's a meta," Manny interjects from in front of them. "Low-powered at best. I'd guess this is how the agency handles his tracking rather than alerting him directly."

"What's his ability?" Cora asks.

"No idea. Hell, he probably doesn't know himself."

They continue to walk, the environment steadily deteriorating around them. Devin disappears and rejoins them several times, making Cora jumpy, but Manny isn't concerned, so she lets it slide.

Then again, maybe she should've been more vigilant.

As they round the corner of 14th Street, they're met by a group of six thugs decked out in matching secondary colors. Cora's heart vomits into her ribcage but she throttles the instinct to leap behind a nearby dumpster. That wouldn't be very FBI-like. She does scoot surreptitiously behind Sofi, though, as the gangbangers step up.

"Yo, Dev, what you doin' with these suits?" spits the short white guy on the end.

Devin scratches his arm and stares at the ground in a pitiful show of submission. "Nothin', C-Dog."

"Sure don't look that way to me." C-Dog lifts the open flap of his puffy coat and rests a hand on the chromed gun stuck down the front of his jeans. The knot of heavies behind him shifts to reveal a plethora of what Cora's positive are unlicensed weapons.

Manny throws his hands up and steps between the gang and his informant. "Whoa, whoa, whoa," he says. "Let's not do anything stupid, guys."

"Shut up, pig," says one of the goons, to a chorus of "yeah"s.

Cora can feel Sofi coiling up beside her. She won't go for her gun—the bear-girl never does—but it's likely seconds before someone gets their face demolished by a curbstone. And while Cora scored well in marksmanship, there's a world of difference between the classroom and the street. Her hands are shaking, and she's not sure if she could draw her weapon if she wanted to, much less aim it with any accuracy. The stab of insufficiency makes her wince.

Manny takes a calm step forward, eyes fixed on C-Dog, and he flashes a broad, warm smile. "Hey, man, ain't no reason to get mad," he says smoothly. "Dev's doing me a favor. Doing one for you, too, bro."

C-Dog doesn't change his posture, but he does raise a curious eyebrow. "Oh, yeah, how's that?"

"Gonna show us where those creed assholes are so we can get 'em out of your territory," says Manny.

C-Dog's face lights up like he'd won the lottery. "No shit?"

Manny laughs and lowers his hands. "No shit."

The hostility pouring off Sofi dissolves, along with the clenched fear in the air. C-Dog turns to his crew with his hands raised in celebration, "You hear that, yo? Suit's gonna give us back our turf."

A baritone cheer goes up. Cora looks to Sofi, who's as stymied as she is. Surely he can't promise that? Can he?

"You need any help, bro?" the ringleader says to Manny.

"Nah." He slaps his hand down on Devin's shoulder, making the skinny man's knees buckle. "Dev's got us covered."

"Right on."

C-Dog opens his arms and embraces Manny in the traditional male hug—one-two-three thumps on the back. They break apart, and the gangbanger makes a whirling gesture with his hand, then the purple and orange thugs sidle their way down a side alley, leaving the three agents and their narc free to go.

When they're gone, Manny turns back to the other agents, who are staring at him goggle-eyed and open mouthed.

"What?" he says innocently.

"How did you do that?" Cora asks. She points at the spot where the armed felons were standing.

"They were seriously going to kill us, then you smiled and lied to them and they let us go?"

Sofi chimes in. "Yeah, what did you do to them? You got mind control powers or something?"

Manny shakes his head with a smile. "What can I say? I'm a lucky guy."

Cora can't help chuckling at that. Understatement, to say the least. His bio—which she immediately dug up after their briefing—lists his metahuman ability as "supernatural luck," citing a hundred-percent case success rate and a poker winning streak that's banned him from every casino in New York. Best superpower ever.

It's another couple of blocks before they stop again, this time for Devin to give them hushed instructions to follow his precise movements. He says they're close to the meeting place, but one misstep could mean the whole thing goes in the toilet.

"Gotta get to the door safe," he whispers, glassy eyes wide.

The agents nod, and Manny gestures for him to lead the way.

It's a circuitous route, to say the least, but they faithfully trace Devin's path. Hopscotch across a parking lot. Climb over an out of the way trash can. Pick up three small stones, then throw them over your left shoulder. Blink six times at a broken window. Push through the middle of an evergreen hedge.

As they emerge from the last obstacle, there's a moment of stunned silence, then Cora and Manny burst out laughing. But Sofi isn't amused.

"Are you kidding me?" she explodes. "It's a goddamn rec center!" When no one responds, she rounds on Cora. "You were supposed to be checking for Otherworld doors, Riley. Why didn't you catch that this was a fake?"

"I thought it was a magic password thing!" Cora chokes out between breaths, too tickled to be threatened. "It's super common in fairytales to have to do all kinds of weird stuff before you can go through an existing door." She wipes away tears of laughter and finds a measure of dignity. "We're lucky he didn't stop to take a leak."

"Besides, you should've seen the look on your face," Manny adds with a snort. "Worth it."

The storm cloud over Sofi's expression subsides as their laughter wins her over. She gives a sheepish grin by way of apology and shakes her head in mock disapproval. "You guys are jerks."

Up ahead, Devin's waving them on, dead serious and hunched over like he's trying to hide in plain sight. The team catches up with him as he nears the entrance of the rec center. It's a warehouse-style building, mostly gray and beige and papered with fliers, notices, and missing persons ads. A basketball court off to the right reminds Cora of high school where the same sounds and smells permeated the air. She absently wonders if all places are connected by interworld threads, giving you déjà vu not because you remember something similar, but because they really are the same place.

A directory listing near the reception desk

blandly lists the facility's available services. It's mostly standard stuff—yoga, meditation, youth sports, arts and crafts—but the bottom line catches Cora's attention.

"'True Believers Recovery Group'?" she reads aloud.

She looks to Sofi with eyebrows raised, but her mentor shrugs, and the three agents gamely follow their drug-addled Sherpa into the nearby elevator. Manny chats casually about how he essentially grew up in a rec center, but Cora's not listening. All she can think about is how much this case is starting to reek of Eris.

SEVEN

It's a short ride to the third floor where the doors open directly into a loft-style space with large windows and laminate flooring. Twenty folding chairs are circled in the middle of the room, every one of them occupied.

The diversity of the group is varied enough that Cora takes note. She fires up her scene analysis skills for a quick estimate. Age range: 18 to 60. Ethnicity: 6 white, 4 black, 5 Asian, 2 Latino, 2 Middle Eastern, 1 undetermined. Gender: 70% female, 30% male. Drug use has its demographics, and the True Believers are totally ignoring them.

"Weird," she says aloud. She meant to whisper, but the word echoes across the high-ceilinged room, drawing the attention of everyone in the group. Twenty heads turn toward them. Months of agency training keeps Cora from lowering her head in embarrassment.

Devin doesn't budge when the three agents step

out of the elevator. "I did what you freaks wanted. Gimme my E," he grumbles.

Sofi's moves to haul their sketchy helper bodily into the room, but before she can grab his jacket, Manny pulls a clear plastic baggie out of his pocket and throws it to him.

"There you go, dude," he says. "Thanks for the help."

Devin snatches the packet from the air, then punches the close-door button. Sofi narrowly avoids having her arm cut off. She stares ruefully at the elevator, then turns on Manny.

"How did you...," she says, letting the question dissolve.

"Took it off C-Dog when he hugged me," Manny explains, giving a one-shoulder shrug. "Figured it's better to pay the guy who helped us than let that asshole sell that shit to kids."

Manny's naturally chill aura must be working its own magic on Sofi because she doesn't explode the way Cora expects her to, red as her face is.

"Guess you guys do it different here in the Big Apple. Back at headquarters, we don't actually pay junkies with drugs, no matter how nice they are," she says in a low, sarcastic hiss.

The senior agent blushes unprofessionally. "Sorry," he mutters, then remembers where he is.

But it's too late. The support group they've come to question has visibly relaxed; the agents' necessary façade of authority is broken. Someone at the back sniggers loudly. Cora sighs. If Jack were here, he'd take back control easy as breathing, command the room, evoke the fear of the law in this motley collection of users. As it stands, they'll have to roll with it.

Manny steps forward, SCD badge held aloft. Cora and Sofi each take a side, trying to look heavy-duty as he addresses the group.

"Good afternoon. I'm Agent 42 of the Supernatural Cases Division of the FBI, and I'm here to discuss the distribution and possession of a narcotic substance called 'creed' or 'reach.' We have reason to believe that at least one of you is a user and/or supplier." He slides his badge back into his inner jacket pocket. "My associates and I will be questioning each of you on this topic. While it is within your rights to refuse the interview, you should know that it reflects poorly on you in the larger investigation."

An elderly woman with enormous purple glasses raises her hand politely.

Manny nods in her direction. "Yes?"

"Are you magic?" she asks.

Cora has to cover her laugh with a cough.

But Manny doesn't miss a beat. "That information is classified, m'am." He raises his chin to address the rest of the group. "Does anyone else have any questions before we begin?"

Another hand shoots up, this one belonging to a young, chunky Latino guy near the back.

"Yes, sir?"

"Uh, yeah, man. Can I go to the john? Kinda sounds like we're gonna be here a while, and I gotta go bad."

Manny partially turns to Sofi and says, "Agent 21, I will accompany this young man to the facilities. You and Agent 6 should begin the interviews."

As the two men head down a narrow side hall toward the restrooms, Sofi gives instructions on not leaving the premises, the consequences of lying under oath—the usual stuff—then they divide the crowd between them.

Cora settles into a couch at the far side of the room, taking a deep breath. Her first subject anxiously takes a seat in front of her as she hits "record" on the memo app on her phone. Her first interrogation.

"Okay, ma'am. Let's start from the top. Are you now using or have you ever used the substance referred to as 'creed' or 'reach'?"

The woman scrunches her over-plucked eyebrows. "Don't you want to know my name first?" she asks.

Shit.

Some guys don't know how to navigate the men's room. Which is ridiculous. It's not like it's complicated. Don't look. Don't talk. One space between urinals. Dozens of microlaws passed down through generations of men the world over.

But this guy is ignoring every one of them.

Manny escorts the kid to the bathroom without incident, but he flat refuses to obey etiquette once they're in there. The agent figured he might as well take a second to attend to his own business and immediately regretted it. The guy, whose name tag identifies him as Paulo, is standing so close to Manny he can feel his body heat. And he's staring. Right at...you know...like he's never seen one before.

Apparently the kid drank a trough full of Mountain Dew today because Manny's finished and zipped while Paulo's making loud noises of relief. Manny scrubs his hands in the sink and tries to surreptitiously observe his charge's behavior in the mirror. Aside from the laughably stereotypical barrio banger gear, he doesn't fit the user profile. His hair's glossy, his skin's clear. Could Devin have put them on the wrong trail? Did 99?

Paulo finishes up, and Manny waits for him by the exit. The way the kid moves seems wrong, too, Manny notices. Like he's not used to his body. A tingle of an idea begins to form. Now that he's looking more closely, he could swear the kid's shimmering like summer heat on asphalt. Could be a possession or manifestation. Though it's just as likely to be his anxiety kicking in.

Without thinking, he reaches into a pants pocket and retrieves an orange pill bottle. The pop of the lid is too loud in the tiled room, and it gets Paulo's attention immediately.

"What you got there, man?" he says, coming over without stopping to wash his hands.

Manny recoils, then realizes what he's done. He shoves the Klonopin back into his pocket and manages not to stammer. "Personal medication."

He tries to change the subject. "If you're finished, we need to rejoin the group. Your interview is important to our investigation."

But Paulo isn't having it. His black eyes shine with interest. "You know, that Xanax shit goes for hella cash, right? I'll give you twenty for the bottle."

Manny's mouth falls open in surprise. "Did you just offer to buy prescription medication from an FBI agent to sell on the street?"

The kid grins crookedly. "Yeah. So fuckin' what? You spooks gonna arrest us anyway, right? All of us done creed."

"No arrests are anticipated unless someone is suspected of trafficking."

"You mean like this?" Paulo plunges a scrawny arm deep into the front of his enormous jeans, and Manny's hand flashes to his sidearm. The kid balks, eyes wide. "Whoa, dude! I ain't got no gun. Just wanted to see if you want some of this...." With exaggerated care, Paulo withdraws a knotty fist from his pants, then unwraps his fingers to reveal half a dozen silver washers.

Manny lets his jacket fall back over his gun. "What is that?"

"Creed. Duh."

The agent gingerly picks up one of the metallic disks and holds it up with thumb and forefinger. It's lighter than it should be—more communion wafer than quarter—and the fluorescent light of the bathroom gives the surface a pearly shine. He sniffs it, but it doesn't smell. He stops short of tasting it; who knows what it could do to him. With his free hand, he retrieves an evidence bag from his other pants pocket and drops the disk into it.

To Paulo he says, "All of it. In the bag. Now."

The dealer groans but complies. Searching various pockets and crevices, he produces over three dozen doses of the drug. Manny's fairly impressed by the kid's resourcefulness.

"Okay, that's it." Paulo shifts his stance back into rebellious teenager mode and sneers. "Shit ain't no good to me, anyway. One-time use."

Manny starts to ask, then thinks better of it. Interviews need to be done in the presence of a witness. You need someone there to make sure you don't, say, beat the snot out of a sarcastic halfling, for example.

He tucks the evidence bag into his jacket with one hand and puts the other on Paulo's shoulder. "Let's go, dude," he says.

The guy squirms as he's pressed back out toward the hallway but not much. Manny gets the impression that he's not that upset about being caught—another red flag.

As he walks Paulo back to the group, he runs a quick tally of their encounter: Found out they've all done creed, resulting in twenty verified testimonials. Bagged a huge sample. Nailed a dealer who's probably in this deeper than he lets on. All because a punk kid had to go to the bathroom.

Lucky me.

Ten hours, a horribly expensive cab ride, and

copious amounts of coffee later, mostly consumed by Manny, the three agents have come to one irreducible conclusion.

"This is bad," Sofi says.

She's sitting at the tiny desk in her room back at the New Yorker Hotel, fingertips pressed to her forehead. The netbook in front of her displays the team's pooled notes from the True Believers' interviews. Despite the remarkable diversity of the group, their stories are practically identical.

The narrative runs something like this:

A non-threatening person approaches the target in public, then has them peel off somewhere private. The dealer says they've got something for them. Even if the target has never done drugs, the offer doesn't bother them, possibly due to supernatural persuasion. The target ingests the drug, which takes seconds to kick in, then they're transported from the mundane world into a meadow. They're met by a tall woman who calls herself "the Mistress." She informs the user that they're special and important, part of her master plans to elevate the human world to heavenly stature. Reports on how long they spend with her vary—from an hour to years—but after exactly seventy-two hours real time, they're transported back with their memories intact.

They also return with a hugely fortified belief in the supernatural. Having experienced real magic, they continually seek ways to get back to the Otherworld. However, the drug doesn't work on the same person twice. This unfulfillable longing strengthens their belief and forces them to find other ways to satisfy their craving, making them vulnerable to less noble beings, such as vampires and demons. Support groups like True Believers have cropped up nationwide for those attempting to overcome their supernatural experience, although most quickly devolve into twisted networking events, hooking up "outcasts" with hosts who promise to provide magic.

"This is bad," Sofi repeats, reading and rereading the collated summary.

Cora leans down to look over her shoulder, and Sofi holds her breath. The close proximity of another person is both comforting and nerve-wracking. Her bear nature enjoys having Cora nearby, but that same familiarity smacks hard against a warning-graffitied wall around her heart.

A polite knock at the door gives her an excuse to move. She slides out of the chair to let Cora read, and her neck hairs relax. A look through the peephole, then she inches open the door.

"Hey, dude," Manny says through the slit. He holds up a brown paper bag riddled with grease spots. "Chinese okay?"

"Perfect."

She swings the door open for him to come in. He spreads the white cartons over the side table between the two double beds, ready to eat after such a long, stressful day.

"What'd you find?" he asks, cracking a Coke.

Sofi gazes longingly at her box of beef and broccoli, then says, "Basically, someone's selling magical kidnapping drugs that up mundanes' levels of belief. Users get exposed to supernatural things they can't deny, which boosts the Otherworld's power. Some kind of cross-dimensional sharecropping."

If he's surprised, he doesn't let on. In fact, it's Sofi who's caught off guard when he says, "Sounds logical—the dealers are from Faerie."

"What? How could you possibly know that?"

He slurps his soda casually. "Paulo was Fae. Couldn't you tell? Walking all weird and didn't quite fit into the scenery?" Sofi shakes her head. He shrugs. "Prestidigitation's a handy disguise tool when you mix it with possession. You learn to spot it pretty quick once you know what to check for. Dude fessed up fast when I started asking pointed questions."

"So," she says slowly. "If the dealers are all Fae, then Queen Mab's definitely involved."

"And Eris," Cora says.

It's barely above a whisper, and Sofi only hears it thanks to her enhanced senses. Manny starts to talk about tracking Fae signatures, but she waves him into silence and turns to Cora at the desk.

"Eris? What about her?" she says.

The chair swivels slowly around until Cora's facing her, gray eyes filled with worry. Sofi's never seen her this way; Cora's always been enthusiastic and light-hearted. Now it looks like she might puke if she says what's on her mind.

She does eventually say something. And it rocks Sofi's world in a bad way.

"You guys don't know about the invasion? Agent 97 didn't tell you?"

"Invasion?" Sofi and Manny ask at the same time.

There's an awkward silence as Cora looks back and forth between them. Then she whispers, "Oh my god," and puts a hand to her mouth. "That son of a bitch."

"Cora, what are you talking about?" Sofi says urgently. "What was Ninety-Seven supposed to tell us?"

Even super-chill Manny is disturbed by Cora's apprehension. He sets aside a takeout carton and scoots to the end of the bed. "Yeah, dude. What is it?" he says with real concern. "Strella and I are listening now, even if Alexander's keeping secrets."

Cora takes a huge breath and exhales through her nose, casting her eyes to the floor. A minute oozes past. Then she takes another breath and pours out a rapid-fire string of sentences that can't possibly be true. Accusations about the goddess of chaos imprisoning and impersonating the ruler of the underworld. How she's plotting to overthrow the mortal world and gathering her forces to tear down the Gauntlet. There are theories involving artificially-inflated belief being part of the scheme and how every case they've worked is directly tied to Eris. There's something vague about Arachne at the end, despite the paragon having locked down in the Roosevelt for ten years.

When she finally stops to catch her breath, Manny speaks up, putting the final pieces in place.

"So, Eris is the Mistress that the users are meeting? And she's shoring up stores of belief, which makes her stronger, so she can make good on her evil plans?" He pauses. "Dude."

"Jack...." Cora falters, then starts again. "Agent 97 said he'd get Ninety-Nine and One Hundred onside so we could investigate, but I guess he didn't tell them."

By the time Sofi's reeling brain catches up, there are fat tears shining in Cora's eyes. Sofi's gut clenches in empathy. Whatever longing she saw thrown Jack's way at the Fifth is a mere snapshot of a deeper truth.

And while she may not understand the fairytale bullshit parts of Cora's story, she does understand that her friend is hurting. The mamma bear in her rises up. Sofi gives Cora's shoulder a quick squeeze before turning to Manny.

"We need to get back to HQ," she says. "Right now."

EIGHT

Three hours and two hundred miles later, Cora is tapping on the glass door of Jack's office. Alone.

Sofi had insisted that Cora be the one to hand in the report since she'd been the one to draw the lines between creed and its potential as a supply line for Eris' forces. She put up a decent fight, arguing that as a rookie she shouldn't be trusted with sensitive information, but even Manny agreed. Despite providing a hefty information download between the hotel and the DC tarmac, she couldn't get out of it. It couldn't be anyone else.

She waits for a response, gripping the manila folder of field reports from New York, but nothing happens. Which is annoying because she can clearly see him hunched over the desk, one hand stuck in his short hair as he pores over a stack of documents. The glow of the computer screen turns his dark complexion sallow, giving him a wasted, sickly look.

Another knock.

This one is followed by a flurry of movement as Jack growls and slams a closed fist down on the desk, sweeping a stack of papers onto the floor and shoving himself up to pace. Cora flinches despite being several feet and an inch of safety glass separated from the outburst. At the same moment, she has an intense desire to rush in and comfort his obvious distress. She crams it down violently, gripping the folder until it bends.

And then, as he turns to stride across the room again, he spots her.

Their eyes meet. Cora's heart flutters.

Movies and TV have taught her that this moment should be magical. The hero and the heroine, separated by time and circumstance and often their own willful pride, finally come together to reconcile their differences and vow never to part again. There's hugs and kisses and tears. Happily ever after.

But if she's learned anything between her trip through the underworld and her SCD training, it's that most fairytales fall utterly short. Like right now, for example. Rather than Jack's face lighting up, then him flinging the door open and gathering her into his arms, he merely nods in recognition and waves her in. She allows herself a quiet grumble at her sappy imagination and pushes the door open. Real life is so much more complicated than stories.

Cora approaches the desk and waits to be addressed. He steps back to his chair and attempts to organize the mess of papers. Files about shapeshifters, SCD procedural handbooks, a yellowed photograph of a woman with a classic Greek profile, a technical sketch. It all pings her curiosity, but the revelations of New York and Jack's nearness are effectively blocking it out.

When the desktop is visible again, Jack sits and gestures at the guest chair. "Have a seat, Riley," he says.

"Thank you, sir, I'll stand," she says stiffly. She keeps her eyes glued to a spot on the wall over his right shoulder. She doesn't have shades to hide her expression, but she's gotten good at the neutral mask.

"As you wish. What did you find out in New York?"

Cora hands over the dossier without comment. When he takes it, their fingers brush, creating a tiny blue spark that drifts onto the desk before winking out. Cora's breath catches. What the hell was that? She looks up to see her surprise reflected in Jack's eyes. But then it's gone. He's better at the mask than she is. She clears her throat, refocuses her gaze on the wall, and stands at ease to wait as he peruses the documentation. That was weird, but she's got a job to do.

After what seems like hours, Jack lifts his head and says, "This is bad."

She can't suppress the smirk at his candor. "That's exactly what Sofi said, sir."

"Do you understand the implications of the report?"

"Yes, sir."

He raises an eyebrow. "You do?"

"Yes, sir. Aside from kidnapping and narcotic violations, evidence seems to point to Queen Mab throwing in her lot with Eris. It's highly likely that the drug's intended to strategically increase belief levels so that members of the Otherworld conspiracy can gain the strength they need to enact Eris' plan." She lowers her gaze from the wall to look him full in the face. "But when I tried to explain that to the other agents, no one believed me because you didn't tell them."

The accusation lands heavily on the office carpet. It takes a moment for the shock to pass, then the stoic mask slips from Jack's face. He inhales deeply through flared nostrils, flexing his jaw. He stands slowly and leans on the desk with both hands. A measured, patient anger. The shift in his manner is so dramatic that Cora immediately wonders if calling him out was a good idea.

"You think I kept it to myself?" he says. "You don't think I tried to convince someone of the truth?" His voice is low with an urgency that makes Cora's scalp prickle, his dark eyes locking her in place. "That I didn't make every effort to get through to Agent 99? That I haven't been practically begging at his doorstep for weeks for approval to investigate what could be the biggest supernatural disaster since the Gauntlet was created?" He cranes forward to drive his point home, his voice rising with intensity. "I've done nothing but tell people. So don't come in here and accuse me of failing because you haven't seen the fruit of my efforts."

Panic grips Cora's throat as she tries to speak. There's a rush to apologize for not trusting him, but nothing comes out. The office's recirculated air is crushing her, his outrage putting a vice around her lungs. Then she realizes she's been holding her breath. It comes out in a rush, along with the words it held hostage.

"I didn't know," she stammers. "When I mentioned Eris to the team, they looked at me like I'd grown a third arm. All I could think was that you'd lied to me or given up or didn't believe it yourself. After months without talking, with you avoiding me...," she says, then stops, embarrassed at her girlish vulnerability, and drops her gaze to the floor. But a voice inside urges her to speak the rest. "I thought you'd abandoned me," she finishes in a whisper.

The sound of expensive shoes brushing over cheap carpeting. The heady scent of cinnamon and sage. The strong hand resting lightly on her shoulder.

It's the closest they've been since he brought her to Washington; to be touching him now disrupts her careful cool. Unshed tears blur her vision as she raises her chin to see he's smiling softly under perplexed eyebrows.

"Never," he says solemnly.

There's no kiss. No tearful reconciliation. A short second of tenderness to reassure her that all is not, in fact, lost. Then the moment's over.

He lifts his hand from her shoulder and steps back, putting precious inches between them. To Cora, it may as well be a mile. But her practical side reminds her of why she came here in the first place. That whole Otherworld invasion thing.

She takes a clearing breath, then asks, "So, what do we do now?"

Jack picks up the New York dossier from his desk. "Now," he says with grim satisfaction, "we force Agent 99's hand."

She doesn't get nervous until they're halfway down the hall. In all her time as an agent-in-training, the sole contact she's had with the upper echelons has been with Jack, whom she doesn't count, and a letter signed by Agent 100 welcoming her to the force. That she's about to walk into 99's office completely unprepared is freaking her out. Agents talk about him like he's a gold-hoarding dragon or wisdom-dispensing sage. Cora's hands sweat as she thinks about how many ways she can screw up this meeting. She's convinced that she's the exactly sort of shit-disturbing whippersnapper who pushes all the wrong buttons on an old-fashioned guy like Patel.

Jack walks beside her, offering no solace whatsoever with his silence. Cora can practically see the black clouds forming over his brow, so she keeps quiet. When they reach the oversized wooden door—one of three offices on this floor — he doesn't pushes his way into the office without knocking, his sparse frame held at aggressive right angles. The room is oddly dark, and the contrast to the bright hallway dazzles Cora as she steps in behind him. It reminds her of their meeting with Azrael in Cloud Nine, which could've gone better. Probably best to let Jack lead so she doesn't cram her foot in her mouth. Again.

The man at the desk looks like a modern Indian Santa Claus with his cropped white hair and generous paunch tucked under a slick suit. He raises his head serenely when the door clicks shut, and he starts to greet them, but Jack cuts him off.

"Agent 6 has something to report," he nearly growls.

Anxiety crashes over Cora. It's completely against protocol. No way should she be addressing 99 at her rank, even with a Ninety standing next to her.

"What?" she croaks.

Jack steps aside to reveal her to Agent 99 who raises his bushy eyebrows expectantly. Cora swallows the sandpaper in her throat, clasps her hands behind her back in the official reporting stance, and moves up to the desk. Deep breath.

"Sir, Agent 21 and I have returned from New York City following an investigation into an alleged narcotics violation. We discovered the drug called "creed" is in nationwide circulation, with the potential for a level six breach if not contained within approximately sixty days. Samples are with forensics now, and Agent 33 should have toxicology results by tomorrow afternoon."

She pauses for an acknowledgment or a question but gets silence instead. She resists the urge to look to Jack for help. If he's thrown her to the lion, she's going to make the most of it. She shifts her gaze from the wall behind Agent 99 to his steely hazel eyes. Anxiety winds around her gut like razor wire around a panicked rabbit. But she continues to wait. She doesn't know what else to say.

The silence ringing in Cora's ears is deafening by the time Patel speaks. To Jack.

"While that is a succinct report of what appears to be good work, Agent 97, I fail to see how it warrants such a violent intrusion and flagrant disregard for standard practices."

"Finish your report, Agent 6," Jack says.

A million details crowd Cora's mind, desperately trying to assemble themselves into a coherent explanation. And a fresh flicker of doubt is making it harder.

Jack said he's been hounding 99 for months to no avail. While she's pissed at the guy for ghosting on her, she does trust him, though they've known each other less than a year. Why wouldn't his boss of over a decade trust him, too?

Eventually, she realizes she's squinting hard at nothing and remembers to breathe. The influx of oxygen brings back her common sense. If Patel's hiding something, he probably has a good reason. He's in charge, and she owes him the truth, even if she's imagining shadows everywhere.

"It appears the intent is to artificially boost belief levels for the Faerie realm and the Mistress they meet there," she says. "We believe it's related to an Otherworld plot to invade the mortal world, spearheaded by the goddess Eris and supported by an unknown number of allies." Her eyes flick to Jack. "I understand that Agent 97 has already briefed you on this information."

Again, 99 speaks past Cora to Jack. A hot spark ignites in her chest at the blatant brushoff, the familiar smolder of Irish temper.

"Explain."

"I've explained it a dozen times, sir," Jack says. "But now we've got a concrete lead." He drops the creed folder on 99's desk.

They wait while Patel peruses the case's summary page. The one Cora wrote herself that includes a description of the potential ties to Eris.

When 99 finishes, he returns his attention to Jack. But to Cora's alarm, Jack takes a step back, leaving her exposed.

"I'd suggest you address Agent 6 directly," he says. "She conducted the New York investigation and was a vital participant in uncovering the Otherworld threat. I understand that she hasn't completed her SCD orientation, but she deserves a modicum of respect."

Agent 99's expression doesn't waver, but he shifts his eyes from Jack to Cora. And waits.

Indignation at being ignored has burned up most of her nerves by now, and her voice is steady as she connects the dots for him. "Creed use coincides directly with the rash of missing persons reports. We believe Eris is the Mistress and that she's using Mab's established drug connections to transport users into Faerie where they're forced to believe what they see, raising background belief levels. The goal appears to be to pierce the Gauntlet or remove it altogether."

No one moves or speaks. Patel gives a long blink, waiting.

All in.

Cora grips her hands tighter behind her back and takes a deep breath. "If I can speak freely, sir, it would be an epically huge mistake to not investigate all facets of this case. At the very least, the drug ring needs to be shut down. It's interfering with mundanes, and if it does turn out to be connected to our allegations about Eris, it can't be allowed to continue."

"I agree."

Both agents on the other side of the desk stare at Agent 99 in amazement.

"You do?" Cora says.

"I do. The potential imbalance caused by creed usage warrants cessation of the drug's production at minimum. It's our duty to investigate. And if, in the course of your assignment, you encounter any actual proof of your—" he hooks two fingers in the air "—Otherworld invasion theory, more's the better."

Jack steps to Cora's side. "You mean for me to go personally, sir?" he says.

"Naturally."

"Very well." He straightens to his full height, repositioning himself as the dutiful servant rather than an angry employee. "I can leave as soon as Thirty-Three returns the tox results and Seventy-Five issues my field kit. I'd estimate no later than seventeen-hundred hours tomorrow."

Agent 99's straight-line mouth curls up on one end. "Oh no, my friend, you won't be going alone. Given the unfortunate events near the end of your previous mission, you require a partner. Or have you forgotten what happens when you're taken down on the job? You're two for two in the last year."

The bitter shift in Jack's energy drops Cora's own temperature from mere proximity. She shivers and wonders what happened to warrant a mandatory escort the first time if last time it took a halberd through the chest to do him in.

With exaggerated patience, Jack says, "No, sir, I haven't forgotten. But there are no other agents available for field work at present, and the drug ring is still my case."

"I'll go."

The words are out of Cora's mouth faster than she could think them. Both men are staring at her now—one startled, the other smug.

"I'll go," she says again. Reasons tumble out, her eyes fixed on Agent 99. "My knowledge of Faerie is extensive, and I'm currently unassigned. I've also been promised specialized sidestepper training since before I arrived, and I have off-plane experience."

"And your relationship to Agent 97?"

The question trips her, but she holds it together.

"We're colleagues, sir," she says stiffly. "I'd go so far as to say we're friends. But that seems a benefit in the field rather than a drawback."

He nods. "An astute observation, Agent 6. You will be assigned as Ninety-Seven's guardian for this mission." Cora's about to thank him, but he continues. "However, Agent 21 must also accompany you, given your lack of full credentials. You're currently on probation, and as your mentor, she is responsible for you."

"Sir, there's no reason...," Jack starts to protest.

But 99 shakes his head. "Either you accept this compromise or postpone your investigation until another agent comes available. The choice is yours."

Cora breaks her visual grip on him to look at Jack. The muscles in his jaw are clenched, accentuating his cheekbones until they're knives under the skin. She makes a mental note to ask Sofi what the hell she did to him to piss him off that bad.

"Yes, sir," is all he says.

Agent 99 nods his acknowledgment, then stands to dismiss them. "Good hunting, agents. I look forward to reading your report when you return."

Jack spins on his heel and strides into the hall without a word. Cora squeaks out a "thank you, sir" in 99's direction before rushing to follow him. She can feel the boss' eyes against her back before the door swings shut behind them. It makes her skin crawl and tugs on her earlier doubts about the boss' motivations.

One thing at a time, though. With the immediate

threats of confronting Jack and then 99 out of her way, another emergency is now free to demand her attention.

Her eyes widen as she remembers what she'd forgotten to share in the meeting. The ding of the elevator's arrival is a starting pistol signaling her to sprint down the hallway. She's got to catch Jack before the doors close—he's definitely going to want to hear about this.

NINE

Jack leans against the railing inside the elevator and lets his breath out in a long, controlled stream. The cool steel feels good, leeching out his aggravation. Finally, 99 listened. Finally, movement forward.

But another part of him isn't so relieved. *After all this time trying to convince him, don't you think he agreed a little too easily?*

His eyes narrow at the unsettling thought. He'd noticed Cora's hesitation to divulge more information to Patel, but he'd brushed it off as nerves. He smirks. Hell, if she could've seen the first time he reported to 99, she'd know how admirably she handled herself. He's proud of her for it. But could she have picked up on something he didn't? He can't rule that out.

Shaking his head, he punches the button for the underground parking lot. He'll feel better after a good night's sleep.

There's a musical chime, and the elevator doors start to close. Before they meet, a hand slaps between them. Instantly, he's on the alert, body tensed and senses balled up for a fight. Then the doors part and Cora's standing there with a wild look in her eyes.

"Wait a sec," she pants. "We need to talk."

His nerves, unclenching after realizing there's no threat, kick him in the teeth again. The computer in his mind tabulates a dozen interpretations of that sentence, each one stickier than the last. He knows he owes her more than a touch and a vague reassurance, but he'd wanted to wait until after this case when they'd have time to do it properly. He definitely didn't want to have this conversation in an elevator.

He attempts a smile, and she steps in, the doors closing behind her. She glances around the metal box suspiciously as it descends. It's such a strange behavior for what he thinks they're about to discuss that it derails him.

"What are you—" he starts.

"Are we being recorded?" she asks.

He nods minutely. There's a tiny microphone and camera in nearly every corner of the building as part of the government's treaty with supernaturals: a dedicated police force in exchange for constant monitoring. It's supposed to be top secret. The only reason Jack knows about it is from dealing with the NSA's accusations of system tampering. Their inability to comprehend that some SCD employees don't appear on recordings is an ongoing battle.

Cora narrows her eyes and nods back, keeping silent for the rest of the ride. It's barely ten seconds, but it's long enough for her unique fragrance of cotton, leather, and blue-tinted energy to find him. When they exit into the heated garage, Jack's mind is pleasantly fuzzy with it. He gulps fresh air like a drowning man and wonders if he'll ever acclimatize to her.

They walk together, Jack leading as he heads for his car, and she waits for the elevator doors to fully close before she speaks again.

"I was at the Roosevelt the other day," she whispers. "Arachne showed me a tapestry she made but doesn't remember doing. It's completely not her usual style. All stick figures and crude symbols. It could be nothing, but I can't shake feeling that it's important."

Worries about a relationship talk see-saw to make room for worries about saving the world.

"What was on it?"

"A figure wearing a crown with a sword in their hand, surrounded by a handful of other people, standing over a crowd. There was a kind of shiny wall between the two groups." She pauses thoughtfully, then says, "All contained in what I'd swear was the outline of an apple."

Jack soaks up the details as they walk, letting the sound of their slick-soled shoes echo until they reach his vehicle, a battered but lovingly-maintained cherry red Alfa Romeo Stradale. He digs in his suit jacket for the keys while his mind scans through volumes of data. Out of the corner of his eye, he notices Cora sizing up the car.

"Don't like it?" he says without turning.

"It's, uh, nice." She pats the trunk lid with the affection of a dainty grandmother introduced to a filthy stray cat. "Very retro."

He chuckles. "A polite way of saying it's old and ugly."

"No! Not what I meant at all."

Now he does turn. He puts his back to the car door and leans against it, smiling at her as she turns pink. "It's fine. I know she's a little strange, but I love her anyway."

A pregnant pause tells him he said something unintentionally meaningful. Fortunately, the mental background processes working on Archne's tapestry throw out a result and let him steer the conversation back to where it should've stayed.

"From what you've said, it sounds like Arachne's been a victim of involuntary augury." She gives him a blank look. "It happens when supernals interfere with fate. They choose someone, either supernatural or mundane, and give them a vision they can't not broadcast."

"Why Arachne?"

His eyebrows scrunch together as he considers it. "I think whoever sent the information knew you'd be at the right place at the right time. They wanted you, specifically, to see it."

"Do you think it was Hel? Or maybe we've got allies we don't know about."

While it's comforting to think there are others on their side, Jack's getting the disturbing feeling it might be too little, too late.

Do not abandon hope, the voice of Ishtar whispers in his mind. You cannot see the shape of things to come. And then she's gone again.

He straightens and forces out the despondent thought. All that's standing in the way of Eris' plans is him and Cora. He's got to keep it together, but the waters are getting too muddy. They need another, wiser mind to intervene.

"Let's keep this between us until after the Faerie investigation," he says. "When we get back, I'll go to the Lorekeeper and see what he thinks. There's ample prophecy going around to make it worth his time."

Cora's face lights up. "Can I go with you?" she asks.

The breathy excitement of the question stirs his blood, but he shakes his head. "I'm not sure I'll be able to get clearance to go myself. The paperwork's approved by Ninety-Nine, and you saw what he thinks of our theory."

The light goes off as quickly as it came on. A defeated "oh" is all she says. He makes a mental note to get her a temporary pass when he applies for his own. It'd be a nice surprise, at the very least.

Neither of them knows what to say after that, so Jack takes the initiative. He pointedly checks his watch, then says, "It's getting late. I'd better head home, big day tomorrow. For you, too." He gives her a somewhat apologetic look. "If you need anything, don't hesitate to call. I promise I'll answer."

She nods a bit sullenly, then heads back to the elevator. "See you tomorrow," she calls over her shoulder.

He smiles as he watches her go. A series of creaks as he climbs into the driver's seat provides an overture to the rumbling roar of the engine as he turns the key. But whatever positive emotions he's been riding drain away as he climbs the garage ramp to street level, heading to his apartment for a long night of anticipation and doubt.

"Absolutely fucking not."

"I don't think you have a choice, Sofi."

"I can go argue with Patel or something. I can't go on this trip. Not with him."

Cora sits on the low-slung IKEA couch in Sofi's living room as her mentor paces the floor in blindingly pink pajamas. She was tucked up in bed when Cora arrived, and it'd taken a significantly longer to rouse her than Cora thinks is healthy. More like hibernating than sleeping. Once she'd gotten on her feet and processed the news about her dubious honor as Jack's babysitter, though, Sofi literally started growling. Agitation pours off her as she strides around, making Cora uneasy, too.

"I don't see what the big deal is," Cora says, gnawing her thumbnail. "I know you've never been off plane before, but it doesn't matter who it's with, right? I mean, he's just a dude." A dude who's three steps from running the agency, can bend interdimensional space, and is part werewolf. But she keeps that to herself.

Sofi gesticulates her frustration, knocking into a table lamp. "Anybody but him. You can't trust that motherfucker."

It stings though it's not aimed at her. Cora's struggled with how much to trust Jack herself, so she's got some empathy. But today put her firmly back on his side, and now she's feeling defensive. She also remembers how poorly Jack reacted when 99 insisted on Sofi's inclusion. Suspicion and curiosity finally build enough momentum that she has to ask.

"You know," she says, dropping her hand and narrowing her eyes, "he had pretty much the same reaction about you. What the hell happened between you guys?"

Sofi stops abruptly at the far side of the room and stares at Cora, blue eyes like whirlpools. Cora's shocked by the anger in them, goosebumps rising on the back of her neck like a dumb prey animal. She's seen Sofi frustrated, annoyed, and even downright bitchy, but she's always thought of her as a good-natured, fun-loving girl. Now she's wondering if she's about to get jumped.

But the danger passes. Sofi's face falls, her shoulders bow, and she leans against the entertainment center, crossing her arms over her chest as if trying to hug herself. She takes a deep breath with a soft, ursine rumble and holds it for a long time. When she finally exhales, she's Sofi again.

Cora wants to comfort her, then thinks better of

it. There's a barrier between them, one of those touchy-feely lines she's not sure how to navigate with new friends. Instead, she stays put and twists her fingers together as she waits for Sofi to talk again.

When she does, it's with a bitter harshness Cora's never heard before.

"The short version is that Jack killed my best friend. She was nineteen," she says. "Back when he was Agent 97 and not a real person. Chased her down like a dog. She was terrified. All she wanted was to figure out how to be happy." Sofi sniffs and wipes at her face. "He didn't care. He had a job to do. And when she died trying to escape, he walked away as if nothing had happened."

The brutality of the accusation hits Cora's heart like a hot iron plunged in cold water. There's no way that the man she knows—the one who protects at all costs, literally falls on swords for others—would kill someone in the cold-blooded way Sofi's suggesting. Especially not a kid.

Quietly, she says, "That can't be true."

Before the last word is out, the predator rises up again, and Sofi advances, fingers twisted into rigid claws of anger. Cora shrinks against the threadbare couch cushions as if they might provide her some protection.

"You weren't there!" Sofi bellows. "You don't know who he used to be! You didn't see how he turned up everywhere and refused to be a human being and fucking walked away when he saw Zara wasn't a threat anymore! All he cares about is the job—not people, not himself, and he certainly doesn't care about you!"

Cora's face burns with shame and fear. She puts a hand over her mouth to stop herself from saying anything more; it's too late for an apology.

Sofi leans over to close the last few inches between them, pressing in so close that her stale breath sours Cora's universe. "I'll go on this godforsaken assignment because I have to," she whispers dangerously, "and I'm even willing to let your bullshit slide because you're a goddamn redneck talking about shit she doesn't understand. But don't you fucking dare try to make him out to be a good guy."

Cora nods mutely, eyes wide. Sofi disengages, shuffling out of attack range. But Cora can't move. She's rooted to the couch, the guilty weight of Sofi's story pinning her down. There's got to be something she can do. Maybe she can take it back. Maybe....

But Sofi's not having it. "Get the fuck out of here," she snaps, then disappears into her darkened bedroom.

Cora bolts. She practically flies the four blocks to her own apartment, tears of fear and shame freezing to her cheeks in the frostbitten air.

TEN

The following afternoon finds Cid Flyneheart, Agent 75 and SCD quartermaster, spraying a fire extinguisher over his latest project, ruining the entire thing and sending him back to square one. He tidied the lab yesterday, but now it looks like the Stay-Puft Marshmallow Man took a dump on his workbench.

Another bomb. Not literally this time, at least. It'll be a while before he works up the nerve to tamper with hoodoo charms again.

Maybe it's the Skrillex playing in the background that soured it. The ghost camera project liked electronica, but maybe this essence scrubber for wishing well pennies is more into Disney tunes. Makes sense. There should be an Aladdin cassette kicking around here. Unless he used the tape to bind that iPad gremlin....

Cid sighs heavily and blows a wispy black curl off his glasses. As much as he loves his job, the "getting to know you" phase of a project is exasperating. His supernatural talent for communing with machinery has made him an indispensable SCD asset; physics and mechanics are his psychology and biology. Equations he never learned in school let him understand, deconstruct, engineer, and optimize nearly anything with moving parts. He doesn't just keep track of the agency's specialized equipment— he invented most of it.

So the fact that this essence scrubber's metaphorically giving him the finger is pissing him right off.

He whispers nastily to the mess on the table. "What do you want?"

"I'd sort of hoped you had a gun for me," replies a voice from behind him.

There's a metallic click in the resulting pause.

"Not that one, if it's the same to you."

It takes a second for Cid to realize who's speaking. When he does, he lowers his arm bashfully, along with the gun he'd automatically aimed behind him, without looking, at the visitor's forehead.

It's only Jack.

The quartermaster slots his gun back into its shoulder harness and leans right, nudging his mobility dock to rotate around. The machine is his own design: part wheelchair, part Segway, and a hefty dose of biomechanical enchantment. While it's not a substitute for working legs, it's damn close.

"Ah, Agent 97," he says with a smile, holding out

a grease-spotted hand as he rolls toward Jack. "Always good to see you. Been a while. Getting ready to perpetrate some new level of badassery, I take it?"

Jack laughs, which Cid's certain he's never seen before. His machinist's mind is delighted at the novelty, making him wonder if he can replicate the expression. There's a pixie AI half-built in the storage closet he can play with. If he could touch Jack's face....

But he resists the urge to put his hands on the man who restrained a centaur without weapons or magic, even if it is in the name of science. Sounds like a fast track to being all the way paralyzed.

"Where you headed this time?" he asks as they shake hands.

The smile dissolves faster than it arrived. "Faerie," Jack says. The tone couldn't be flatter if he'd run over it with a steamroller.

Cid pretends not to notice. "Ooh, tricky business. I got you covered, though."

"You always do."

Jack follows the quartermaster's lead toward general equipment. Cid's section of the SCD building is long and narrow, containing an odd combination of spaces. There's the experimental machinery lab, the weaponry development area, a magic safe-disposal booth, and the agent equipment storage closets, not to mention his personal workbench. It adds up to a lot of junk in tight quarters, but Cid's arranged it expertly for ease of navigation in the standing dock. He's not anxious to tip over again; once was plenty.

When they reach the gear cabinet, which occupies an entire wall, Cid holds up a warning hand to Jack, and the senior agent obediently reverses a full stride. Once he's out of the danger radius, Cid tugs open the door and braces himself for impact. But there's no avalanche of equipment—this time. Both men exhale with relief, and Cid reaches into the overstuffed middle shelf to retrieve a small black canvas bag. The muffled clink of glass against metal echoes against the hard surfaces of the lab.

"Here you go," he says, handing the bundle to Jack. "One standard Faerie field kit, all packed and ready to go."

Jack takes the materials in one hand and holds out the other. "Actually, Cid, I need three today."

Black wiry eyebrows shoot up in curiosity. "That so?"

He hands over two additional packages without pressing further. He's been here two years now and long since learned there's not much point in asking why. The answer, at least with Agent 97, is always "classified."

So when Jack volunteers the information, to say Cid's surprised is an understatement. "Agent 99's assigned me a handler," Jack mutters, shaking his head. "And a handler for the handler."

"No effing way," Cid breathes. He knows he sounds like a cheerleader hearing a friend's been knocked up by a teacher, but he's fairly confident Jack doesn't notice. Besides, how else is he supposed to react?

The senior agent nods, a well-worn crease in his brow all that indicates he feels anything about the situation. Cid's heard rumors about 97's "miraculous transformation" since his hiatus, though some things apparently haven't changed.

"It's fine," Jack insists. "But I'll need you to give these girls the kit rundown before we leave. I can't be holding their hands every step of the way."

Cid doesn't make the obvious joke about holding girls' hands. Any other agent, maybe, but not this guy. Instead, he simply nods and slides over to the clearest workbench. He's unrolling one of the field kits when the lab doors slide apart and two rather small women stride in.

What comes next is the most basic expression of his abilities. He's never been able to control it, and up until he was sixteen, he thought everyone's mind worked this way. Mathematical formulas spin across his vision, writing themselves into ratios and measurements, proportions and power distributions, forming complex systems into data. Within seconds, he knows each woman's body's mechanics—how they walk, approximate age, how much they can lift, and yes, their bust size.

"Take a picture, it'll last longer," sneers the blond girl, whom he recognizes as Sofi when she gets closer. The red-haired woman snickering at the jibe is a stranger, though.

Cid clears his throat and blinks with embarrassment. "Sorry, sorry," he mutters. "Can't help it."

The two cross to where Jack stands next to the metal worktable, and introductions are made. "This is Cora Riley, Agent 6, sidestepper. She's shadowing Agent 21." He dips his head toward Cid. "Riley, this is Cid Flyneheart, Agent 75, quartermaster and machinist."

Cid shakes Cora's hand, noting the strength of her grip. "A shame we haven't met yet, Riley. Ordinarily, I get a day or two with rookies for equipment briefings and special marksmanship training, but given the insane caseload, I've barely had time to sleep, much less do anything fun."

"What, you don't count building spy gadgets and blowing up faulty wands as fun?" Sofi says. He returns the sass with a playful sneer. He can never tell if she's flirting, but he'd like to get his foot in the door. Metaphorically, anyway.

Cora releases his hand with a dismissive shrug. "You probably wouldn't want me as a student, Flyneheart. I shot my instructor at Quantico while trying to clear a jam. In the leg, but still."

"On purpose or on accident?"

"The report says accident, but it could have been on purpose. He had a wandering hands problem."

He laughs. "Well, once you get back from this assignment, we'll give it a whirl. Firearms training is somewhat different here."

"I should freaking hope so," she says.

There's a moment where they're smiling at each other, which is broken by Jack emphatically clearing his throat. "Can we get back to the task at hand?" he says, "We've got a lot of work to do."

Cid nods. "Sorry, boss." If he didn't know better, he'd think the guy was jealous.

"Agent 6," he says, turning his attention to the unrolled canvas bag on the table, "this is your field equipment. It's standard issue for away missions, plus extras designed especially for work in Faerie."

He's about to start explaining the individual items when there's a sound like a wasp trapped in soda can. It hums for several seconds before Jack dips into his pants pocket and retrieves a vibrating phone. Cid shoots him a dirty look; one thing he can't abide, it's technological rudeness, especially in his own lab. But Jack doesn't notice. He ducks into the hallway, phone pressed to his ear, muttering something about forensics.

Cid waits until the automatic doors glide shut behind him before continuing his briefing.

"This is all basic stuff," he says of the left side of the kit. "Two extra clips for your sidearm, mace, cuffs. No surprises here, although the electronics won't work on the other side. Might as well leave your phones, radios, and flashlights here. But this," he says with professional pride, "is where it gets fun. Stop me if you have questions." He points at each item on the right side as he names them. "Cold iron clip, six shots. Honeyed cream. Music box."

Sofi raises her hand at the last one. "Wait, what's that for?"

Before he can respond, Cora's answering. "Faeries and elves love music. Not sure what the belief flux has changed, but in traditional folklore, you could stop them dead in their tracks with a good tune."

"Well, I'll be damned," Cid says, breaking into an impressed smile. "Excellent, Agent 6, that's absolutely right. Some of the old ways have stayed true, thanks to folks like you, though you're right to be cautious. The last time we had an agent on that side was three years ago when Agent 57 went native. Who knows what's changed since then?"

He rolls up the case, then hands the bundle to Cora and its mate to Sofi. "I don't think you'll need any of this stuff while you're gone, but it sounds like if you do, you've got it under control."

"Wait, that's it?" Cora says, looking disdainfully at the kit. "I thought there'd be more James Bond gadgets. A garrotte watch or a rocket cigarette or a homing pill or something cool."

Cid chuckles. "Sorry to disappoint you, Six. While I've certainly got some of that stuff kicking around here, this isn't that kind of assignment." He winks slyly. "Better luck next time."

"There better be," snarks Sofi. "Honeyed cream is hardly a cool gadget. Hell, it's not even a good snack."

Always thinking with her stomach, this one. "If you're that worried about food," he says, wheeling to the lab fridge and digging in the crisper, "take this. Can't hurt to have provisions, right?" He tosses her the brown paper bag containing his lunch.

Sofi catches it with a wink and says, "Thanks, Cid. You're a peach," then tucks the bag into her field kit.

Dammit—he was being sarcastic. Now what's he

supposed to eat today?

The girls are packing up as Jack strides back into the lab, ringing off whatever important conversation he'd been having.

"Got it. Thanks." Jack pockets the phone and says, "That was Agent 33 in forensics. As far as they're able to tell, the key ingredient in creed is definitely of Fae origin, so we're on the right track. Toxicology and horticulture resources say we're looking for ergot."

Cora's forehead creases. "Wait, like *The Crucible* ergot? That hallucinogenic, LSD fungus crap?"

Everyone turns to look at her.

"What?" she says, reddening under their combined stare. "Didn't anyone else wonder how the witch trials started?"

Sofi snorts. "Not enough to do actual homework, you nerd."

Jack smirks but continues in his usual professional way. "Thirty Three said it's probably being cultured on short-grain rye. Assuming they're holding true to standard Fae patterns, it'll be in a centralized field. They aren't brilliant planners."

"If you're looking to raze crops, then you might need this," Cid chimes in.

He guides his rig to a glass-fronted cabinet near his personal workbench and lifts out an antique amber bottle, which he hands to Cora. She holds it up to the light, tilting the contents to see the morphing, fluid glob inside. He grins at the agents' intrigued expressions. Figuring out how to manufacture the real thing without magic took over a year, and he's proud of his handiwork.

"Greek fire?" Cora says after a moment.

"Exactly!" he crows. "Super impressive. Not many newbies know as much about mythology as you do. You're a lucky girl, Agent 6."

He doesn't miss the lightning-quick glance at Jack. He shoots his own questioning look to Sofi who shrugs. Odd.

"If you say so, Cid," Cora chuckles as she tucks the bottle into her field kit. "All that storybook knowledge is taking up space that could've been used to cure cancer."

He makes a tutting sound. "I think you'll find it's more helpful than you ever imagined."

She gives him a strange look but doesn't reply. Jack fills the gap in the conversation. The guy seriously cannot deal with small talk.

"We need to get moving. Riley, Strella—you ready to go?"

Both women nod, and he nods back. To Cid, he says, "See you soon, Seventy-Five."

"Good hunting," the quartermaster says, waving as they leave. Then, almost to himself, he adds, "You'll need it."

The doors on this side of the Gauntlet aren't the same as the doors on the other side. In the real world, they rely on magical intervention to exist. They're created, kept open, moved, and closed by a combination of emotional resonance, background magic, and rituals. The only influence mundanes have is whether or not they blunder into one. On the Otherworld side, though, doors are building blocks of the universe with all the complex rules that entails.

Sadly, that's pretty much all Cora knows about sidestepping since discovering her powers. And she learned it from a battered, handwritten tome delivered anonymously to her DC apartment. She likes to think Jack sent the book, but when she braved asking him, he denied it. He knows about it, of course—he wrote the recent pages himself—but it's supposed to be confined to the restricted section of the SCD library. It holds centuries of collected knowledge of sidestepping and is believed to be the lone existing textbook on the subject. Too bad it's half destroyed, most of the pages smudged, worn, burnt, drowned, or erased. What a pity. She's cried more about that than from homesickness and bruised ribs combined.

Weeks of fruitless study later, she's standing in the stark white Interdimensional Staging Room, sandwiched between Jack and Sofi, getting ready to use her powers as if she's been through months of grueling trials to perfect them.

The performance anxiety makes her want to hurl. She takes some comfort in having raised the sensor circle at the Smithsonian, but opening interworld doorways is a whole different ballgame. A treacherous part of her is convinced she can't do it. So many stories go that way. The hero discovers their magical powers, which come from being tormented or pure, then the instant they're healed or tainted, their power dries up. Mythologically speaking, there's a super high chance that the end result of her underworld quest wasn't to grant her wish for specialness but to take it from her.

Cora shakes her head to dislodge the thought, and Sofi squeezes her hand gently.

"You okay?" she asks with genuine concern.

Cora had been worried about coming to work this morning after their blowout, but there's been no sign of the defensive rage Sofi turned on her last night. They met in the bullpen at nine, went over case files, ate lunch together, even had a bit of a gossip about Manny's relative hotness compared to the DC crew. It's like nothing ever happened. Cora's not sure if they're okay, the incident forgiven and forgotten, or if Sofi's laying a professional veneer over a wound in their friendship. Either way, in this uncertain moment, it's comforting to know her mamma bear is still looking out for her.

"Yeah, I'm cool," Cora says. She knows she's radiating fear, but Mom taught her how to maintain an unflappable façade. Sort of. She lifts her chin and gives Sofi a wan smile.

Another squeeze on her hand. The one Jack's holding. The gesture's platonic, but she can't deny the tingle is generates under her ribs.

"It's exactly the same as the 'step we made from the Hunting Hall," he says, low and reassuring. "It's nothing you haven't done before. In fact, it should be easier now. You're familiar with the person we're carrying along, and we're not fleeing for our lives. The energy will be more stable." He gives her hand another squeeze. This time, she squeezes back. Their eyes meet, and he gives her a small, private smile. "You'll be fine."

Cora nods and exhales sharply, turning her attention forward. Even with Jack's encouragement, she feels a bit of a fool standing in an empty room preparing to walk face-first into a blank wall.

The Interdimensional Staging Room is one of a handful of permanent doorways on this side of the Gauntlet, established by Jack shortly after he signed on with the agency and tinkered with later by Cid. When Jack explained it on the way from the lab, she'd imagined a magic-powered Holodeck. Which isn't far off from reality. Because there's so much built-up supernatural energy in the SCD wing of the Hoover building, Jack and Cid discovered it could be corralled and focused, creating an invisible tether to the Otherworld. When they built the doorframe—a rectangular arch made of a classified alloy of legendary metals—it amplified and enhanced Jack's door-seeking powers within the room. As a result, a sidestepper using the ISR can bring destination doors to them instead of taking their chances in the wild. Provided they've got US government clearance and forms signed in triplicate, of course.

On either side of her, Sofi's grip tightens and Jack's relaxes. They refused to stand next to each other, leaving Cora in the middle. A pretty metaphor, if she thinks too hard about it. She takes a deep breath and squeezes both their hands.

"Let's do this," she says.

There's a visible cerulean glow as she pools her energy with Jack's, creating a circuit between them. A rush of endorphins fills her veins with fizzy syrup; the polar opposite of the violent, fear-filled leap of the last time they 'stepped together. This time, it's an insinuation of one person into another. A phantom breeze blows through the room, carrying saffron and coriander notes. She grips Jack's hand tighter.

"Ready?" asks Jack. Cora wonders if the huskiness she hears is real or wishful thinking on her part.

"Ready," says Sofi.

Cora says nothing. He knows.

One, two, three.

Step.

There's no movement, yet they move. Floor to grass, central heating to warm breeze, ceiling to sky, walls to trees. DC to Faerie.

ELEVEN

Everything's the same as when Jack left ten years ago. The grass in the clearing is the same impossible emerald, the sky the same unthinkable blue. The sun is bright but not scorching, and the flowers are so lush they'd make a devoted gardener faint from envy. Pure and perfect, reflecting the collective belief of mankind about what it means to look upon Faerie. Vast and hyper-real.

Sadly, he can't enjoy it. The second after the sidestep likely comes off as disorientation, but it's the time it takes to reswallow his coffee as old, familiar magic washes over him, turning his stomach. The faded green triskelion tattoo at the small of his back crackles to life the instant his feet touch the ground, the brand calling his name in a building song only he can hear.

The land remembers him.

But there's no time to dwell on it. That same

second is all he's got to process the scene they've jumped into.

Four faeries lounging on a tapestry nearby watch the three agents that have interrupted their picnic, gray eyes like street lamps in fog. They're practically identical, naked and unashamed with royal blue skin and willowy frames. One of the picnickers, apple-sized strawberry raised to his lips, tilts his head in curiosity but doesn't rise. He murmurs to his companions, and they titter like popular girls gossiping, revealing perfectly white, razor-sharp teeth. The casually cruel lords and ladies of Faerie.

Jack ignores the tingling from his tattoo and steps forward. Cora and Sofi don't move, likely shaken from the 'step and reorienting themselves. Fine by him. He can already tell something's not right. Back in Agent 57's day, the Fae would've been respectfully on their feet in the presence of authority by now. Maybe everything isn't the same after all.

He reaches into his jacket for his badge, purposely holding it open to reveal the cold iron clip at his belt. It doesn't have the desired effect, though. They should sense the nearness of their bane and cringe, even at range. Instead, the four continue to watch him with amused grins. Jack adds it to the growing list of suspicious behavior as he raises his badge.

"I am Agent 97 of the Supernatural Cases Division of the FBI," he says, looking to each of the Fae as he speaks. "Behind me are Agents 21 and 6.

We're here on an official investigation."

The female Fae turns to the strawberry-holder and says something in a lilting, lyrical tongue. High Fae. It's one of the few languages Jack's been unable to pick up, but you don't need to understand the words to hear sarcasm. His anger is a shotgun blast to his chest, using the magical tug of his faerie brand for fuel, but he forces it down with a heavy breath. Not yet. Suspicion isn't enough. More information required.

He tries again, using the faerie language he did learn. *"You are required by Interworld law to assist in our inquiries,"* he says. *"You will address us in English or in Low Fae, and you will afford us the respect that is due to us by the rules of decorum."*

That shuts them up, though there's whispering behind him between the other agents. Let them talk. He can explain later.

The strawberry-eater, whom Jack pegs as the alpha, narrows his eyes, then nods to the other three. They unfold from their languid postures on the ground and come forward to form a tight line about ten feet away. Up close, Jack can see further differences in the Fae. They're taller—perhaps eight feet—and tattooed with gold spirals that cover their arms and legs. An air of unpredictability clings to them. They're more their true selves now, less what humans invented for them. The results of an influx of controlled belief, courtesy of creed.

Fae and man size up one another, then the ringleader speaks in clipped, accented English.

"What do you want, mortal?"

"We are investigating an alleged narcotics operation in the area. We need to ask you some questions."

There's a subtle shift in their collective posture. A little weight shifted, the twitch of a hand, a tilt of the head. From spiteful to suspicious. Not good.

"That sounds like a human problem. That is no concern of ours."

"The Avalon Treaty contains provisions requiring denizens of both the Otherworld and Perat to assist in pursuit of any alleged violations." He allows an iron edge into his voice. "You will answer our questions or face consequences."

They laugh. All four of them. A full-throated, melodious sound, showing their teeth and tongues. It makes Jack's fingers itch to put that special clip to his gun, but he sticks to the book. For now.

He waits for the laughter to subside, then presses on. "Where is the ergot field?"

"You wish to see plants, mortal?" The leader throws out an arm at the wildflower-speckled field. "There are many in this place to enjoy." He smirks. "Perhaps you should sit down and join us while you take in the scenery?"

It's a Call, the last sentence edged with the harmonics of an order, demanding he do what he's told. This motherfucker just used Faerie magic on him. It cranks up the volume of the song sung by his brand, and he wonders if Cora and Sofi can see it glowing under his jacket. It feels like it's visible from space. With gritted teeth, he shoves aside the yearning to comply; he worked too hard to escape this place to let it reclaim him this easily.

Cora and Sofi step to either side of him in the tense space, closing rank and forming a line of their own. Three agents in black suits against four faeries in blue nothing.

"You think that's funny, Faerie-Boy?" Cora says. She leans over to speak to Sofi across Jack. "Attempting to coerce an agent with mental magic is technically assault on an officer, right, Agent 21?"

Sofi nods, shades masking her expression. "That's correct, Agent 6."

She can sense the magic, Jack thinks. She probably doesn't know that's not normal. How is she doing it?

The distraction breaks the Fae's concentration, and he turns his focus from Jack to Cora. He stares daggers at her, then sneers, "You cannot threaten me, half-breed. Not in this place." He takes a challenging step forward, flexing twiggy fingers.

The other three Fae don't look as sure as their leader. They whisper amongst themselves, eyes crawling over Cora. But before she can ask the question broadcast across her face, Jack steps back in. Now's not the time for that conversation.

"Since you refuse to cooperate, I have to ask that you clear the area so we can make our way to the queen's court at the Waterfall Court."

There's an arm's length between Jack and the ringleader now, and the promise of imminent violence crackles the air. A lightning calculation of the situation flashes through his mind. Their odds are good—unless the amplified background magic has changed more here than he suspects.

The Fae leader gives Jack an unnervingly flawless grin. He leans down until they're eye to eye, and with quiet relish, he says, "No."

The word is followed by an explosion of motion.

It's Sofi that acts first. Maybe it's her supernaturally-enhanced animal instincts, maybe she's always ready for a fight. Jack isn't sure. All he knows is that the moment he expected his fist to connect with the midsection of the faerie leader, the target's already on the ground.

The bear-woman growls deep in her throat, standing triumphantly over her victim for half a second before another Fae attacks her. She throws him off as if he were a crazed child and is quickly reengaged by the leader who grabs her ankles, slamming her to the ground with him. Jack's instincts beg him to intervene, but a snarl from Sofi as she bounces the Fae's head off the ground tells him she'll do fine.

He turns his attention to the remaining two combatants, eager to punish their insubordination. Cora's engaged with the female, knees bent low in a defensive stance and bobbing. The remaining faerie, at the end of the line and slower than his companions, is crouching to spring into the fray.

Target acquired.

A horrible grin spreads across Jack's face. SCD training and a mild case of lycanthropy have made him a savage combatant. When he chooses to use it. Of all his talents, it's the one he most hates using, primarily because his opponents rarely recover. The FBI requires a certain amount of asskicking, though, and he's nothing if not dutiful.

Two leaping strides brings Jack's fist smashing directly into the Fae's delicate cheekbone. The faerie cries out and stumbles back but keeps his feet. Jack waits patiently for the next attack. The Fae obliges by lunging again, arms outstretched and nails flashing. The agent easily avoids the move, stepping behind and grabbing the faerie's right elbow as he passes.

It's too easy. High Fae are known for their poise and grace, which makes Jack wonder if there's an invisible price for their new, defiant freedom.

He twists the arm up behind the Fae's back with a sickening snap of tendons, followed by a howl of pain that resonates around the glen with supernatural harmonics. The other faeries instinctively look to their keening friend, which provides helpful openings for Cora and Sofi gain the upper hand in their own fights.

Jack presses down and forward on the limb he's holding, forcing his victim to his knees to avoid a broken bone. The faerie is openly weeping and babbling incoherently. Behind him, Jack smirks, the thrill of the fight singing in his bones. Years ago, he'd finish the job—press down, shatter the arm, win definitively. The man he is now, though, values mercy over victory. Most of the time.

He's about to release the faerie as a neutralized threat when a swift foot sweeps Jack's out from under him. Suddenly he's snorting turf, mouth filled with the sharp tang of copper as his jaw clacks against the ground. He ignores the pain, rolling over in an attempt to spring up and re-engage, but a bare blue foot shoves into his chest and pins him down. His former victim grins triumphantly over him.

"*Things have changed since last you were here,*" he sneers, using Low Fae to ensure Jack understands.

Jack spits a mouthful of blood onto the faerie's chest, squirming against the ground in a desperate try for purchase. Anything to get him on his feet and back into the fight. But for all his wiry strength, he's pinned fast.

What has creed done to these people?

He risks a glance at the other two agents. They haven't fared much better.

Sofi's taken out one; he's clutching a mess of ruined flesh and white bone where his shin used to be. But the ringleader has stayed on his feet and in control. He's got a fistful of long blond hair in one hand and Sofi's left arm twisted behind her back with the other. Blood streams down her nose, and one eye is starting to darken.

Close by, Cora and the female Fae are circling each other, evidently pausing for reappraisal. Her shirt is torn, her face is scratched, and she's wheezing from effort, but her opponent is unscathed and light on her feet, seconds away from pouncing for the kill.

This is no longer about winning the fight or controlling the situation. They need to escape.

Jack's ribcage creaks as the faerie lording over him presses down harder. White sparks of pain force him to start over every time he tries to formulate a plan.

But before anything else happens, the world goes abruptly silent. The pressure on his chest is lifted. He gulps a breath and turns his head to see Cora training her gun directly on the forehead of the female faerie.

The rookie agent's posture is perfect, and although she's sweating and bleeding and wobbling, her target is shaking with fear. The cold iron bullets—she must've swapped her clip before they jumped. Six inches apart, the faerie can obviously feel the effects.

"Now listen here, asshole," Cora breathes. "I am all out of fucks to give for whatever attitude problem you have. You and your buddies get down on the ground right now or I swear I'll unload this entire clip into your brainpan."

Checking that his opponent is thoroughly enthralled by the scene, Jack carefully gets to his feet. He takes a couple of steps in Cora's direction, senses sharpened by throbbing pain and a thorough understanding of what will happen if an agent guns down member of the Fae Court, in self-defense or otherwise.

"Cora...," he starts.

Approaching hoofbeats cut him off. Everyone turns toward the sound, momentarily forgetting themselves in curiosity.

An enormous white mare gallops at full tilt

toward the knot of combatants, its rider flat against its back. No one moves, everyone mesmerized by the odd interruption. Horse and rider pound across the glen with incredible speed, coming to a halt directly in front of Jack by rearing high with flailing hooves.

When the horse settles, the rider rises and throws back the hood of the billowing violet cloak to reveal another High Fae, her face decorated with gold spirals and crowned with intricately braided sea-green hair. The four faeries on the ground immediately drop to their faces as she casts her gaze over them, their rebellious quarrel forgotten. She surveys the situation, taking in the two human women with casual disdain. Then her eyes fall on Jack.

With a voice like a tinkling silver bell atop a wedding cake, she says, "Welcome home, Jack Alexander. I have been waiting for you a long time."

The Call she pours into the words is too much. His mind short-circuits as the tattoo on his back ignites with power in the presence of its creator, filling his head with memories he's begged to forget. Flashes of blue and brown, sweat and sugar, laughter and screams, nails on skin and broken twigs underfoot.

Jack hits his knees in the grass, eyes welling with tears, but refuses to bow, using up the dregs of willpower she's letting him keep.

TWELVE

Looking up at the elegant blue woman on her ridiculously oversized white horse is giving Cora flashbacks to high school. Not that they had an equestrian team—those are hard to come by in the Ozarks—but it's the way this woman holds herself. Like she owns everything, and you definitely fall into the category of "everything." Short-legged, red-haired, weirdo Cora Riley had no chance in hell of being popular, and she's too familiar with the sort of haughty stare that comes so naturally to this lady she probably doesn't notice she's doing it. She hasn't dismounted, forcing the three mortals to crane their necks to look up at her like ants in the path of a goddess. Glory and hauteur prom queens would cream their panties for.

When the woman's gaze sweeps over Cora, there's a brush against her mind, the same sensation as when Eris rifled through her brain in the underworld. Fear of a repeat episode drops her heart into her stomach and twists it.

This time, though, rather than her utter helplessness under Eris' gaze, when Cora locks eyes with this High Fae, she feels nothing. The potential mental assault is reduced to a pissy knock on a firmly closed door. There's no intrusion, no sense of submission. It's no different than looking at any other person she's met, blue skin aside. It's as if her mental shields came online all by themselves.

But they're not up—she'd forgotten to erect them in the flurry of the fight. Her rational mind demands an explanation. Could it be that she's strong enough to withstand a telepathic beating without magic?

The impatient shifting of the white horse snaps her back to the moment without an answer. She takes a deep, grounding breath. Whatever it is that's saved her from mentally drowning, she can second-guess it later. All she needs to know right now is that she doesn't have to be afraid. She can resist the psychic invasion. She's safe.

As Cora refocuses herself, the rider narrows her gray eyes, creasing her delicate features. As if she can see Cora's inner monologue and disapproves. There's a tense half-second where Cora's not sure what to do. Then the faerie's face clears, and her attention sweeps away, leaving Cora deflated with relief.

"Attention!" the woman barks.

The prostrate High Fae leap to their feet and pile into an obedient line in front of her. Their eyes lock straight ahead at nothing in what Cora recognizes as the universal stance for addressing a superior officer. Being a mook is the same no matter what world you're in, apparently. She clamps down on the accompanying smile. Gods forbid she should giggle in the middle of whatever serious business is about to go down.

The woman turns in the saddle to address the waiting faeries with a voice like a whip crack. "You are dismissed. Return to the Waterfall to attend Her Majesty before I report the lot of you for abandoning your posts."

Four blue bodies scatter in four different directions. Cora actually admires their tactics. Their apparent panic must be purposeful. Can't let the stupid mortals divine the direction of the Waterfall. Smart.

The woman watches them go, then rearranges herself in the saddle as if her horse were an incredibly large armchair. She even props her elbow on the animals' neck.

"Now. Let us discuss your purpose here, agents," she says with a pedantic smile. "Mr. Alexander—Jack. To what do I owe the extreme pleasure of your visit?"

The way she says his name turns Cora's stomach. It's all sweetness and familiarity and "hey, sailor." She's suddenly hyper-aware of Jack, his kneeling position, his cowed expression, the texture of his energy across yards of open space. It prickles the hair on her neck and balls her hands into fists.

Jack's response is curt, borderline rude. "SCD investigation."

The faerie woman half pouts, which would look ridiculous on a human adult's face but is stunning on her fine-china bone structure. "What a pity. I'd hoped you'd come back to play for a while." As an afterthought, she brightens and says, "But you haven't introduced me to your friends, Jack. Who are these lovely young things you've brought along?" A mischievous smile. "Are they here to play, as well?"

"This is Agent 6 and this is Agent 21." He points to Cora and Sofi in turn. "Agents, this is Limerence, chief handmaiden to Queen Mab, the ruler of Faerie."

Cora's textbook memory pipes up. *Limerence (noun): The initial feelings of infatuation and desire that precede love.*

Her petty side follows immediately with: *Oh, hell, no.*

As if reading her mind, Limerence gracefully inclines her head to Cora and gives her an imperious smile. She's seen this look before, too, when Carol Hartwick won the heart (and pants) of a guy they'd both been after. It's a look that says, "I win."

Jack barrels ahead. "We don't want any trouble, but we are here on official business."

Limerence turns her attention back to him with a melodramatic shiver. "Ooh, official. Going to show me your badge, agent?" It's practically a purr.

"If I have to."

She laughs and waves a hand. "No, no. Continue. Tell your sweet Limerence what you desire."

There's a ripple in the air, almost too faint to get Cora's attention. When she follows the tug with her mind, it leads directly to Jack. His energy's thick with hot anger and strange weakness, making Cora want to run to protect him. If she were less pissed off, less spun around, she'd think this was weird. They're sidesteppers, not empaths; they shouldn't be able to connect that way. But for now, she clings to the connection, desperate for a sign she's reading this relationship all wrong.

For his part, Jack doesn't give any indication he's tapped Cora's mind. His eyes stay locked on Limerence with every semblance of desire, but the struggle in his voice and darkness of his energy tell Cora a different story.

"We need to locate the ergot field that Mab's using to manufacture creed," Jacks says.

Limerence freezes, amusement evaporating in an instant and replaced with hard lines. Her horse feeds off her agitation and whinnies pitifully. The three metahumans look to one another surreptitiously, anxious about the shift.

"I will not help you with this," Limerence says.

"As I told your friends, you're required by law to assist us in the investigation or be charged with obstruction of justice." Jack lowers his voice, the timbre of his energy hardening. "Don't make me drag you out of here into an iron-barred cell."

The threat sends an icy shiver along Cora's spine, but it makes Limerence recoil in the saddle, her perfect features a twisted mask of horror.

"You wouldn't," she whispers.

"Try me."

The faerie woman scowls at him, then says, "Fine. If that is the way you wish to play, then that is how we shall play." She swings her legs back into riding position. "These are my terms, Jack Alexander: I will tell you the location of the field on the condition that you accompany me to my home— alone.

"Your companions," she sneers, "are free to continue their 'official business' while we reacquaint ourselves with one another." She grins cruelly, and Cora can't help feeling like it's directed at her. "I'll be sure to return you in one piece. Eventually."

Jack turns to look at his fellow agents, his face unreadable. Cora's connection to him wobbles, then drops, leaving her mildly disoriented. They glance at each other, and she tries to shake her head, but he either doesn't notice or doesn't care.

He looks back at Limerence. "Fine," he says, then starts toward the horse.

Cora gasps involuntarily, then slaps her hand over her mouth, as if that could retrieve the sound. Stupid girl feelings.

But Jack pauses, then turns on his heel and walks back to her. She chokes down an embarrassment-flavored knot and forces her face neutral. He bends down to close the height gap between them. This close, his scent of bay and cinnamon makes her lightheaded, but she keeps it together.

"I owe you an explanation, but there isn't time,"

he says under his breath. "I'll answer any questions when we get back. And we will—she doesn't break her word. But the mission comes first. You and Sofi have to finish the investigation." He gives a half-hearted smile. "Don't worry about me. I'll be fine."

"And if you're not?" she says, matching his low tone. Not that she cares if Sofi hears, but she'll be damned if she lets that Fae bitch eavesdrop. "I'm supposed to be watching out for you. Ninety-Nine will have my ass if you get hurt."

"I'll be fine," he repeats firmly.

He gazes at her with those huge, dark eyes, and she wonders if he believes what he's saying. She reaches out and lays a hand on his arm as reassurance, wanting to do more. To her surprise, a single blue spark leaps from where they touch, and both watch it fall. Bewildered, Cora slowly takes her hand back, but Jack folds it in his.

"Trust your training. Trust yourself," he says. Then, softly: "Trust me."

Cora nods, pulling her hand back and squaring her shoulders. Jack gives her an approving nod, then he's back across the field, climbing up behind Limerence, who's holding herself like the queen of queens bringing home a prize concubine.

"The field you're seeking is due north, past the forest and the Deep Mine," the faerie woman says, pointing a beringed finger to her right. "Good hunting, girls," she trills. "Don't get lost."

She laughs and nuzzles her back against Jack's chest with a satisfied grin, then spurs her horse hard in the flank. The creature whinnies and rears dramatically before thudding off toward the nearest treeline, disappearing as quickly as it arrived.

When the sound of hoofbeats is completely gone, there's a tap on Cora's shoulder. She'd been staring after the horse, off in her own world of panic and jealousy, and the gesture makes her jump, ready to fend off another spiteful faerie. But it's only Sofi.

"I could hear about half of what he said. Anything else I need to know besides, 'it's fine'? Pretty vague instructions for a big case."

Cora sighs. "Not really."

"Hey, he'll be fine. He wouldn't have left us if he didn't know what he was getting into." She laughs sarcastically. "Pretty sure he's happy to deal with whatever sexlympics chickface wants to throw at him. Dude could stand to get laid."

Inwardly, Cora winces as if Sofi had stabbed her in the stomach. Outwardly, she returns the laugh. "No kidding. Besides, he wouldn't be Ninety-Seven if he couldn't handle himself." Pause. "Right?"

"For sure."

Sofi glances at the sky to note the position of the sun, then turns to the north. Cora follows her gaze. A dense forest lies ahead with trees taller than she'd ever imagined they could grow, bigger even than pictures she's seen of the Pacific Northwest. What lies beyond is completely hidden. Aside from Sofi's fieldcraft skills, the folklore she's absorbed from her father may be all they have to navigate by. And mythology isn't exactly the best map.

"You know where we're going?" Sofi asks her.

"Hell no."

"Awesome."

The two women set off in silence. Cora's heart keeps trying to drag her off to the west, down the path where Jack disappeared, but her mind keeps her feet pointed resolutely forward. She's got to trust he's got this handled, that he meant what he said. There's work to do here that, if abandoned for the momentary peace of assuaging her jealousy, could unbalance the delicate worlds forever. There's too much at stake. She takes a deep breath and moves closer to Sofi as they walk. Time to focus on the job.

Miles away from the interrupted picnic spot, Zeal, the leader of the disbanded foursome, drops to one knee on the sandy riverbank near the throne, head bowed, weight pressed into his right fist planted on the ground. He sprinted from the meadow directly to the Waterfall, though a human bystander could never tell, his breathing is so steady.

"My Lady."

"Yes, Zeal." The voice is musical, mingling with the rushing falls behind it. "What have you discovered?"

"They've arrived. Perhaps an hour ago."

"Are they alone?"

"There is one other. A young female, another metahuman but not a sidestepper."

"I assume Limerence has been alerted?"

"Yes, my Lady. She arrived shortly after the agents."

"Excellent." There's a swish of fabric and the pat of bare feet against stone, followed by a touch on his shoulder. "Rise."

Zeal does as he's told, shifting from kneeling to standing in one fluid movement. But he doesn't look directly at the queen; the taboos are too great. He rests his eyes instead on the complex gold swirls tattooed across her left forearm. The contrast with the midnight blue of her skin is practically hypnotic. Then the arm lifts, a delicate hand raising his chin so he's forced to look at her face. His entire body shudders with a mix of delight and terror.

Lightning flashes in her thundercloud eyes as Queen Mab says, "It is time to fetch our champion."

THIRTEEN

The Faerie landscape reminds Cora of a mix between where she grew up in the Ozarks and the Garden afterlife she visited on her quest through the underworld. Everything is lush and green; the sun shouts into the azure sky; the background hum of critters and water plays a daydream serenade. The only real differences she notes are that most plants sparkle with organic glitter and she doesn't recognize any birdcalls. The entire place is the idyll of serenity and tranquility.

Which is clearly a trap.

She learned her lesson in the Garden—don't trust anything or anyone off-plane that isn't actively not trying to kill you. The bushes she's passing could contain any number of vicious beasts or flesh-hungry brownies vibrating with anticipation for unsuspecting travelers. Between her personal experience and what she's learned in SCD training, she knows better than to let her guard fall for a second.

After a solid five minute walk, the two women are standing at the break between the meadow where they arrived and the forest Limerence directed them into. Sunlight filters through the shimmering leaves and dapples the ground with rainbow effects. There's no path to speak of, and the trees go on for as far as Cora can see.

"So...," she says. "Now what?"

Sofi squints into the woods, then as she crouches down to examine the underbrush, poking twigs and leaves with an intense look of concentration on her face. This goes on in total silence for several minutes, and Cora starts to get bored. Even when she'd go on faerie hunts with her dad, it never took this long to pick up a trace. Finally, Sofi rubs a hand in the dirt, lifting it to her nose and inhaling deeply. She's rewarded with a sneeze, and Cora stifles a laugh.

The senior agent stands again, pointing straight ahead. "There's a trail through here, about a day old. Probably elves on rounds. They did a good job of staying light, but it hasn't rained in a while, so there's a scent I can track."

"You want to follow them?"

"Might as well. We've got no map, no leader, and no idea what's changed in this world since the last agents came through. Faerie shifts constantly, and the changes are probably way worse with creed on the market. We're going to need help."

Cora nods. Sound advice.

"You ready?" Sofi asks. "I know you probably

think you're hot shit after your little adventure through hell with Ninety-Seven, but this is a whole different ball game. I mean, I've never been here myself, but you just had your first field assignment last week."

The briefest of internal arguments.

Her first thoughts are proud and indignant: *Of course I'm ready. I've literally been through hell and back before I took this job. I can handle whatever this place dishes out.*

And then a more logical set of second thoughts: *Faeries are dangerous. Maybe more dangerous than that house where I nearly lost myself. Who knows what we'll find here. And what I'll do about it.*

And, to Cora's surprise, a third voice. This one quieter: *Maybe you'll find something you've been wondering about for a long time.*

She wants to dig into that, but Sofi's staring at her impatiently with those big, blue eyes. She puts a careful mental box around the thought and tags it "for later pondering," throwing into the pile with other boxes marked "Jack and Limerence?" and "automatic shields?" among others. She's getting better at focusing on the job instead of what she wants. Sort of.

"Yeah, I'm good," she says aloud. "If you're worried, maybe you can quiz me on field procedure while we walk. Although I'm pretty sure you'll be too busy with your nose to the ground."

She means it to be funny, but Sofi doesn't laugh. She narrows her eyes and nods curtly, then heads into the woods without looking back.

Cora sighs and follows. Friendships outside of her small town take a lot more finesse than she thought. The sarcasm and teasing that flew so hilariously well back home are definitely not working. She decides to cut that shit out before she winds up "accidentally" abandoned in the middle of a fictional landscape.

Sofi takes point as they trace the practically invisible trail through the woods, hopefully toward a friendly face. Cora couldn't know that she's reliving the day Zara died. The day she came face-to-face with Agent 97 and saw herself in his unshielded eyes. Tracking through the woods outside that cave, using her then-new bear instincts to hide away the tool of Zara's destruction, to return before the agent found them. Things are different now, but those memories are painfully fresh. The rustle of leaves reminds her too much of circling helicopters.

It's not that she minds Cora's total lack of tact. Honesty is one of the things she likes best about people. It's that Cora wants so badly to be her friend and has no clue about boundaries. Sofi likes to think there's one sore spot in her entire being, but in the dark hours of the night, when she lies awake staring at the ceiling, she has to admit that one spot has swollen until it touches everything else about her. Zara literally left her mark on Sofi's life, and her death created a gaping hole in it. Losing

your best friend makes you hard. Cora doesn't
know that, and Sofi's good at smiling like nothing's
wrong, but the damn ginger keeps poking at that
one spot, completely blind to the pain it causes. She
wants to give Cora a break, but she's not ready to let
go of Zara. Not yet.

There's a sudden change in the trail as she's
mulling over her hot thoughts, and she pulls up
short. Cora slams right into her back.

"What the hell?" she grumbles. "Did you lose the
trail?"

Wordlessly, Sofi points at the faint imprint in the
loose soil. A perfect, humanoid foot—a woman's
size six, if she had to guess—accompanied by the
circular divot of a walking staff alongside.

Both women raise their eyes to scan their
surroundings, but there's no break in the tree cover,
and there's no sound to indicate immediate danger.
Not much to go on. Although, now that Sofi's
geared for contact, she thinks she can hear water
nearby. A creek?

"They've got to be close," Cora says. "What do
you think we should do?"

The answer is obvious to Sofi, so she takes the
opportunity for a teachable moment. "What do you
think we should do?"

Cora's red eyebrows furrow as she thinks. She's
sharp enough to cut herself sometimes, if her
training record is anything to go by. Always trying
to discern every shade of gray, usually forgoing her
gut and choosing wrong from overthinking. Seeing
all angles is a good quality in theoretical problems,

but out in the field those lost seconds can be fatal.

"C'mon, Riley. This isn't a classroom."

Annoyance flashes across her face, but she answers promptly. "Let's follow. We probably won't be seeing any High Fae after Limerence ran them off, and we're prepared for a fight this time. If something goes wrong, I'm pretty confident we can take them."

Sofi grins. Maybe she' starting to trust her gut after all. "Free up your sidearm, but don't draw it yet," she instructs. "Don't want to spook any friendlies if we can avoid it."

Cora nods and does as she's told. Sofi notices the wince as she touches her gun but ignores it. Wouldn't be the first time a rookie got their thumb caught in the safety catch.

Together they pick their way over fallen logs and around large stones until the beginnings of a real path appear. The soil is sandier here, traveled often in recent days. Several different sizes and weights of people—beings, she corrects herself—must live nearby.

"What do you remember about faerie settlements, Riley?" she asks in a half-whisper as they walk.

A mild groan. "I thought you said this wasn't a classroom?"

"No better classroom than the field. Answer the question."

"Uh, they don't have buildings? Most of them don't use fire because of the sacred tree thing. They have lots of parties. And they're segregated by type.

Fae don't live with elves and pixies don't live with dryads. That sort of thing." Then, as an afterthought, "And humans aren't welcome."

"Right."

The path cuts off to the left, but Sofi leads them into the bushes behind an enormous redwood where there's cover and a good vantage point. She pulls aside a supple branch to get a good view of where they're headed.

"Well, fuck me," she breathes.

A clutch of beings sits in a close circle, talking freely and eating out of shallow dishes made of leaves. It wouldn't be cause for swearing if the group didn't totally fly in the face of the data that Cora recited. From what Sofi can see, she counts three Low Fae, two forest elves, six gnomes, a dryad, and three pixies sitting together around a large central fire pit. When she strains her hearing, she picks up others in the distance. Not good.

Cora pops up at her shoulder to see. Her eyebrows shoot up in surprise, and she looks to Sofi for an explanation. Sofi shrugs. This shouldn't be happening. Maybe creed's influence did more than make the Fae cocky and belligerent.

"Now what?" Cora says.

Sofi eases the foliage back into place and takes a deep breath. As much as she hates to admit it, she wishes 97 were with them. He'd know exactly what would cause this kind of fraternization and have zero qualms about walking in badge raised and balls out. Metaphorically, anyway.

But he's not here, and with him gone, she's the

senior agent in charge. Cora's counting on her. The agency's counting on her. And she's counting on herself, she remembers. Can't let a tiny thing like a pixie get under her skin. Figuratively or literally. Between her field experience and Cora's fairytale brain, they've got this.

Sofi squares her shoulders and fishes out her badge. "Now, we try to make some friends."

FOURTEEN

Rain is different in New Orleans. It insinuates itself into your bones and never dries; everything shines from unending days of slick humidity. At night, it's beautiful, though. Seen through the particular lens of a native, it's downright gorgeous. Neon light sparkles in the dew, making sequins out of sewage. The rain coming down is an ephemeral curtain that hides a wealth of sumptuous delights and evil deeds.

Like the one being perpetrated right now in the French Quarter, on a landing that overlooks the river.

She's cute and knows it. The city's winter warmth encouraged her to dress lightly, and the hurricanes he's been plying her with have brought an extra flush to her olive skin. The light drizzle makes beads of perspiration heavy on her skin, running in tiny rivulets into her cleavage. He can't help tracing their path with hungry eyes. Though he's supposed to be the hunter, he's dangerously close to being captured himself.

He moves closer, respectful but ensuring she feels him there. She leans over the railing trying to get a better look at the revolving Carousel Bar, her eyes glassy from drink and hair mussed from dancing. He'd picked her easily out of the crowd in her all-pink getup, clearly not from here and enjoying the freedom of not knowing anyone. She'd been eager to get to know him, though.

What's her name again?

"You ever been up there, Nathaniel?" she says, her Northeastern accent clanging against his refined Southern ears.

"Many times, cher."

She turns to face him, putting her back to the railing and jutting her breasts out like she doesn't notice them. But she knows exactly what she's doing. And she knows that he knows, too.

A sly grin. "Ever take a girl up there?"

"Only the ones that are worth the wait."

She lays a hand on his arm, caressing the white linen jacket as if she's never seen one before. She probably hasn't. The touch is electric even through the fabric, and he has to suppress the shuddering urge to take her right here, right now. The life pulsing under her skin calls out like a siren on a far shore, begging him to crash into it. But he masters the impulse as he's had to do a thousand times. Patience is a skill he's been forced to learn after more than a century of this miserable existence.

He moves in closer, sliding an arm around her

waist, drawing them together until they're face to face. She grins in what she probably thinks is an alluring way, but the seduction is marred by her blood alcohol content. They must do nothing but drink up in Boston; she ran through his bankroll faster than he could've. Fortunately, what he's after isn't tainted by the trash humans inject into their bodies to feel powerful.

"Am I worth it?" she purrs.

"Definitely."

He grins, showing perfect teeth, and bends low to kiss her thin, pink lips. The urge to take everything he's after right now is pounding on the doors of his willpower. But all he does is kiss. She inhales faintly, turning it into a lustful growl in the back of her throat. It continues to amaze him that young girls get hot for men in their fifties. At least, ones that look like they're in their fifties.

"Although," he says through another kiss, "I ain't entirely sure I can wait any longer."

She's breathing heavily and nods. He's got her. He kisses her again, biting her lower lip as a promise of things to come. She doesn't know what darkness follows.

He takes her hand in his, leading her from the damp landing toward the private lot where his car is parked. Soon he can to satisfy his every desire without worrying about being seen.

"Ahem...."

It's a tiny, apologetic noise, but it rockets through his mind, trailing angry red flares. He drops the girl's hand and spins to face the intruder.

When he sees who it is, the anger is tempered by resigned recognition. With an aura like that, it must be the messenger.

"What do you want?" he growls at the wispy white guy coming up the stairs.

The man wrings his hands together. "I've got a piece of business to discuss with you, Mr. Wexford." His eyes flick to the girl. "In private."

He clenches his jaw to avoid screaming at the pitiful servant, exhaling hard through his nose. Of all the times. When he'd agreed to the alliance, this sort of egregious violation of his privacy is not what he had in mind. But duty calls.

With practiced ease, he turns his face into a mask of sincere regret and addresses his companion, who's straightening her clothing and looking miffed. "Darling, I'm afraid we must part for the evening." He smiles and hands her a card with his number on it. "Next time, we'll meet at my place. Pick up where we left off."

She huffs dramatically before snatching the card out of his hand, then tilts dangerously on her stiletto points back toward the myriad bars of the Quarter. Off to try again with some other handsome sugar daddy.

Once the click of heels is safely out of range, he's on the messenger with supernatural speed. The drain of magic doesn't bother him, despite being hazardously low on energy—he'll refuel soon. He grips the man's neck and spins him around, lifting him off the ground with one hand. The faerie's aura ripples as his human-suit contacts the side of the cannon monument, but the possession holds.

"What on earth could possibly bring you here at this hour?" he hisses. "Surely the Mistress doesn't need my services so desperately that you'd interrupt my evening with anything less than a call from the Lady herself."

The messenger's gray eyes bulge, and he points feebly at the hand closing off his throat. He's dropped with a grunt of disgust.

"Her Majesty requests your services as champion," he gasps out. "The sidestepper and two metahuman females have arrived in our lands and are snooping about. The Mistress will not tolerate their intrusion, lest they disrupt her plans. She instructed Her Majesty to send for you if the agents appeared in order for you to prove your loyalty."

The sidestepper.

Fourteen years ago, he stood on this exact spot in the pouring rain, arguing as his heart broke, praying to every deity he knew to keep his brother-from-another-mother safe in New Orleans and to stop him from leaving. Other memories rush to join it. Discovering the limits of their powers together, dawn filtering into their shared room, the Aphrodite incident. Followed by betrayal, condemnation, and abandonment. The pang of nostalgia mixes with an upwelling of resentment.

Jack.

He wills his face neutral. "And what, exactly, does the Mistress intend for me to do?" he says.

The messenger stands on shaky legs. Faeries never do well in human bodies; they're so much more fragile than Fae. He reaches into his shirt pocket, and produces a round tablet the size and sheen of a quarter. A single dose of creed.

Although he's been moving creed through this town for months—he's sitting on five keys back in his apartment—he's never taken the drug himself. Why bother going to Faerie when everything he wants is on this side of the Gauntlet? It's pointless.

"You want me to take that?" he snorts. "I thought the rule was 'never get high on your own supply'?"

The messenger persists, holding out the disk and reciting the formal proclamation: "Nathaniel Wexford. Her Majesty, Queen Mab, and the Mistress of the Otherworld, Lady Eris, hereby request your aid in ridding their lands of the human intruders and protecting their interests. Of primary consequence is the apprehension of the sidestepper known as Jack Alexander. Should you accept and succeed in this duty, the Mistress wishes it to be known that you will be handsomely rewarded."

"Meaning?"

An uncertain waver. "I am not privy to that information, sir. I was told that you and Lady Eris had previously agreed on terms."

That's true. Perhaps this interruption has been worthwhile after all. The promise of Eris' blessing holds far greater reward than a drunken hookup. Another step toward his ultimate goal. Plus, there's the added bonus of meeting up with Jack again—this time, on his terms.

He grins and says, "Of course I'll come." The

disguised faerie exhales with relief. Oh, what a mistake. "But first, I need to prepare for the journey."

He waits a fraction of a second before striking, relishing the look of terror that crashes onto the messenger's face as he realizes what those words mean. Then he's clutching the man's shoulders with both hands, shoving their mouths together in a gross parody of the kisses he'd been planting on his previous victim.

This time, he takes exactly what he wants.

Sizzling yellow-orange waves of living energy stream from the helpless faerie's mouth, absorbed directly into the soft tissue of his own. The changes in him are instantaneous and so pleasurable after weeks between feedings that it makes his eyelids flutter. His flesh fills out and darkens to its original ebony, no longer dry and faded with age; his hair darkens from a distinguished gray to jet black; his grip strengthens as his muscles rebind.

But he doesn't stop there. If Lady Eris intends for him to be her champion, he'll need every last drop of power he can muster. Once his youth is restored, he continues to draw out the pulsing life from his victim, ignoring the panicked cries and pleading in the gray eyes. Magic fills him to the brim, making his blood dance with the overflow.

By the time he's sated, the faerie has long since stopped struggling. All that remains of the unfortunate messenger is the hollow-eyed husk of an elderly man. He releases his grip on the corpse and lets it fall in an undignified heap.

"That'll teach you to interrupt a sourceror on the hunt," he sneers. Even his voice sounds younger. Faeries are good for at least twenty years; supernatural vitality gives their life force extra kick. That waifish girl would've given him five at best.

He reaches down and picks up the single dose of creed in the man's open hand. Best to take it now before the Cleaners arrive to tidy up the scene. Nothing like a supernatural death to upset the mundanes. Not that such things concern him.

Lifting the disk to the sky in a sort of narcotic toast, he places it on his tongue.

The effect is immediate. It's the titillation of falling fast and unexpectedly through open air while the world dissolves with flicker-frame speed. Dark, light, city, forest. The fresh magic in his veins sings with building excitement. He's waited long enough; it's time to claim his rightful place among the gods.

There's time for one final thought before the drug takes full hold and thrusts him across the Gauntlet. Closing his eyes against the flashing lights, he whispers to himself, "See you soon, Jackie." Then there's an audible pop, and Nathaniel Wexford disappears.

FIFTEEN

The hum of conversation around the fire pit stops dead as Cora and Sofi step into the clearing where the assorted beings are eating dinner. A dozen faces of different colors and constructions turn silently to them. The fine hairs on Cora's neck and arms rise to attention, the intensity of the faeries' focus begging her to run and hide. Right on top of that animal instinct, though, she can feel their collective power in her own pulse. She locks eyes with one of the Low Fae, a greeny-gray boy with twigs in his hair, and he dips his head politely.

Curious.

It's Sofi that breaks the standoff. Cora thanks providence that there's a seasoned agent with her; she has no idea how long she would've stood there looking stupid.

"We're here on official business of the Supernatural Cases Division," Sofi says authoritatively as she holds up her badge for the crowd to see. "This is Agent 6, and I'm Agent 21. We'd like to ask you a few questions, then we'll be on our way. We don't want to cause any trouble."

No one moves or speaks. They just keep staring.

"Maybe they don't speak English," Cora suggests.

"Yes, they do," Sofi replies out of the side of her mouth. "Humans believed it long and hard enough to make it true. They have to speak it."

"But they prefer not to."

The new voice comes from behind the gathered faeries, and Cora's attention snaps up. A woman wearing the barest minimum to retain any sense of modesty steps between overgrown ferns, the walking stick in her right hand covered with tied-on trinkets. She's older, maybe in her late forties, with waist-length brown hair bound in a gray-streaked braid. Her skin is darkened from sun exposure, but she's not blue or green or pink like her compatriots. A human.

"I'm surprised you found us," she continues as she approaches. She stops behind one of the elves and puts a hand on his shoulder protectively. "We take great care to avoid being located. We'll have to move again because of you." It's a statement of fact, not an accusation. Her tone rings with professional familiarity in Cora's ear.

Beside Cora, Sofi is openly staring at the woman. Cora elbows her, and she shuts her mouth, then clears her throat.

"Kerowyn?" she asks.

The woman grins, revealing perfectly straight

white teeth with over-long incisors, giving her a wolfish expression. "I haven't gone by that name in a very long time, agent."

"Everybody said you defected, but I don't think anyone actually believed it." Sofi casts a glance around the area. "What are you doing here?"

Kerowyn moves from behind the circle of faeries to stand in front of the two women. Up close, Cora notices the trinkets attached to her walking stick are from the mundane world. Mostly plastic costume jewelry and bottle caps. Including an SCD badge with "57" stamped on it.

"You were an agent?" Cora says.

"I was the agency's Faerie specialist. At the time I was hired, a civil war was on the verge of breaking out between the different races that inhabit this world. The SCD felt that my skillset was best suited to counteracting it."

"What do you do?"

The woman smiles and waves a hand in Cora's general direction as if she's wiping fog from a window. Every muscle in Cora's body loosens. Tension slides from her bones, her mind following suit, and her eyelids flutter. She lets out an audible sigh. It's like slipping into a scalding bath after a hard day's work pulling rocks from Mom's garden. Everything turns into hot butter and nothing can possibly bother her. She distantly wonders what she was stressed about in the first place.

Then there's a snap of fingers, and the brain fog dissipates, letting her forgotten worries flood back into their old gaps. Cora's body responds by adding rebar stakes back into her muscles. She whines pitifully at the change, then shakes her head to finish clearing it and gives Kerowyn a suspicious look.

"So they sent you to calm the natives?"

"Precisely."

"Seems sort of manipulative. I mean, the peacefulness goes away when you're not controlling it anymore." Cora looks around at the hodge-podge of faerie races gathered by the fire, totally out of synch with their traditional ways. "But it looks like it worked."

Kerowyn shakes her head, her amused expression falling straight into sadness. "What you see isn't what stopped the war. I'm afraid something much more insidious than my parlor tricks is to blame."

Both Cora and Sofi start to ask a question, but Kerowyn is already walking to an empty place by the fire between a blue-skinned High Fae and a six-inch- gnome sporting a red hat and bushy white beard. They respectfully scoot apart to make room for her to sit.

Cora does a social calculation and reasons that Kerowyn's set herself up as the group's leader. But if humans aren't allowed in faerie settlements, how did that happen? What did she do that allowed her access, and what could she have done to stop the war? There are so many questions.

Kerowyn waves a hand in the agents' direction, indicating that they should sit on the ground in the gap of the circle of tree trunks. They oblige, settling down cross-legged in the ring of faeries.

"You must be hungry and tired after crossing over," the former agent says. "I invite you to eat with us and get what rest you can." She squints up at the sky, where the setting sun is painting washes of crimson and tangerine. "But you must leave in the morning so that we can move our camp."

"Of course," Sofi says.

"Thank you," Cora says. But what she thinks is, *Shit. No help here.*

Kerowyn claps her hands. Two tiny pixies float up from their perches and disappear into the woods. They return with large, bowl-shaped leaves and deposit them into the mortals' cupped hands. They giggle in a register so high Cora wonders if she's part dog to be able to hear it, then flit away to settle on Kerowyn's shoulders.

The smell of wet grass and cornmeal tickles the inside of Cora's nose, and her stomach rumbles its approval of the food despite her brain's disinterest. It looks like she's been served a smooshed mud pie, topped with grass and doused in milk. And she's salivating over it. She glances at Sofi, who's doing her level best not to look sick.

"What's the matter, Twenty-One?" Cora says under her breath, elbowing Sofi in the ribs. "Do bears not eat fairycakes?"

Sofi elbows her back. "Not if they look like cow poop." She ditches the leaf bowl behind her when no one's looking. "Besides, I thought off-plane food is a no-no."

Cora pauses with a scoop of mush halfway to her

mouth. She lowers it thoughtfully, kicking herself for not remembering, especially after the lavender lemonade incident in her heaven. But where she'd been ignoring warning bells that time, there aren't any now.

"I think that's an underworld thing. Something about the living eating the food of the dead." She takes a confident lick of the food. "And besides, do you think Kerowyn would tell us to eat if it wasn't safe?"

Sofi's brow furrows as she considers it. Then she shrugs, digs in the field kit at her waist, and pulls out Cid's lunch. "Either way, I'll take a soggy turkey sandwich and busted up apple over that runny mulch, thank you."

Kerowyn doesn't seem to have noticed the exchange. "Enjoy the food and the music, agents" she says, picking up her own leaf bowl. Others around the circle, having finished eating, are bringing out instruments. "We will have plenty of time to speak afterward."

Cora lifts her bowl to Kerowyn in acknowledgement, then scoops more of the organic mess with her fingers and rolls it around in her mouth judiciously. Tastes like raw honey and lavender and somehow sparkly. She sighs, eyes rolling heavenward with pleasure. She's dined at some of New York's finest restaurants, and once she ate a deep-fried Twinkie at a carnival, but this brown, lumpy paste has got to be the best thing she's ever eaten.

Cora gratefully leans her weight against the

rough end of a tree stump as she eats. The combination of the low, crackling fire with the breath of twilight settling over them is soothing her jangled nerves. The musicians play a haunting tune with minor notes thrown in at odd times, producing a decidedly Celtic air. Some of the pixies fan their wings to create a humming harmony. Between the atmosphere and the food, Cora's not sure she's ever been in a happier place.

If only Jack were here....

The thought produces a twinge of guilt that boots her psyche back into work mode. Her common-sense voice worries about the food, the music, and the beings surrounding them. What danger is she overlooking? Was she too quick to trust Kerowyn and her motley band of faeries?

But something deeper down reassures her. It's probably normal to feel this way in Faerie. She remembers the odd strength she felt during her visit to the underworld; like she belonged there more than in the real world. Maybe it's the same here. As long as she knows who she is, she'll be fine.

Dinner over, the three women adjourn to the bank of a small creek nearby. The music was starting to swing, other beings coming in from afield to join the merriment, dancing and whooping as the tempo ratcheted up, and Cora had wanted to stay. After all, she's not in charge; she doesn't know all the intel. But Sofi insisted. Needs the experience, she said. There was a small amount of pouting. Behind

Sofi's back. Quietly.

Kerowyn sits on a boulder with her tiny, bare feet dangling into the cold water as it rushes past. Cora and Sofi both stand, unsure of how to comport themselves in the presence of someone who's both technically a senior agent and the leader of a roving band of misfits. They revert to official stance: at ease, hands behind their backs, respectfully attentive.

"I know why you're here. And I can't help you," says the older woman.

The flatness the pronouncement jars Cora hard. "What? Why not?"

"I want to, Agent 6. There's nothing more I'd like than to help with your investigation." She gazes across the water, her voice wistful. "Some days I miss the agency."

"So, what's the problem?"

Kerowyn lifts the hem of her short skirt by way of an answer. The rising moon is bright enough in this unpolluted landscape that Cora can see the large, stylized knot etched into her hip. Like the raised tattoo on Jack's back but different somehow.

"I've been given the brand," she says matter-of-factly.

"Meaning...?" says Sofi.

The hem goes down, and Kerowyn sighs. "I did jump ship three years ago, like you said, Twenty-One. When it became clear that the war here was beyond the scope of my powers—beyond any of our powers—I had an epiphany. The problem wasn't the fighting; the problem was why they were fighting."

Tears are standing in her eyes now. "Faerie was dying—the land and the people—because no one believed enough." She gestures to the other side of the creek. "These woods used to be full of brownies and pixies and owlbears, but now there are hardly any. They...," she clears her throat, "ate each other to survive. They used up their friends and relatives to stay alive that little while longer."

The silence that follows is too heavy for anyone to interject.

Kerowyn continues after a choked breath. "I couldn't stand to watch. My talents would never be sufficient to stop the war, and even if they were, everyone here would die of starvation anyway. It was simply a matter of time. But I couldn't go to One Hundred with that answer, so I stayed to work with the High Fae to solve the belief problem. I'd studied organic chemistry before I joined the SCD and thought it would be easy to find a solution by mixing science with magic. " She lowers her head. "It got out of hand."

Sofi's hand flutters to her mouth. "You created creed."

"It wasn't supposed to be used this way," Kerowyn chokes out. "It was supposed to be given to mortals who found their way here by accident, to boost their belief naturally and help them remember their experience when they got home so they could tell people and raise belief levels gradually. By the time I realized the Fae were dosing and kidnapping people on the other side, they'd already 'rewarded' me with the brand, which made me Fae myself. When Mab's proclamation went out that citizens of Faerie were no longer allowed to assist humans, it bound me, too." A shimmering tear splashes into her lap to punctuate the end of her sentence.

Cora wants to hate her. The bile of resentment is bubbling as the story's rolled out. How could she be that cowardly? Or so blind as to not see that a race of tricksters would turn on her? Especially when looking down the barrel of extinction?

Then again, she didn't know. For all her naiveté, Kerowyn wanted to do the right thing—add magic to the mundane world and preserve a supernatural race. Blaming her for being an unwitting pawn in Eris' game is unfair. Cora's stomach unclenches as she imagines herself in her shoes. She's been the fallguy for Eris before, too. A modicum of sympathy is in order.

Cora takes a step forward and puts a hand on the former agent's bare shoulder despite Sofi's muted protest. She looks up, startled by the gesture of kindness.

"It's okay," Cora says. "You didn't know. This place messes with your head. You were trying to help."

Kerowyn's entire body shakes violently as she lets out a sob, dropping her head into her hands. There's a long, awkward moment where the two younger women watch her cry out her relief. It's several minutes before she composes herself to speak again. She sniffs and uses the end of her long braid to dry her face, then straightens up, dignity regained, as if she'd never broken down.

"You see why I can't help you," she says, voice husky from tears. "I can tell you the history, but that's all. I'm sorry, agents."

Sofi huffs unprofessionally. "There's really nothing you can do for us? Not a map or a guide or anything?"

Kerowyn shakes her head. "Every faerie is bound by the Queen's command, and there are no maps of the land as it currently exists. Part of the belief system of this place is that it's always shifting; it's been that way for centuries. Because of creed's influence, Faerie is more fluid than ever."

"Great. Frigging awesome. How are we supposed to find the field, then?"

"From what I've observed, the changes are daily. It's too late for you to set out again tonight—you don't want to be on the move when things shift—but if you leave after midnight, you'll have a full twenty-four hours to find your way. As long as you don't take longer than that to find what you're looking for, you should be safe."

"Still doesn't answer how we find the field in the first place. Limerence pointed us in this direction, but that could be on the opposite side of the valley by morning." Sofi kicks the dirt, sending a clod bouncing into the lazy creek with a splash.

There's a peaceful tingle that starts at the base of Cora's spine and crawls its way up to her scalp. Something about the sound. The water. The land. The complete lack of concern about getting lost. The ease and familiarity of this place.

"Uh, Cora?" Sofi says.

Cora looks down and sees that she's glowing softly in the dark. Her entire body pulses with blue light in time with her heartbeat and the tempo of the creek. It freaks her out immediately, and she shakes herself hard to break up the fuzzy aura. She stares at her hands, feeling her magical energy dissipate, and shudders.

What the fuck was that?

Kerowyn's eyes widen, then narrows them shrewdly. "You're a sidestepper," she says flatly. "And you're one of us."

"Well, this is only my second real case, but yeah, I'm one of you."

The expression on Kerowyn's face twitches into careful reserve. "That's not what I meant." She doesn't elaborate. Instead, she turns her attention to Sofi. "You found our settlement by yourself, so I don't think you'll have any trouble finding the field. It'll be getting to Mab herself that'll give you problems—she doesn't want to be found, especially not by agents." She casts a meaningful glance at Cora. "But this one can get you there. She'll figure it out sooner or later."

"What does that mean?" Cora demands. This veiled talk like she knows something she doesn't is pissing her off.

Kerowyn doesn't reply. Of course she doesn't— that's how stories work. She simply stands and walks back toward the sound of drums and flutes, leaving the two agents on the banks of the creek, wondering what morning will bring.

SIXTEEN

The place where Limerence finally stops is not the place Jack expects. Compared to the simple willow-twined bower he remembers, this new home is practically palatial. Sturdy oaks line the boundaries, rowan and ash trees marry near their tops to create a long corridor of cool shade, ending in a nave barely visible from the entrance.

Judging by her robes and residence, Limerence has been promoted close to the queen; she's entitled to roses, lilacs, and orchids by the flower laws of the court. Instead, she's kept the wildflowers of her past. Rings of lilacs and daisies encircle her home. The scent of these more humble blossoms wafts to him through the breeze. It combines with Limerence's own spun-sugar smell and the warmth of the brand on his back, making him lightheaded. Memories he's sealed in the lowest parts of himself scratches at the door. But he fights back while he can.

The snow-white mare trots to the side of the bower's open front and waits patiently while its riders dismount. Limerence alights with a feather's ease; Jack practically falls on his face. He's never gotten along with horses. It's their eyes. And their hooves. And everything in between. Limerence watches him struggle, an amused grin on her face, then sweeps inside without looking back. She hangs her cloak on a handy branch, and starts to busy herself with what passes for a kitchen in Faerie.

He toys with the idea of running. It's a mad hope borne of fear he'd rather not admit. If he goes inside, anything could happen. The work he's done over the last year to free his emotions will work against him in there. The things she's done, the history they share....

But a pull from the triskelion tattoo crushes any idea of escape. It leads straight to her, and he must follow. He takes a deep breath, winding his energy as tightly as he can, shoring up his mental defenses before stepping across the springy grass and into the house that's not a house.

"Sit, sit," Limerence says, gesturing to a pallet on the ground littered with silk cushions. She turns back to the wooden table as she talks. "I'd lose my position as Her Majesty's handmaiden if I neglected to offer you proper hospitality."

The unmistakable smell of fairycakes and wine clench Jack's stomach into sickly knots. Like the revulsion to a particular liquor after a truly raucous party. Too much indulgence followed by a regrettable morning. Times a thousand, in this case.

Jack shifts his attention from the sourness in his gut to the woman herself. It's a desperate choice to avoid being sick. The last thing he should be doing is admiring her; it enhances the magical bond. As if on cue, the brand warms, the aroma of sugar and wildflowers increases, and his resolve slips a notch.

It's been ten years since he last saw her. In mortal time; he's not entirely sure how long it's been for her. But she hasn't aged a day. Fortunately, she's not completely naked—it's unseemly for high-ranking Fae—though the wisps of clothing she is wearing hide nothing. The royal blue of her skin has deepened up to the edge of midnight, and the new golden spirals accent every beautiful curve and edge of her body. Hair the color of a Caribbean sea trails down her back in a braid thicker than his arm. A touch memory of winding his fingers through its loose waves breaks free, quickening his heartbeat.

And what about the other woman in your life, hrm? comes a whisper from inside.

Instantly ashamed, Jack slams the memory back into its hiding place. He's here because it was the surest way to ensure the success of the mission and the safety of his.... He stumbles over the label. Agents, he decides, though it's not the word he'd wanted.

Lowering his gaze breaks part of the spell, although his brand is blushing warmer than before. He reaches behind himself and traces the green knotwork gingerly. It's hot to the touch, making him wince. Limerence's mark is taking hold faster than he'd anticipated. He must stay vigilant.

The faerie woman turns, a tray in her long-fingered hands, and crosses to where Jack's sitting, delight in her gray eyes. She places the tray of food and drink in the center of the palette, then draws herself to Jack's side.

"You must be exhausted," she says. "It's been a long day for you, I imagine." She lifts a stone cup and offers it to him. "Drink. Eat. Whatever your heart desires." There's an unmistakable purr in her voice that slides right up Jack's spine. He represses the shudder as he accepts the drink, although he's not sure if it's from desire or fear.

"Thank you," he says.

Limerence ignores the dull tone. She takes her own cup and raises it in a toast, a smile spreading across her lips. "To us."

He taps his cup to hers but doesn't drink. It's inevitable that he will; he's merely delaying it. Once he drinks, there's no making up the ground he'll lose to her control. He doesn't reciprocate her sentiment either, for the same reason.

That seems to irk her—a twitch of an eyebrow, a curl of the lips. Things he'd never notice on anyone else, but in this too-familiar face, they're as clear as if she'd shouted. She covers her displeasure by leaning in until their shoulders touch, propping herself against him while she swirls the potent faerie wine in her cup.

"I've missed you so, dearest one. It seems like yesterday you left me, but my heart aches as if a century has passed."

"It's been ten years, two months, and twenty-two days."

"See? Far too long." She sighs contentedly and lays her head on his shoulder. His brand sings out again, now soothingly warm, like a hot water bottle pressed between sheets on a winter's night. The sensation of melting at her touch.

Resist. Don't let her enchant you again. You may not be able to escape this time.

Jack adjusts his weight, shifting until she has to sit up to stay stable. This time, she gives him a full-blown frown. Hairs on the back of his neck stand to attention.

"What's the matter, my love? Aren't you pleased to see me?"

Her frown morphs quickly into a pout. On anyone else, he'd find it ugly. On her, though, it's bewitching. He inhales sharply against the impulse to apologize and comfort her; the willpower is quickly draining out of him as she tugs on his brand. Her brand. The vigilant, logical part of him is forced to watch as fingers of enchantment coil and tear at his resistance.

"I am," he lies. "But I have work to do here, and you're obstructing my investigation." He looks down into the golden liquid in his cup. Maybe he should drink. Get it over with. It'll hurt less when he inevitably tells her to go to hell and she breaks every one of his bones.

The pout continues. "Your womenfolk are doing the work. You're responsible for nothing except what happens here." She switches to a sultry grin, reaching out and tracing a finger down his cheek. "Shall I remind you of what you left behind?"

He wants to lean in, to relish her touch. All that saves him from such a fatal error is the mention of Cora and Sofi. His subconscious throws out horrific scenarios of them lost in the changing wilderness, trampled by pegasi, or eaten alive by a redcap tribe—anything to keep him detached and logical. But those powers are considerably weakened, by his own design. They're no longer a match for the magic Limerence has burned into his flesh.

"Tell me the story," he says. The voice is his own, but it echoes strangely in his head, like that of a much younger man.

She grins, then takes a long pull on her drink. He follows suit. What remains of Agent 97 tries to stop him with data about the dangers of combining booze with magic, but he's stopped caring. Let it happen. He needs to give his agents time to complete the assignment; the mission is more important than his safety. Right?

If she senses his internal turmoil, she doesn't show it. Instead, she curls up close against him and begins the tale.

Once upon a time, there was a beautiful faerie maiden who lived alone in her simple willow bower in the middle ring of Queen Mab's kingdom. She loved wildflowers and honey, excelled at storytelling and riding, and wanted nothing more in life than to one day become the queen's chief handmaiden. She grew her hair long so it would catch in the breeze as she rode across Faerie, granting the wishes of mortals and planting flowers wherever she could.

One day, as she lay sunbathing by the queen's waterfall, having attended her first day at court by Her Majesty's invitation, the maiden was startled by splashing in the pool. She leapt up to rescue yet another hapless human from drowning, diving into the water and retrieving the sodden mortal. Already her mind was spinning with new games to play and plans to tease their desires from them before sending them back into their own world with wild tales to tell.

But when she looked at the man she had rescued, all thoughts of faerie tricks fled from her mind. He was the most beautiful mortal she had ever seen. And though he was drained from the journey between their worlds, she could see the power within him.

'This is no ordinary human,' she thought to herself.

And she was right.

Over the next little while—days to her but months to him—she nursed him back to health. His memory of who he was or how he had found Faerie was vague and broken. Occasionally, he would mention that he needed to get back, but she shushed his protests. "You are here now. Be here," she would say. He soon saw the wisdom of her words—and the beauty of his benefactor.

For weeks after his recovery, neither could bear

to untangle themselves from the other. Their love had grown wild and fast. She loved his earnestness and the deep magic contained in his fragile mortal life; he loved her beauty and irrepressible joy. They explored Faerie together many times over, hunting through its hidden places, making love by moonlight, and telling one another tales of their disparate worlds.

Then one night, after a year and a day of inseparable love, the man came to the maiden and asked if he would be allowed to leave. The maiden was heartbroken.

"Why would you want to leave?" she sobbed. "Do you not love me? Do you not wish to be with me always?"

He said he that did but that he missed his home. He could no longer bear to be apart from his world or his people. But the maiden had a plan.

"I can take away your sorrow," she said. "I will bind us together for always. Your heart will never again long for your old life. We will be as one."

The man agreed.

The full moon and many fair folk oversaw the ceremony of the brand. She shed tears for his pain when he cried out at the searing of his flesh, but after, there was no time for tears. Only love.

They remained together for many years, blissful and unendingly passionate for one another.

Until one night, when the maiden woke up alone. The pillow beside her was cold. She knew he had fled; she could feel the enchantment of his brand weakening. The maiden howled her rage into the starry sky and ran after him.

Though she pursued him for hours in the same forest they had once shared, he eluded her capture. He was too fast, too far ahead, too afraid, too decided. The door opened at the edge of the queen's waterfall, and he disappeared.

The maiden's heart shattered into a thousand pieces that she could not collect.

Limerence's voice trails off, tears thickening her voice until she's forced to stop. Diamond tears stand in her huge eyes as she looks up at Jack. There's hope lingering there, but the spell of the tale is woven so tightly that he can't reassure her.

Not that he can't—he won't.

"A pretty story," he says. "But you left out the part where you enslaved me with that enchantment. And how you turned me into a series of prey animals for the Hunt to track through the woods. And how the whole ordeal traumatized me so effectively I haven't touched another woman since." It's a cruel, desperate ploy. Anything to keep him in the real, to stay in control.

She waves a hand nonchalantly and sets aside her empty cup. Both hands now free, she snakes her arms around Jack's neck and pulls her tall, thin frame fully into his lap. There's hardly any weight to speak of, yet he feels crushed to the earth with the gaze she gives him, mere inches from his face.

"I'm afraid such things do not make for a good

fairytale, my love."

She leans in to kiss him. The spun-sugar scent of her skin envelops him, taking the headiness of the faerie wine in his blood and lifting it to new heights. His entire body, warmed through by his brand, thrums with longing. She's both familiar and unknowable. His first and, if he lets this moment happen, perhaps his last. A home to rest in. A woman who needs him. A life where he wouldn't have to keep struggling to stay above his own waterline.

His shoulders bow as he moves to meet her lips. The heat of her body pressed against him shuts out all thoughts except of her, here, now. She slips her hands inside his open suit jacket, ready to push it aside, a demand for further pleasures.

Then a quiet memory breaks the surface, no more than a pin dropping.

She eases the jacket down over his shoulders. It drops to the floor next to his boots, leaving him with nothing but his khaki pants. He looks down at her, over a full head taller than she, but she doesn't meet his gaze. Her hands move to the exposed scars that bisect his chest, her fingers delicately tracing their path from collarbone to bottom ribs.

There's a susurrus of resistance in his heart. It's all he needs.

"No," he says.

Limerence stares at him in shocked silence, a thunderstorm gathering in her eyes. "What?" she whispers. Her lips are millimeters away, and the temptation to breathe his way into the kiss is overwhelming.

But he doesn't. "No," he repeats.

The crack of her hand against his cheek reverberates through the bower and rolls out across the field. A whinny from the startled horse punctuates the intensity of the blow.

"How dare you toy with me?" Limerence hisses, suddenly standing over him. "Do you think you have a choice in the matter, foolish man?"

She lifts her chin with a triumphant smirk that sets his back on fire. She doesn't flinch when he cries out through clenched teeth or when he collapses to the ground. Instead, she waits until he's drenched with tears of agony, then reaches down and strokes the welt on his face where she struck him. A juxtaposed, tender gesture.

"Don't worry," she croons. "I'll break your mortal pride. I have the perfect place for you."

SEVENTEEN

The two agents are bedded down for the night a good distance from faerie camp, tucked under the low branches of a tinkling silver tree. An elf brought them reed mats to sleep on, which they were polite about but have zero lumbar support. The field kits balled up as makeshift pillows are more comfortable. It does feel good to rest after the day they've had, though.

Sofi lays near Cora, the sound of dancing feet and drums permeating the background and lulling her to sleep. Being a city girl has its advantages; when you come across a bunch of drunk, partying faeries, it's easier than ignoring fire engines. Cora shifts restlessly on her mat, and Sofi imagines she must be having a harder time. Country girl can't sleep with noise.

Despite the ease with which Sofi could drop off, though, her mind is revving. They've got less than five hours before the scenery shifts and they need to head out. Analytics don't come naturally to her; she's an action agent, she tells herself. It's a good excuse for leaning on brighter, organized minds to formulate plans. Minds like Cora's.

"You awake?" Cora whispers, as if hearing her name.

"Yeah."

"You shouldn't be."

"You either."

"Do you have a plan for tomorrow?"

A pause. Does she tell the truth or try to fake it? Common sense pushes her toward honesty. Pointless pride can be more dangerous here than back in the real world. Cora looks up to her as a boss or mentor or whatever, but pretending to have all the answers gets people killed.

"None whatsoever. I sort of figured we'd go out there and wing it."

Cora groans. "That's a shit plan."

"You got a better idea?"

"Uh, yeah." There's a rustle as Cora sits up on her mat to face Sofi. She can see the rookie outlined against the moon-brightened sky, her excitement practically visible. "You've got tracking and scent abilities; I've got damn good direction sense and Faerie knowledge. Between the two of us, we should be able to avoid getting lost. I say we head north again, then see what happens. If the ergot field is as busy we think, there's got to be a path or a trail for us to follow."

Sofi smiles in the cover of darkness. Of course. She should've thought of that.

"I like it. Good job, Riley." Sofi rolls over to put her back to Cora. "Now get to sleep. Kerowyn's coming soon to wake us up, and it's been a weird day."

A rustle behind her says that Cora's laid back down, too. But less than a minute later there's another question in the dark.

"Sofi, do you trust me?" she says tentatively. "I mean, with this assignment. Faerie's a dangerous place, and we're not exactly veteran agents. Hardier and smarter people than us have been lost here forever. Lifelong friends have turned on one another trying to escape." She pauses, then says, "I just want to make sure we're okay."

There's no sound except the distant music of the faeries at the fire, but the simple question rings loud in Sofi's ears.

Do you trust me?

The screen of her mind shows her image after image of a wild-haired girl with skinny arms and legs laughing and crying, tortured by her longing for happiness, followed by the shameful memory of her own explosive outburst when Cora doubted her story about Jack.

A hot tear rolls into the corner of her mouth. Bitter.

The fear of being vulnerable, of letting another person into her trust after what happened to her dearest friend, rolls her stomach like a stunt plane, making her want to vomit. But deep down, she knows of the cost of holding everyone at arm's length.

Do I want to follow in Zara's footsteps?

Thoughts of being lost and alone, in the mundane world or any other, for the rest of her life threaten to push her directly into the darkness she swore she'd never visit again.

There's only one choice she can make.

"Yeah, we're okay," she says. "I trust you." The words croak out around a lead block of grief jammed in her throat.

The silence that follows puts Sofi's heart in a vice. The reassurance she needs for this simple admission, one that's a leap of unbelievable faith for her, doesn't come. Seconds tick by. She starts to panic.

And then, "Thank you."

Rigid muscles soften, nerves unwind. She takes back the cynical, mean things she'd been thinking. She readjusts herself on the cold ground and finally drifts off to sleep, the sound of faerie drums playing along with a phantom heartbeat that isn't hers.

Cora's dream about eating ice cream in a Jacuzzi is suddenly full of earthquakes. She struggles to stand and calls out, but no one's there. Her Ben & Jerry's tumbles into a lava pit, and she shouts again.

"Somebody help me!"

"I'm here!" shouts a voice from far away. "Wake up!"

Her dreaming self follows the voice up to the surface, and Cora gasps, starting awake to see a soft face surrounded by loose brown and gray waves.

Kerowyn has her by both shoulders, her eyes concerned and searching.

"You're fine," the former agent says. "You were sleeping so soundly I couldn't wake you without shaking you. I apologize."

She lets go as Cora blinks away the last of the dream. Sofi's mat is empty, and Cora has another moment of panic. Kerowyn shakes her head reassuringly, the bright moonlight bouncing off the white streak at her forelock. "She's fine. Talking shop with the duende about talismans, I believe. Shamus never sleeps, and he loves a good fight. It seems they have a lot in common."

Cora's pulse slows with relief, and she laughs. Leave it to Sofi to harass a leprechaun about his lucky charms.

Once she rubs some life back into her arms, she stands and joins Kerowyn in looking over the serene landscape at the edge of the camp. It did change in the night.

A protective circle had been drawn before the party got too out of control, spells chanted over it to keep their bit of land out of the change lottery. But everything else is different. There's no creek—Cora can't hear any water nearby—and the majestic forest is replaced by a breezy prairie, the trees now several hundred yards away. The stars overhead are no constellations Cora recognizes, and they dip close to the ground, lending their glitter to the plants below. Will-o'-the-wisps dance in and out of the high grass, mimicking the stars with their dance.

"It's beautiful," Cora breathes.

Kerowyn nods. "And deadly." She turns to Cora, worry lines visible as shadowed valleys in her face. "You and your friend must leave at once to give you the maximum amount of time before the next change. The longer you stay in Faerie, the easier it is to be enchanted." She gives Cora a cryptic look. "But you know where you're going. It would be practically impossible for you to get lost here."

Again with the predictions and trust-your-gut speech. Ugh.

"What does that even mean?" Cora asks with more bite than she intended. "I'll buy that supernals and paragons can look into my soul and see the future, but you're mostly human."

"Emphasis on 'mostly.'"

Cora huffs, but Kerowyn smiles gently. "It's not my place to explain your life to you, agent. We must each discover our own destiny." She touches Cora's arm, sending a jolt of longing for her mother straight into her heart. "I doubt it'll be long before you understand," she says. "Don't despair yet."

Cora takes a deep breath and lets it out again, loudly and slowly. "Fine. No despair. Just constant confusion about where I'm going and what it all means and what makes me special."

"Precisely like everyone else in existence."

She can't help laughing.

Kerowyn gestures back toward the camp. "Agent 21 is waiting for you. I've given her food and clean water. I'm sad to say that's all the help I can provide."

"I understand. It sucks, but I understand."

As she turns to walk away, a lightbulb goes off in Cora's head, and she ducks back to her pile of things, retrieving the SCD field kit. She unrolls it, then returns to Kerowyn, holding out two small objects. The older woman takes them with polite curiosity.

"Thank you," she says, though it's obvious she has no idea why she's being given a plastic squeeze bottle and miniature wooden box.

By way of explanation, Cora lifts the lid on the box, and a tinny tune wanders through the pre-dawn air. They let it play. As it starts over, a slow smile grows on Kerowyn's face.

"*Over the Rainbow*. How appropriate."

Cora laughs and closes the lid of the music box, then points at the plastic bottle. "That's filled with honeyed cream. Should be good—we haven't been gone long." There's a hungry flash in Kerowyn's eyes that tells Cora she's made a good move. "Considering how long you've been away and what with the faerie brand and all, I figure you'll appreciate these more than the SCD does."

Kerowyn's amused smile spreads to the rest of her face, and she tucks her new treasures into a leather satchel attached to her staff. "Thank you, Agent 6. That's very kind."

Cora holds out her hand. "And thank you for your help and hospitality. I'll let Ninety-Nine know you're safe and sound."

Kerowyn shakes. "I'd like that."

They part, the former agent left staring out over

the open field of glittering grass, while Cora heads toward the fire, wondering if her desire for specialness might be more sinister than she imagined.

"Are you sure about this?" Sofi huffs.

They've been walking for hours, but it's the third time they've passed this particular fir tree. Cora knows because it's got a knot of her hair snagged in it. She's sweaty, tired, and terrified they're what her ex-boyfriend, Jeremy, would've described as "butt-ass lost."

Still, she can't help being amused. Growing up in the country gave Cora plenty of outdoorsy skills and a high level of comfortability off asphalt, but Sofi's stepped in two rabbit holes and nearly twisted her ankle on a rock. Turns out daylight is more important to her tracking abilities than she thought.

"Pretty sure," she says. "The sensor circle wasn't meant to pick up anything except doorways, though. I'm basically cobbling together what I've read about auras and background magic with instinct. Kind of a 'square peg, round hole' thing: It'll work if you screw around with the peg."

The lone upside to not having official sidestepper training is that she isn't locked into someone else's plan for how she should use her powers; learning on her own affords her the freedom to explore new ideas. Between curiosity and the old book she's been studying, she's cooked up a few already. Like using the radar to detect different energy signatures. If her theory's right, softening her focus and actively seeking living creatures instead of interworld doors should turn up readings when a supernatural is nearby.

But this is the first time she's tried it—until now it was a scribble in a margin—and nothing's pinged besides Sofi. Could be working, could be fucked. All she can do is hold the circle and see what happens.

"When the sun finishes coming up, you can take over," Cora reassures her. Maybe once it's fully light out, Sofi won't feel useless.

Sofi grumbles and takes a swipe at a fern, so Cora changes the subject. "Do you know anything about fairytales?" she asks.

"Not really. My folks were more interested in headlines and stock markets than bedtime stories."

"Want to?"

A reluctant sigh. "Sure, why not? It'll pass the time."

Cora checks the sensor circle for integrity. It's spread over a limited area and isn't demanding much concentration. Talking and holding it up shouldn't be a problem.

"So, there are seven basic stories in the world," she starts, "and they're not limited to books or movies—they play out in the real, too. They're written into the fabric of the universe. The quest format is far and away the most common and popular. We're actually living it out right now."

"Huh? How?"

"Think about it. Every SCD assignment is a

quest. You're sent out into the world to change something, and you always come back different. This quest, we're setting out to destroy an evil plant and stare down the Faerie Queen so we can go home to a better world."

Sofi *hrms* thoughtfully, latching onto the idea. Cora smiles. Nothing like a good story to draw a person out of themselves.

"There are always allies along the way," she continues, "trials and obstacles, and, of course, enemies. We got in a fight with High Fae, lost Jack, and the landscape is shifting; there's our setbacks. We met Kerowyn; there's our ally. All that's missing is enemies."

"Not counting faeries hopped up on creed-belief, the prom queen who stole Jack, and the inevitable angry monarch?"

"Okay, fair. See, you're catching on."

"So then what's next in the story?"

Cora ponders that. It was suspiciously easy to find the settlement, and Kerowyn said things are different in Faerie these days. Maybe the stories she's familiar with aren't true anymore.

"Well, if I were writing it, this is about where there'd be an attack on the hero. Some kind of obstacle to reaching the big goal. Maybe a vicious monster or highwaymen or an oubliette?"

Of course that's when the underbrush starts to rustle.

It's a fair distance away—it hasn't been caught in Cora's sensor yet—but it must be big to make that much noise. They've wandered into an area of the woods where the trees aren't crammed so close together and ferns are dotted loosely across the sandy ground. Ruddy sunlight is starting to sneak through the leaves, heralding the arrival of dawn. It'd be peaceful if it weren't for the fast-approaching crashing.

The agents slip behind a handy bush for cover. Sofi drops into a low fighting stance, hands bunched into waiting fists. Cora draws her sidearm and aims over Sofi's right shoulder, forming a high-low turret, a move they've discussed but never used in the field before.

Aside from the scuffle on their arrival, this is the first time Cora's been worried about getting hurt on the job. Her heartbeat thuds in her ears, and her palms itch where they touch the metal of her gun. It's a mild irritation, but it effectively distracts her from the sensor circle. It wobbles, and she has to drop one hand from her gun to scratch. Sweat starts to bead on her forehead.

The disturbance in the underbrush gets more violent, the noise becoming more thunderous. Cora strains her ears, flicking through her mythological Rolodex for an ID but the sound's too muddy. Hearing failing her, she refocuses on the sensor circle, which makes her gasp out loud.

One, then five, then more than a dozen points, all clustered together and moving fast toward them. The intensity of the energy reading sags her shoulders with its magical pull.

Below her, Sofi says, "Get ready! They're about to break through."

Cora grips her weapon with both hands and steels herself for the attack.

As the approaching cacophony reaches its apex, a single unicorn bursts through the thick ferns, careening between trees at top speed, tossing its ivory mane and brandishing a three-foot horn. Fresh sunlight dances off its perfect snow-white coat as it bolts directly in front of the two stunned agents.

Then another one races out.

And another. And another.

An entire herd of unicorns bears down on the clearing, charging madly and totally oblivious to the humans in their path.

Cora reacts without thinking. She drops her gun and grabs two fistfuls of Sofi's shirt, throwing them both to the side as hard as she possibly can. Dozens of slashing hooves crash down in the exact spot where they'd stood, ripping up and flinging huge chunks of turf as the herd continues its frenzied dash through the woods. The sound of falling saplings marks their passage, white flanks and silver manes moving fast in an easterly direction.

When the first bird starts singing in the eerie silence that follows, Cora lets go of Sofi's clothes with an apologetic look. They both stand, brushing dirt and ruined greenery off their clothes. Cora moves to retrieve her abandoned weapon and finds it crushed inside a hoofprint the size of a dinner plate. Sofi steps up beside her and looks down.

"Oh, snap," she says.

Cora bursts out laughing. The rollercoaster of

adrenaline plus the slang over the beauty of seeing real, live unicorns is too much. The delicate grip she had on her sensor circle totally fails, and it blinks out, leaving nothing for her to feel except the sweet relief of laughter. Tears squeeze out of her tightly closed eyelids, and she has to bend over to catch her breath. By the time she recovers, gasping and sputtering, Sofi's laughing, too, and Cora starts again. They go on like that for a while, the built up stress they've been carrying melting away in a wash of giggles.

"Okay, okay" gasps Sofi. "We need to get going. That was close, but damn you had me scared with all that story talk."

"How was I supposed to know unicorns aren't rare anymore?" Cora chuckles. "I guess we should give My Little Pony more credit."

Sofi reaches down and picks up the ruined pieces of Cora's weapon. "Might as well save this. I'm sure Cid can fix it for you. And who knows if those cold iron bullets are useful for anything else."

Cora reaches out to take the bits of metal, but when they touch her hand, she hisses and drops them, clutching her palm to her chest.

"What the hell?" Sofi says.

Cora gingerly opens her hand, revealing a palm full of bright red welts in the shape of bullets. She shows Sofi, who raises her eyebrows in confusion.

"What. The. Hell," she repeats.

The marks throb with the dull ache of a burn. Like she touched the stove and didn't take her hand away in time.

In the shape of bullets.

Cora looks at the detritus at her feet, inspecting it from a safe distance, then reaches for the bullets. Her palm starts to itch before she touches them. Experimentally, she pulls the spare clip of standard ammunition out of her kit, weighing it in the palm of her good hand. Nothing.

"The cold iron," she says after a moment. "It burned me."

Sofi's forehead creases hard, giving her a unibrow Cora would find funny any other time. "That's only supposed to work on faeries," she says, catching Cora's eye. "And it's supposed to kill them dead on contact. I've never heard of anything like this."

Another rustle in the bushes cuts off Cora's response. She curses herself for not relaunching the radar right away, but it's too late now.

This new threat is closer than the unicorns and moving much more slowly. Patiently. The fine hair on Cora's forearms lifts in response to the approach of a predator. Sofi must feel it, too, because she tries to pull Cora away from the gap left by the herd and into a safer hiding place, but Cora's entire body tightens, the confusion of the moment paralyzing her. All Sofi can do is draw her gun and aim it at the gap.

But instead of a monster, a man in a white linen suit steps carefully into view.

He's tallish, maybe in his mid-30s, dark skin, shaved head, hands already in the air. Clearly human and clearly disoriented. Which means there's two ways he could've ended up here: he accidentally wandered through a door or he's on creed. Hard to tell which.

The man looks from Sofi to Cora and back again with the speedy assessment of someone who's been on the wrong end of a gun too many times.

"Whoa, hey, sorry," he says with a molasses-sweet drawl. "Spooked a mess of unicorns on accident when I turned up. Didn't mean to spook y'all, too." He gestures with his chin at Sofi's gun. "Mind putting down that peashooter long enough for us to chat? I'm not packing or anything."

Sofi doesn't lower her weapon. "Who are you?"

"I'm late of New Orleans, assuming I never figure a way home." Keeping his hands in the air, he makes a small bow. "Nathaniel Colin Wexford. At your service, ladies."

EIGHTEEN

The short blonde girl doesn't lower her gun after he's introduced himself. He pegs her immediately for the protective goody-goody type. The redhead looks stunned—obviously the rookie, despite being maybe ten years the blonde's senior. He suppresses a smile. They don't know they're practically oozing "cop." Besides, guns don't belong in the Otherworld. Only visitors have them, and the only people that visit are either accidents or agents. It's obvious which category these matching black suits fall into.

He opts to keep up the charming Southerner routine. He could give two shits about whatever these girls are doing, but there's no way they're here without Jack's sidestepping help, no matter what their powers are. Stretches in the Roosevelt taught him that much about the Supernatural Cases Division and its agents.

It'd be easy enough to read their minds for

everything he wants to know, but where's the fun in that? His dose of creed is fresh, so he's got time; no rush. Anyway, it's not worth drawing on his power reserves to get information with magic that he can get with patience. Far more entertaining to play up the lost soul angle.

"Ladies," he begins, adding a touch of helplessness into his baritone and taking a step forward.

Blondie cuts him off. "Nuh-uh, mister. Keep 'em up and stay put." She's got big brown doe eyes with steel underneath.. "You're not a faerie, so how'd you get here? Fall into a hedge?"

He chuckles. "Sort of. Took a wrong turn down Bourbon Street with too many daiquiris under my belt. Thought I was opening my car door."

"Bullshit. I'd bet a hundred bucks you're a creed user, suit or no suit."

Red nudges her friend but clearly agrees. They're not buying it. Can't have that; he has to secure their trust if they're going to take him to Jack.

"Actually," he says, looking down theatrically, "I tell a lie. Didn't want to shame myself in front of strangers, but Momma taught me to fess up when I'm caught." He scuffs the dirt with a wingtip. "Yes, I succumbed to the lure of altered consciousness— one of my many weaknesses. The promise of delights I never could imagine was too tempting to resist." He takes a moment to admire the Faerie landscape with its purple-green trees, glistening creeper vines, and outrageously colored flowers. "Lived in Nawlins my whole life—you'd think I'd've seen everything by now. But that girl was right: I never seen nothing like what I woke up to."

Blondie looks smug. Red's glare softens. Perfect.

He inclines his head, careful not to incite a shot to the gut, and says, "What about you? How'd you ladies end up in this place? Same?"

Now Red pipes up. She's got a honey-sweet voice with a blur to the vowels. Southern enough he'll have to watch his mouth; she'll see through him if he spins up too many yarns. And those gray eyes mean trouble if he's learned anything from the Mistress' allies.

"We'll ask the questions, Mister Wexford," she says. "You're the one who barged in on us."

"Mister Wexford was my father. Please, call me Wex," he says with a tinge of hurt. "And I certainly didn't mean to scare anyone. I'd hoped that finding a couple other humans in this place, maybe we'd put our heads together and find a way back home."

The women exchange a glance, then Blondie waves him to the nearest tree with the end of her gun. "You stay put. We're going to have a conference."

Wex obliges, not bothering to eavesdrop as the girls huddle together a short distance away. He doesn't need heightened senses to get the gist of their conversation. You learn a lot about body language after fifty years trolling bars for willing victims.

Blondie's half-turned in his direction, face concerned. Swayed by his honesty, most likely. But Red's not convinced. Holds herself at an angle, back to him. Making stabbing motions as she talks. There are raised voices, bits of sentences coming to him like "dangerous to take on a stranger" and something about stories. It doesn't take long for Blondie to pull rank, though—she squares up and says one sentence with a very specific cadence. Red sighs, but then she squares up, too. Good girl. Listen to your boss.

They break and come back, Blondie holstering her weapon. She smiles with a lot of teeth and gums, genuine, and holds out her hand.

"My name's Sofi, and this is Cora. Sorry about the welcome, but you never know."

"I understand, cher. Been on both sides of that, myself."

He takes her hand, and they shake, but he holds on a second too long. There's immense strength hiding under that petite, plump frame. Oh, what he could do with that power in his veins....

She clears her throat awkwardly, and he lets go with an apologetic smile.

"There was some disagreement," she says, "but we're happy to have you along, Wex, as long as you don't get in the way. We're trying to get home, too, but we've got business to take care of first."

Eyebrows raised, he says, "You're here on purpose?"

"Yes, but it's classi—," Cora coughs pointedly, and Sofi stumbles, "—private business."

"Understood. Never was one to pry into the secrets of women."

He flashes Sofi his best smile. It's won over a

hundred stronger-willed women, and the steel in her eyes melts obligingly. There we go. A tiny bit of magic well spent for her compliance.

Cora must notice the relaxation in her friend's posture because she breaks in to take over. "We're burning daylight here, Soph. Dudeface can come with us, but stay focused."

Good observational skills—this could be entertaining, indeed. What a fun challenge the Mistress has arranged for him. He'll have to thank her when he collects his reward.

Sofi nods. "Right. I'll scout ahead. You and Wex follow at a safe distance." She starts walking northward. "Stay alert, Riley."

And then she's gone, disappeared into the thick, shining ferns.

Wex turns to his companion and says, "Shall we?" motioning for her to go first.

Cora gives him a sharp, critical look that feels familiar. She's sizing him up with calculated curiosity, reading him for hidden information. Only one other person he's ever met has looked at him with such scrutiny. This girl definitely knows Jack.

"Go ahead. I'll bring up the rear," she says. It's not unfriendly, but it's not giving him any leeway, either.

He nods and smiles, taking a couple of long strides to put a safe gap between them, and they begin walking in silence. He's not worried. There's yet to be a person's heart he can't worm his way into. No one he can't possess.

Except him.

A lightning strike of anger evaporates the thought instantly. He's closer to rectifying that mistake now than ever. If he plays his cards right with these soft, mortal women, they'll lead him exactly where he needs to be. Jack won't slip through his fingers a second time.

Cora's sweating under the high noon sun by the time Wex speaks again. They've been following Sofi's trail markers through the forest for hours in pursuit of any sign of the ergot field. She's peeled off layers down to her undershirt, exposing her blindingly pale arms to the sun and partially revealing the SCD gear on her belt. Her jacket and shirt are wrapped around her waist to keep it hidden from Wex. The less he knows, the better.

"You ladies never did answer my question," he says without turning around. "How'd you wind up in this place?"

Cora and Sofi had agreed not to tell this guy what they're here for, but she's not sure how long she can keep it a secret. Practically anything that happens between now and getting back to the real world will give them away. And Sofi wasn't exactly guarded earlier; if he's smart, he's figured out they're not normal people. Telling mundanes the whole truth isn't always the best idea, though. They usually freak out. But Wex did take creed willingly, and he isn't losing his mind about being in off-plane. Maybe he can handle it if she feeds it to him a bit at a time.

"We're part of a supernatural investigation team," she says.

He seems nonplussed. "You don't say? Didn't know there was such a thing outside of ghost hunters and exorcists."

"I'd think that, being from New Orleans, you'd know all about voodoo and spirits and other dimensions."

"True say. Just never expected to wind up in one. Especially not one this sparkly and full of unicorns." He lets a beat pass. "And pretty ladies."

Cora rolls her eyes behind his back. She'll admit he's charming, but why do guys try this flirty shit when they first meet you? What would he do if she actually threw herself at him right this second, anyway? She ignores his clumsy pass and hopes he takes the hint to knock it off.

They walk a bit longer in silence, letting Cora's thoughts turn to how she's fared on this case. When she volunteered for the assignment, she'd assumed it'd be Jack in the lead and her as backup, the way it had been in the underworld. But with him gone, she's pleasantly surprised at how well her own approach is working. Between her and Sofi, she's starting to feel confident that they'll both complete the mission directives and retrieve Jack safely. She grins as she thinks about saving his ass for a second time. He'll hate that.

"You got a sweetheart back home, cher?" Wex asks, derailing her train of thought.

This time she huffs loud enough for him to hear. "Not that it's any of your business, but no." A pause as she considers what she does have. "Well, sort of."

He laughs softly. It's a slick, resonant sound completely out of place in this wilderness. A bird even calls back.

Cora's not impressed. "You ask an awful lot of personal questions for someone who's supposedly lost and scared," she says. "Why aren't you acting like it?"

He shrugs like a cat stretching to get up from a nap. "Guess I've seen too many strange things in my life to get bent out of shape by a little magical travel. Once you find out your best friend can move between worlds at a whim and you've had relations with a couple of vampires, the novelty wears off."

Cora stops dead in her tracks. A series of data points runs through her stunned brain as she parses what she's heard.

One: He's not surprised about Faerie or a supernatural investigation.

Two: He knows about metahumans and vampires.

Three: There are two documented sidesteppers in the world today, and I'm one of them.

Four: Jack said he went to college in New Orleans.

Wex must notice the lack of footsteps behind him because he stops walking and turns around with an eyebrow raised.

"I say something wrong? Figured you'd seen your fair share of weirdness, too, what with being on a supernatural investigation and whatnot." He makes a contrite face. "I do apologize if I shook you up, Miss."

She waves a hand dismissively. As much as she hates to tip her hand, she's got to ask: "Mr. Wexford," she says slowly, "do you know a guy named Jack Alexander?"

His face lights up like a surprise party birthday cake. "Jackie Alexander? Hell yes, I do, girl! We're college buddies. Ol' Loyala pals." His chest inflates slightly. "I taught him that radar trick after he caught hell for popping out of a doorway in the ladies' locker room."

The texture of the air changes as this information sinks in. This random stranger not only knows Jack, he's claiming to be a meta himself. She hastily flicks on her makeshift supernatural detector. A gently pulsing, bright orange dot appears. She has no idea what the color means, but he's definitely magical.

Well, I'll be damned, she thinks. *You find friends in the strangest places.*

She starts to reach out and shake his hand, ready to tell him how she met Jack and what they're doing here. But a quiet voice reminds her she's not in the country anymore—not everyone's trustworthy. Given Jack's high SCD case rate, it's as likely that this guy's a former collar as he is a long-lost buddy. He may not be on their side. While she wants to trust Wex, it's better to play it close to the vest. At least for now.

"Any friend of Jack's is a friend of mine," she says with a smile. "I've worked with him for a while, and he's a stand-up guy."

The grin he gives her is blindingly white. "I haven't seen that sonofabitch in nearly ten years. Thought he'd died in a fiery car accident or something."

Cora flinches with the memory of the wreck that nearly killed her earlier in the year. But the friendliness Wex radiates is reassuring and keeps her present. He does seem absolutely genuine. She wonders if Sarah would miss her that much after ten years away.

"Definitely not dead," she says. "He gets caught up in his work is all."

Wex chuckles. "That sounds like him. I can't tell you how often I had to bribe that bookworm out of the library for a bit of fun." Then his forehead scrunches with thought. "You said you worked together. He join you on this expedition?"

Dammit. That discretion thing lasted a whole ten seconds before she blew it. The way he's suddenly hyper-focused makes her feel like an ant under a magnifying glass. She tries to recover her fumble.

"Yeah, but he's following up a different angle." She points at the trail Sofi left to get his attention off her. "Once we get back to the world, I'm sure you two will have a great time catching up. He's probably as anxious to see you as you are to see him."

"I'm sure you're right," he says, springing back to his friendly manner again.

The rapidity of the change raises the hair on the back of Cora's neck—a sign of a practiced liar. Or a sociopath. Either way, she needs to keep an eye on this guy.

Wex's eyes get foggy with nostalgia. "Man, I remember this one time. We holed up in this abandoned Victorian house, and we brought in this succubus girl...."

She tries to keep her face straight, but judging by Wex's reaction, she's failing.

"Oh, I'm sorry, cher. Are you...?" He lets the question hang.

Cora drops her eyes to her shoes, then looks back up sharply. Why should she be embarrassed? That's Jack from ten years ago; she didn't know him then. By all accounts, he's a much-changed man.

Then again, her personal life isn't this guy's business no matter whose friend he claims to be.

"Couldn't tell you, man," she says with a shrug.

He takes a cautious step forward and puts a broad hand on her shoulder without malice or flirtation. "That's a shame, cher," he says. "He's a damn fool if he's passing up on you."

Southern manners are an obscure dance of respect and affection, or at least that's what Cora's learned from her mother. And affection time is over. It's time for respect.

She takes a protective step out of Wex's reach, careful not to offend him. He nods in acknowledgment, then turns around and begins to walk down the trail. Cora follows at a polite distance, her thoughts once again whirling in the shared silence.

Aside from wondering whether or not she can trust Wex and how the mission is going, what's bugging her most is the fact that her experimental supernatural radar actually works. Of course she's excited that it does, but it shouldn't. From what she knows about metahumans, it's one talent per person, with a handful of wildly exceptional cases. You have powers, they do specific things, that's it. There's no reason she should be able to detect magical signatures apart from interworld doorways.

Then again, maybe it's got nothing to do with her. Maybe it's this place; maybe the trick won't work back home. She remembers the easy resistance that saved her from Limerence's mind-skimming, the strangely elusive things Kerowyn said, the cold iron burns on her palm. Does Faerie do something weird to visiting metahumans?

Cora sighs. When she'd wished to be special, she hadn't imagined it'd come with so many damned unanswered questions.

She's about to raise the magical sensor for another test run to pass the time, but a crashing rustle ahead steals her focus.

Wex freezes, and Cora rushes up beside him to drop into a combat stance, whipping the can of mace off her belt with one hand. Her eyes dart around, mind on high alert. They've wandered into a less forested area near the foothill of a mountain; high stone walls gradually lead down ahead of them, as if they're walking into a canyon. The noise seems to be coming from everywhere as it bounces off the rocks. As it gets closer, she can distinguish several sets of footsteps, but her damaged hearing can't tell what sort of creatures they belong to. She wishes for the comfort of being properly armed and curses the herd of unicorns for crushing her gun.

Then, from around the corner, Sofi appears. Both Cora and Wex relax.

But as she approaches, it's obvious something's wrong. She's holding herself stiffly, and her expression is both embarrassed and apologetic.

"I may or may not have failed my spot check," she calls out.

Cora and Wex look at each other, confused, but it's promptly explained as four stocky figures with beards you could camp in appear behind Sofi, armor gleaming and axes shining in the bright sunlight. Possibly the easiest of all faerie creatures to recognize, given the insane resurgence of *Lord of the Rings*.

"Dwarves," Cora breathes.

A black-bearded dwarf with beady eyes to match. He calls out, his thick brogue bouncing off the stone. "Yer prisoners of the Deep King and will be comin' with us, whether ye likes it or no. I suggest comin' peacefully lest you arrive one or two limbs shy of how we found yer." He brandishes Sofi's confiscated SCD equipment at them.

Cora glares at Sofi, "What did you do?"

The failed tracker shrugs. "Tripwire in the dirt. I got about fifteen feet before these guys turned up. They said I'm trespassing on their lands and took me prisoner. They think we're Queen Mab's spies."

"Seriously?"

Another shrug. "I tried explaining that we're humans, but they don't give a shit." She turns to the dwarf holding her things. "If I wasn't such a nice girl, I would've beaten the snot out of them when they stole my field kit." To Cora, she says, "But maiming the vertically challenged isn't politically correct, and I'd like to keep my job."

Cora sighs. To Wex, she says, "Let's go. It's got to be a misunderstanding. Whoever this Deep King is, I'm sure we can clear it up before sundown."

The two join the posse at axe-point. Cora makes a disapproving face at Sofi, who has the decency to look ashamed. Their diminutive captors form up around them, two in front and two in back, and lead them into the stone canyon.

Cora shakes her head at the situation as they descend into cool, dry air. Chalk it up to another plot twist in the story of their quest. Though whether it turns out to be the end or not remains to be seen.

NINETEEN

Rain down the back of my shirt cuts like ice. I'm not sure if it's my conscience or it's starting to freeze or if he's messing with my mind.

I look up into a blur instead of a face. I know it's him. The insinuation of furious eyes and a snarled mouth. Directed at me. Screaming at me.

I back up, hands out, terrified. My foot slips. A crumbling ledge over a crater where there should be street.

He storms forward, bringing the rain with him. Hands reaching out. I'm not sure if it's to save me or push me over the edge himself.

Words in a language I've never heard appear in physical form, red-hot and searing the air. They hang for a moment, then fall on me, burning my face, my arms, my chest. I scream, but there's no sound.

A familiar, flat voice laughs. Not his. Not mine. Hollow echoes in my mind, burning as badly as the

curse he's laid on me.
A familiar face. Not his. Hers.
The rain stops. I reach out. I fall.

Jack starts awake with a gasp, long limbs spasming and heart pounding like a freight train. How long has it been since he dreamt about Wex?

He pushes himself up to sitting, slowing his breath. For a moment, head in his hands and eyes closed against the echoes of the nightmare, he's lost. Spinning between reality and dream, past and present, enemies and friends.

Then he remembers where he is.

The adrenaline evaporates as he opens his eyes again. Whatever Limerence slipped into his wine, it knocked him out effectively enough for her to move him from the house. A cursory glance at his new surroundings shows him more of the forest, the sky, and clumps of overgrown lilac bushes. There's yards of clear space around him before it runs into forest. A path runs through the trees, but the foliage is too dense to see where it leads. He shifts his weight out of the pile of springy grass and feather down he'd been sleeping on and stretches. Smells like a disused pegasus nest.

The oddness of the environment plucks a note of suspicion. She's far too clever to leave him out in the open if she's truly angry with him. What's she playing at?

"The sort of game I can't lose."

Her voice comes from directly behind him, and,

though startled, he refuses to give her the satisfaction of seeing it. He deliberately turns, as if he'd already been going that way.

Limerence sits on a rough stone bench nearby, now wearing a sheer flowing gown. Her eyes sparkle with amusement, a wry smile on her lips. Jack wonders how long she's been watching him.

"I was afraid you might not wake," she says. "You've been sleeping for hours—much longer than I intended." She gives him a lascivious once-over, "Your body has changed much since the last time I had to drug you."

He walks toward her without rising to the bait. He doesn't remember her slipping substances to him, but perhaps that's the point. Another footnote in the "what the hell was I thinking?" file on this woman.

She holds out a warning hand when he gets within a couple feet of where she sits. "Ah, ah," she warns. "I wouldn't."

"Wouldn't what?"

Jack takes another step forward, but the instant his foot touches the ground, there's a rush of sugar-scented air, followed by a tiny pop, and he's standing back in the nest where he started.

"What the hell?"

Her silver-bell laugh tinkles across the glade. It grates against the Jack's mind even as it warms the brand on his back. He stands and gives the area another, more magical scan. Grounding himself, which is difficult under layers of faerie enchantment, he reaches out with his sensor circle in the vain hope of finding a doorway out.

But the circle stops dead at ten yards, right where the clearing stops and the forest begins. It snaps his energy back like a cut rubber band. His pulse quickens, and he tries again, raising his circle over and over as data collates into a definite picture. And it's not a good one.

Invisible walls twice as high as he is tall meet in a closed dome overhead, every inch charged with energy-deadening magic. And there are no doors out. Not normal ones, not magical ones, not interdimensional ones. It's the ideal cage for a sidestepper.

He lets his sensor fall, mind grappling for a solution an unsolvable problem.

"I made it especially for you," Limerence says.

Wordlessly, he turns to her. The look of utter triumph on her face stirs the angry beast deep inside him, but he pushes it down. It won't serve any useful purpose now.

She stands and puts her hands against the invisible barrier. There's a shimmer, then an inward dip of pressure, and both her hands pass through, creating odd circles in the air around her wrists.

"No way in or out without me," she grins, wiggling her fingers on his side of the wall. "No doors. No magic past the barrier." She withdraws her hands, the air ripples, and the barrier reseals, once again completely invisible. "It took months of spells, rituals, and sacrifices to create. All for you, my love."

Years of field experience and research filter through Jack's mind like numbers through a computer program. But nothing he's aware of could create something like this. Not even at the heart of Faerie where the background magic is strongest. An iron knot forms in his stomach as he realizes how much power the Otherworld is getting from creed. This is far more serious than he'd thought.

But....

If the belief levels are amped this high, classic myths and legends can't be all that's influencing the world. Or him. Other sources of human belief must be at work.

A scrap of his childhood floats up to him. As a boy, Jack would huddle under the blankets late at night with a flashlight in one hand and a comic book in the other. Comics were forbidden in his father's house, but his love of them ran deeper than simple rebellion. Reading the adventures of mutants and aliens and magical beings with the power to change the world—for better or worse— made him feel like maybe he could, too, someday.

In particular, he loved Nightcrawler, a circus acrobat with teleportation powers and a heart full of family torment. The X-Man's story spoke to Jack's own desperate yearning to be anywhere but where he was, to have the power to think of a different place and instantly be there.

Little boy Jack certainly believed superheroes were real. He was invested enough in Nightcrawler to dress up in costume, take on his persona, and wish him into existence. Does adult Jack, a jaded and scarred man with powers of his own, believe in him, too?

Maybe. Maybe not. But the uncertainty makes him curious.

Jack moves to the boundary where Limerence stands, stopping an inch from resetting his progress. The faerie woman's arms are crossed in front of her, amused at his frail human grasp of the situation. They could touch if it weren't for the invisible barrier. His brand thrums pleasingly at her nearness, and he grits his teeth with the effort of forcing rational thought through its urgings.

"There's no way out?" he says. "What if I teleport?"

The smug grin drops from her face. "You can't."

"I can't because you designed this prison to prevent it? Or because you don't think I'm capable?"

A flicker of uncertainty. "You haven't the skill."

Now it's his turn to grin. "You're right. I don't," he says. "But now I know it's possible. Your poker face has slipped, my dear."

"Even if it is," she snarls, "you can't do it. Magic doesn't move in you. You keep it locked inside your mind and think you own it because you can test it like a scientist." She spits on the ground in disgust. "No heart. Dead magic."

"What does heart have to do with it? Magic's inborn. You have it or you don't."

Limerence rolls her eyes. "Mortals. You always think it's one thing or the other, no shades of gray. No room for new ideas."

"Because in ninety-nine percent of cases, that's true."

A pitying laugh. "What a narrow view of the world. If you would widen your gaze a fraction of an inch, matchless power could be yours." And then she turns to leave, hitching the hem of her gauzy dress out of the grass.

Panic grips Jack's heart. For years, he's known down to his bones that his abilities are incomplete. Despite the praise and amazement of other supernaturals, it's never felt right. And now this hint that his suspicions are correct. He can't let it go—no matter how dearly he wants to escape this deranged faerie who's captured him for a second time.

"Wait!" he shouts after her.

She stops and half-turns at the desperation in his voice, smiling like a cat who's lured the mouse into her den. "Yes, my love?"

"Tell me what I need to do."

Limerence purses her lips as if considering it, then picks her way back to him. Thundercloud eyes set his brand afire as tendrils of her familiar mind brush against his own. Her lips part with concentration, and Jack catches his breath while she tills up his memories. Pressing, caressing, insisting. He sinks into the embrace, unable to resist.

When she does untangle her mind from his, it leaves him feeling hollow and spent. She blinks with a slow, languorous wave of eyelashes. Bedroom eyes out in the open.

"Beneath your mask of logic, I sense a fragility," she whispers. "Such intimacy with your own depths is beyond your capabilities. Perhaps it is better if you continue to imprison magic in your mind rather than opening your heart." A haughty smirk. "Even if knowledge of your full powers is the cost you must pay for that ignorance."

He thinks of his years as an emotionless machine. He thinks of the passionate man he sacrificed in an attempt to save his own life—and the life he lost because of it. He thinks of the treasonous plot he's trying to stop, of the battles to come. He thinks of Cora, the power she intuitively wields, and the walls he's put between them.

Limerence gazes dreamily at him as he thinks. A long curl of turquoise hair has fallen across her face, accenting her sharp cheekbones and highlighting the golden spirals on her sapphire skin. There's a flicker of envy when he pictures Cora, but the faerie woman says nothing, supremely confident in her ownership of him. It chases away every other thought except the desire to please her. And to prove her wrong.

"Teach me," he whispers.

The invisible wall shimmers as she puts her hand against it. Tentatively, not wanting to be sent back to the filthy pegasus nest, he puts his own hand up as if they were lovers on opposite sides of a plate glass window. She smiles, this time with sincere happiness, and flexes her fingers through the wall to grasp his hand.

But before she can say anything, there's the

sound of something approaching fast from the west. She breaks away too quickly for Jack to react, and he's snapped back to the center of the cage.

By the time he catches his breath, two High Fae mounted on gryphons have arrived, trailing feathers and smelling strongly like wet cat. They pull up in front of Limerence, who's stormed over to meet them. Even from this distance, Jack can see their swords and bows; one has a great horn strapped to the side of his mount. He can also tell the damned faeries are drunk. Which takes some doing. They must be bored—likely a side effect of too much power and not enough brains.

"Lady Lim'rence!" the first one slurs, making a half salute. "Her Maj'sty bade us request quarry from you. Says you've an int'resting specimen."

The handmaiden's aura erupts to life in angry, volcanic streaks of crimson fire, upsetting the gryphons into rearing dangerously. Their riders sway but keep their seats despite the sparking air.

"How dare you invade my home and make demands for your brutish Hunt!" she yells.

The second man finds courage to answer, if meekly. "But, t' Queen…"

"That is no concern of yours, footman." She pronounces the title as one would say "peasant" in medieval times. "This mortal is mine and is not to be used for base sport, regardless of what the queen may say." Waving a dismissive hand, she shoos them off. "Return to your drunken reveling, and keep your weapons well secured, lest someone lose an eye to your idiocy."

There are muttered apologies and a messy about-face, followed by thundering hooves in the opposite direction.

Limerence watches them go, then takes a deep breath and lets it out in a rush. Her aura shrinks and fades with the subsiding of her temper. Muttering about stupid underlings, she squares her shoulders and resumes her sultry beauty attitude before she sashays back to Jack.

"Terribly sorry about the interruption," she purrs. "Now, where were we?"

Jack takes her outstretched hand as she crosses the barrier into his invisible prison. The sensation of finally touching her, skin-to-skin, after so long, bursts within him like soft lightning. He can't imagine why he'd ever resisted, why he'd ever run from her. He wraps an arm around her tiny waist and pulls her close, inhaling her cotton candy scent.

"Right here, I believe," he says with a smile.

Limerence lifts her chin triumphantly and slides her hand to rest over the small of Jack's back, caressing the enchanted tattoo that bonds them. A confusing mix of memories and sensation spreads through him: a pallet on the floor and a four-poster bed, sea-green and fire-red hair, two sets of gray eyes without bottom.

And then, a sandy voice cuts through his reverie. *Do not give in to the charms of Faerie, Jack Alexander. You have not yet fulfilled your oath to me.*

Reality slams into focus. He knows what he needs to do. The interruption of the Hunt doesn't matter. In fact, it was exactly the time he needed to formulate his escape plan.

TWENTY

The SCD's files on dwarves are surprisingly scanty. But what Sofi's learned about them is definitely not what she's seeing. Where a typical dwarven community should be congregated deep down in a rough mineshaft or natural cavern, this place is a shallow system of caves leading into an architecturally impressive underground castle. The inhabitants are all wearing elaborately-forged armor and carrying decorated axes rather than sporting the traditional soft leather clothing and digging equipment. And there's an awful lot of gold laying out—it should be carefully sealed up in a vault. Sofi thinks back to what Kerowyn said about belief levels altering Faerie's residents and wonders what's happened to dwarves since the rise of creed.

The three captives are marched between cave walls intricately decorated with runes and scenes of battles that human scholars have never heard of. Torches illuminate most of the long, sandy path, but there's a background glow coming from somewhere that Sofi can't pin down. She sniffs the air, noticing an abundance of oil and steel. Not good.

And what she sees when they stop concerns her even more.

King Brolin Stonehammer is known to the agency as a larger-than-average dwarf who specializes in sounding gold mines. His techniques informed advances in human excavation over the last century, marking the transition from sending men to their doom with a terrified canary in hand to tuning fine machinery that reads the dangers during digging. He's also provided neutral ground for potentially explosive summits between supernaturals, hosting summits to avoid all-out war four times. His dossier paints a picture of a trustworthy being who's slow to act but almost always right.

The dwarf in front of the marble throne wearing full chainmail, however, is apoplectically red in the face and gripping his war axe as if he means to hurl it. His eyes are wild with rage, and he paces in short steps as he waits for them to approach. A far cry from the reasonable ruler Sofi expected.

One glance at Cora and Wex tells Sofi that neither of them know what's happening either. She risks a step toward the volatile king to make herself the most obvious target. At least if she gets hit, the other two will have time to run away. Besides, she's pretty confident she can take at least one axe. It's the other dozen from the surrounding guards that'll be a problem.

Sofi tries to get the first word in, but Brolin's faster.

"Who're ye that trespass on dwarven lands as if you owned them?" he demands. His words are heavy with a rumbling Scottish accent, but his agitation makes them shrill.

There's a moment of indecision. There are two paths she can take. On one hand, she could opt for the truth. He's an ally of the SCD, after all; he wouldn't know her, but she'd bet he knows Jack or at least respects the badge. On the other hand, with the changes she's already seen, there's no telling what's been done to their minds. When supernaturals fall prey to shifts in belief, unstable isn't the word for it. Take a normal human going through an existential crisis and add magical powers—dangerous. She needs more information before it's safe to trust the king with the truth.

"We're three humble mortals who lost their way, Your Majesty," Sofi says, lowering her eyes with artificial fear. "We had no idea we'd done anything wrong."

"Lies!" Brolin screams. "You're spies of the queen!"

Stick to your guns, Strella. She flinches and lets a tremble into her voice. "Queen?"

There's a guttural gurgle, followed by stumpy legs approaching. Then there's an axe blade under her chin, forcing her to look up. Relatively, anyway—she's short, but she's looking at the top of a plain helmet. Up close, she can see intricate braids in the king's dusty hair and beard. Another unusual touch.

The king's voice lowers a hiss, his agate eyes glinting with undisguised glee. "Queen Mab's flunkies have been crawling over this land fer the last year, lookin' for the entrance to our caverns so she can destroy us for resistin' her rule. But you've been caught, my girl, and you'll rot in my dungeons for yer pains."

Now the fear is real. Sofi can sense the guards closing in around them, and the look on the king's face broadcasts sheer madness. This is way worse than she thought. And she already thought it was bad.

Brolin gives Sofi a shove in the gut with the handle of his axe, and she's caught by two dwarves who chuckle as she stumbles backward. She lets them hold her, too shocked by the king's reaction to resist.

Glancing around, she sees Cora and Wex in the same predicament. The new guy isn't struggling with the two guards seizing his arms—in fact, he's oddly serene—but Cora's putting up a massive fight. She flings elbows and insults with the proficiency of a bar fighter. The rookie stomps on toes to no avail; they've always worn steel-capped boots, at least that much hasn't changed. Two additional guards head toward her, one with a length of metal wire to bind her hands. The four guards together manage to subdue her, and the three humans are half-dragged, half-marched out of the throne room.

As the massive stone door starts to swing shut

behind them, Cora shoulder-checks one of her guards and spins around to shout, "I know what Eris did to you!"

Everything stops. The guards freeze, holding the door open. The king slowly turns to face them.

"I know what her plan is," Cora continues. She's speaking softly now, but the words ring off the walls like a coin dropped into a canyon. "We're not lost mundanes, Your Majesty. We're here to stop her, if we can."

Sofi's mind swings through such a wide range of predictions and emotions she's not entirely sure she's sane.

What the hell is she thinking? We're going to get killed. I need to protect them. There's no way the king believes this. How do we know he's not a bad guy? Do I even believe in this Eris/Gauntlet crap? Does the king?

She breaks the shocked guard's hold and moves to stand next to Cora in the doorway, ready for a fight.

But rather than frothing at the mouth and ordering their messy deaths, King Stonehammer is silent for a long time. The flush drains from of what Sofi can see of his face around that beard, and he lowers his axe.

"Grag," he says to a dwarf to the right of his throne, "show these three *tkaar* to my chambers."

Sofi gawps at the king, utterly amazed at the transformation caused by Cora's outburst. She barely notices the walk to the king's private office. One thought plays over and over in her mind as she tries to adjust.

That should not have worked.

That should not have worked.

Cora's still impressed with herself by the time they're seated in lumpy rock chairs in King Stonehammer's study, a close room lined with bookshelves carved directly into the walls. Sofi likely had a reason for hiding their identities, and she'd wanted to roll with the senior agent's call. But things got desperate. She threw out that piece of information as a last-ditch attempt to avoid another Otherworld dungeon. She hadn't expected such an abrupt and positive reaction, though. Everyone else she's mentioned Eris to has been either dismissive or patronizing.

Brolin hasn't joined them after a several minutes of waiting, so Sofi takes advantage of the break for an agent huddle. She turns her back to Wex, who's standing at the back admiring a painting a six year old could've done better, and hunches over conspiratorially as she whispers to Cora.

"Dude, that was incredibly stupid. But it kept us from getting our heads put on a pike, so good job."

Cora gives a half-embarrassed grin. "Yeah, I know. Looks like he's interested, at least."

Nod. "It's on you, now, Riley. I can't help with the conspiracy theory."

A pang of hurt. "You seriously don't believe me? You saw how it all fits together back in New York. How can you still not see that Eris is up to something awful?"

"I want to," Sofi says, backpedaling, "but you have to admit it's pretty far-fetched."

"It's so obvious!" Cora hisses loudly. "Even a half-witted dwarf living underground his whole life believes it after one sentence."

"You ladies do I know I'm sitting right here."

Cora winces. She'd been too wrapped up in trying to nail down Sofi's support and hadn't noticed the king come in. She turns to face him, grimacing apologetically.

"Sorry, Your Majesty."

Brolin nods patiently. With him sitting in the taller chair on the other side of the marble desk, they're roughly the same height. Cora feels faintly guilty that she's more comfortable this way. Maybe now they can see eye-to-eye.

Speciesist, she thinks.

The king removes his helmet, hanging it on a hook behind him and rubbing a red-knuckled hand over his bald spot. Off comes the shining breastplate and away goes the axe. Without the trappings, Cora notices he looks a great deal more like the dwarves she learned about in old stories and SCD files. And much more comfortable.

He takes a gravelly deep breath, then says, "Before we get down to hard grit, I'd like to offer apologies for how I acted earlier. These spells come over me at the worst times. I wasn't myself." A pause. "Haven't been for a limestone's age."

None of them responds. What could they say?

The king shakes his bushy head as if to clear it,

then trains his unblinking gaze on Cora. "Now, human. Tell me what you know."

"Well, Your Majesty," she begins, casting a sideways look at Wex. She'd rather he not hear this, but it's too late now. So much for keeping a low profile. "We're on assignment from the Supernatural Cases Division." She shows him her badge and puts it back. "The agency's learned that Queen Mab is drugging mortals to boost belief levels in Faerie. Our objective is to destroy the ergot field that supplies the active ingredient."

Brolin nods approvingly. "And the mad goddess?"

Cora chews the inside of her cheek, nervous under the combined weight of three sets of judging eyes. How much does she reveal, particularly in front of Wex, a stranger who literally came out of nowhere? She briefly wishes Jack were here to explain the situation so she doesn't make a fool of herself, but she stifles it. He wasn't the only one who heard what Lady Hel said. Cora's got as much authority on this as he does.

She clears her throat and straightens. "I'm ninety-nine percent sure that Mab's drug ring is being puppeteered by Eris as a branch of her plot to bring down the Gauntlet. She's shoring up belief on this side to make a full breakthrough and take over the mortal world, probably soon. Information's scanty right now, but it's our secondary reason for being in Faerie. I—we mean to stop her."

By the time she finishes, she's not sure the king is listening. He's stopped moving, his eyes are closed, and one hand has disappeared into his beard, presumably on his chin. Several seconds pass. Cora can't hear him breathing. Maybe she's given him a heart attack or bored him to death. Do dwarves turn to stone when they die?

She's about to poke him to check when his eyelids slide open and he speaks again, his slow voice faraway and sad.

"Humans have changed my people so much. If you are truly agents, then you've undoubtedly noticed the difference. The last ten years have sent us down a path from which we haven't been able to turn. There was a time we lived solely underground, content to build our mines and families and live simple, peaceful lives without involving ourselves in Faerie as a nation. But as mortal belief changed us, we craved sunlight and adventure—our quiet existence was no longer adequate. We forged fine jewelry, armor, and weapons though we'd never seen or desired such things before. The gold and gems we harvested from the earth became more precious than our love of digging or of one another, and we hoard it to the detriment of our society. We grew short-tempered, jealous, and vain." He sighs. "This isn't who we are."

Cora wants to ask a question, but Brolin continues. "If it is Eris' desire to bring down the Gauntlet, to merge the worlds, we want no part in it. As much as it hurt dwarves to be separated from Perat in the beginning, the barrier is all that keeps us—and you—safe from the perils it was constructed against in the first place. Should it be destroyed, the changes humans have wrought in us will be permanent. Dwarves will forever be what you have made us."

"But you're dying," Wex interjects. Cora snaps her head around to stare at him. "If the worlds merge, then belief isn't an issue. You won't have to rely on flaky humans to survive because they'll have to believe what's in front of them. Don't you want to save your people from wasting away into nothing?"

The king shifts his stony gaze to Wex, measuring him up. As much as she wants to argue the point herself, Cora lets the king take the lead. Maybe Sofi will finally get it through her thick bear skull that she's telling the truth about Eris if it comes from someone else.

"We are. And I do," Brolin says evenly. "But we understand when other lives are more valuable than our own. It is not worth my people's survival to have supernals enslave the human race on our behalf."

"Who said anything about enslavement?"

A crack appears in the king's beard. The dwarven version of a smile. "Has an invading army ever not enslaved the people they conquer? Wholesale slaughter is the alternative—I doubt that option is preferable to you. Mankind is to supernals as cows are to humans, my friend. If the Gauntlet comes down, the lost world will be reclaimed, and humanity's rule will end."

Wex's brow furrows, but he doesn't reply.

Good. He's out of his league, anyway.

But part of Cora doesn't like the way he's talking.

Even if he's a metahuman himself, how does Wex know so much about belief and the Gauntlet? And why isn't he surprised by their real identities?

Doubt tugs on a suspicion she ignored when they met Wex, and she decides now's a good time to test it. She flips on the supernatural radar, using as little magic as she can and focusing directly on Wex with one burning question in mind. The answer is thrown back with resounding surety, so clear and fast that the senor crashes immediately, leaving her stunned.

Wex isn't just a supernatural; he's the most powerful one she's ever seen.

The vast difference between her first scan and this one makes his motives even more suspect. If he was obscuring his magic levels before, what else has he lied about? And why isn't he covering up now?

Possibilities career through her mind, crashing into one another like bumper cars, until she notices that the room has gone dead silent. Everyone is staring at her expectantly. Including Wex, whose eyes are subtly narrowed in her direction.

Cora blinks and clears her throat apologetically. She'll have to worry about Wex's intentions later.

"Sounds like you're on our side, Your Majesty," she says. "Are you willing to help us bring down the creed ring?"

"Aye."

"Wait, you can't, can you?" Sofi butts in. "Mab put a ban on faeries helping humans."

The crack in the king's beard widens. "Dwarves are not faeries."

All three humans stare at him in dumb silence.

Cora squints at the effort of wrapping her brain around that one. "But you live in Faerie. Doesn't that automatically make you faeries? I mean, elves aren't Fae, but they fall under that," she waves her hands vaguely, "supernatural heading."

"Our own belief counts in the balance, and ours is simple and all-consuming." He points at himself. "I am not a faerie because I am a dwarf. That is all that matters."

Talk about your obvious statements.

"Then we'd be happy for your help, Your Majesty," she says with a smile.

The king rests his forearms on the marble desk, leaning in with a sparkle in his agate eyes. "And I will be happy to give it. On one condition." Cora groans unprofessionally, and the king chuckles. It sounds like pouring cement. "Nothing comes for free in the Otherworld, agent, particularly not here. Faerie or dwarf, a deal must be made."

"I know. But I'd sort of hoped it'd be easier this time."

She shoots a quick look to Sofi, who nods. As the junior agent, Cora's not supposed to be talking to the king, not to speak of brokering deals. If she had to guess, though, Sofi's more comfortable with the mythology expert doing it instead of the muscle. Besides, Cora's had some experience with Otherworld oaths.

"What's your proposition?" she asks.

"I will give you the location of the field you seek, and I will send a unit of my soldiers to accompany you. In return, I require your solemn oath that you and your agency will help my people return to their true selves."

Cora's eyebrows bunch together. "How are we supposed to do that?"

Brolin shrugs and spreads his hands. "That is up to you. I cannot pretend to know the ways of humans. I'll know you've fulfilled your end of the bargain when I stop losing my *grezzkn* mind six times a day."

The king puts out his thick hand for her to shake, and she hesitates, completely unsure of how she can fulfill her end of the bargain. Images of Lord of the Rings protests and bonfires of World of Warcraft discs flash though Cora's mind, and she shudders. There's got to be a way to counterbalance the pop-culture power contributing to the dwarves' change, though she's damned if she knows what it is. But Sofi's pressing gaze on her back tells her it doesn't matter right now; what's important is the task at hand, and they can't do it without the dwarves' help. Cora takes Brolin's hand, a rough thing with the texture of asphalt, and shakes it solemnly.

The king sits back in his chair, looking satisfied. "You're good people. I can tell." He snaps his fingers, and Grag enters. At least Cora thinks it's Grag. Could be any dwarf with a mossy beard. "Have a map of the ergot field's current location drawn up, and ready Khalin's unit. They'll be accompanying these humans in their quest."

Grag eyeballs the three non-dwarves with an

acid glare, then says, "Yes, Your Majesty," and scuttles out of the room.

"Out of curiosity, King Stonehammer," Sofi asks, "how many warriors are you sending with us?"

"Seven."

A small miracle—none of them laughs.

TWENTY-ONE

There's no conversation on the trek between the caverns and the large X marked on Brolin's map. No one has much to say. The humans are exhausted, and these dwarves either refuse to or doesn't know how to speak English.

The last breath of sunset greets the party as they approach the ergot field, the trees thinning closer to what passes for civilization in Faerie. The light stings their eyes, a significant problem for everyone except Cora and Sofi who don their SCD shades while Wex and the dwarves squint. Fortunately, the way they've organized their plan of attack, the sun won't matter soon.

Sofi scents the field before she sees it. A damp, organic aroma laced with a compound that fills her mouth with the taste of tar, making her gag. The smell of something toxic. They've definitely found the place.

She holds up a hand to halt the posse, then motions them into a nearby clump of bushes to review before it's too late to do anything except fight and hope for the best. The map goes down on the ground, and she squats over it, using a stick to direct her motley crew.

"We've got one shot at this, and we've got to make the best of it." She taps on the map. "Cora, you and Wex and these three dwarves stay on the east side of the field," tap, "while me and the other four will take the west. If you guys' tower shields do their job, it should a quick in-and-out hit. Nobody gets hurt, nothing to it."

One of the dwarves raises a hand crusted with iron shavings. Sofi raises her eyebrows. "Yes?"

"What if they call for help?"

She tries not to look surprised. Puny jerks apparently can talk after all.

"We'll roll with that punch when it comes," she says. "Don't think there'll be any problems, though. The king's intel says there are only two Fae at any one time. It's the basilisks we've got to worry about."

The questioner nods, apparently satisfied.

"Anybody else?"

Silence.

"Okay, then." She looks to Cora. "You ready?"

The rookie looks uncertain but nods anyway. She's probably lost without her gun. Sofi'd happily give over her own sidearm if it'd help, but the reaction Cora had to the cold iron bullets could throw the entire thing. Fortunately, in addition to the map, the soldiers, and returning their SCD gear, King Stonehammer also generously outfitted the unarmed mortals with short swords. Even if Cora doesn't know how to use hers, Wex and Brolin's three soldiers will be there back her up.

As if reading her thoughts, Wex catches Sofi's eye and smiles. "Ready when you are, boss."

Her heart gives an excited flutter that she writes off as battle nerves. No matter how many stings she's run or perps she's beat down, that adrenaline rush never goes away. The warrior bear lurking under her skin is itching to get out. They haven't moved into position yet, but her vision is already narrowing. Better go now before instinct takes over and she's useless as a leader.

Sofi stands and examines her team in the fading light, each member nodding their readiness. Without further commentary, the two groups split, heading opposite in directions.

As she heads off to the western end of the ergot field, part of her wonders how many they're going to lose tonight. And who.

After the party breaks up, Wex promptly discards his sword, wedging it into the crotch of a birch tree as they pass. The two of them are making for the eastern edge of the ergot field, taking care to avoid breaking twigs or rustling the underbrush too badly. The element of surprise is the crux of Sofi's plan, and Cora will be damned if she's the one who blows it. But Wex chucking out his weapon is too crazy to let go without commentary. She looks at him like he's grown a third arm.

"What are you doing? You can't go in there unarmed," she whispers.

"Relax, cher," he says.

And lights his hands on fire.

Cora's eyebrows shoot up in alarm. It's not the magic that surprises her—she knows he's a meta, albeit not what type until now—it's the casualness of the gesture. Like he does this all the time. Most metahumans, including ones who've been "out" for years, are reserved with their power. It's not good PR, and it's an easy way to get the SCD crawling up your ass. Him throwing it around like it's nothing gives her the willies. Although maybe all mages are like that.

Wex's mage flame is a coal-fire glow, and it warms her face an arm's length away. He lets it burn for a second or two, then clenches his hands and douses the fire.

"I'll be fine," he says, grinning slyly.

Cora purses her lips but says nothing. They've reached the treeline around the field, and the three dwarves are in position. No time for talk. Time to do something for a change.

She steps up behind the middle dwarf and surveys the scene, the stink of rampant mold packing her nostrils like shoes in a debutante's closet. The two Fae handlers on either end of the closely-planted acre of black rye are easy to spot. The basilisks, on the other hand, take longer to find, primarily because she's looking for something completely different. Rather than the smallish, feathered dragons she expects, they're enormous cobras on chicken legs with huge fangs and golden scales. More Harry Potter than Pliny the Elder. Either way, though, she has to assume they'll still kill you dead—whether by poison or petrification doesn't matter much. It's too late to change the battle plan; all she can do is add the information to her mental files and keep going.

Cora draws her sword, keeping her eyes on the nearest basilisk, and motions for the dwarves to lock ranks in front of her. They respond immediately, sliding their square shields together to form a wall of shiny steel. She trades places with Wex, putting him behind the line to deal with the basilisk. Then, using the tall grass for cover, she slinks off to the right where the High Fae handler is neglecting his charge. Once she's in position, she signals to Wex. The mage nods, then ignites his hands.

"Go," Cora whispers.

They all step out at once.

The battle cry of the three dwarves shatters the calm of the newly-fallen night and draws the basilisk's attention immediately. There's a hiss as the monster's gaze bounces off the over-polished shields, and Wex's triumphant whoop rises above it all as he engages the monster.

Hearing the ruckus, the Fae handler whips around with a rapier in his hand, ready to charge, but Cora steps up and shouts, "Over here!"

There's exactly enough time to put her back to

the basilisk skirmish before the faerie changes direction in mid-air and heads for her, eyes ablaze.

Cora grins and crouches down, choking up on her sword like a baseball bat. She hasn't had SCD sword training yet, but it's a pretty simple principle. She'll learn as she goes.

On the west side of the field, Sofi's taking advantage of the noise Cora's detachment is making. Her team of dwarves formed their reflective shield wall before they reached the gravel edge of the field, and now they're proceeding relentlessly forward.

She darts ahead into the rye, staying low while fishing in her field kit with both hands for her faerie bait. She stomps down moldy stalks, then dumps the pocket-sized music box onto the flattened circle and squeezes the entire bottle of honeyed cream over it. A soggy rendition of Over the Rainbow tinkles out when she pokes it on with the toe of her shoe.

She grins as she backs up towards the dwarves, impressed by her own cunning in devising the faerie-attracting mess. It'll bring that nasty Fae directly to them. Why work hard when you can work smart, right? She's already concocting the humblebrag she'll tell Cora when this is over.

Trap set, Sofi unholsters her sidearm and clicks the safety off, sighting for the Fae handler. If she can pick him off with an iron bullet before the basilisk goes down, she won't have to fight him hand to hand. Although that would be more fun.

"There 'e is, lads!"

Instinct wants Sofi to turn, but she keeps her eyes forward. One look at that nasty lizard would murder her in half a second. Instead, she glances around at the three outbuildings arranged along the north side of the field for any sign of the Fae handler. But there's not a lick of blue skin to be seen.

In fact, everything's quiet on this side. She can hear the clang of metal on metal echoing from Cora's end, but nothing is coming from her own honor guard of dwarves. That's either very good or very, very bad.

Keeping both hands on her weapon, Sofi screws her eyes shut and turns to where she knows the line of shields is. Tentatively, she peeks under the barest crack of an eyelid to see a dwarf waving at her, trying to get her attention.

"We got 'em," he says with gruff satisfaction.

She opens one eye at a time, then lowers her gun as she takes in the scene.

Sure enough, there's a frozen basilisk standing mere inches away from the dwarves, claw outstretched and ready to strike, completely petrified. And off to its right, a blue statue decorated with golden spirals and its sword hand raised for an attack. That Medusa-reflection trick Cora came up with totally worked. Sofi may conveniently forget to mention the Fae sneaking up behind her when she tells the story later, though.

Sofi holsters her gun and smiles at the dwarves. "Well, that was easy," she says.

Elsewhere, Limerence is pressing her body to Jack's, running her tongue over her teeth like a hungry animal. They fit together as if made in a set, both tall, thin, and angular.

Tendrils of her mind wrap around his, touching dark places she created, drawing him in. He knows she's doing it. But holding her again now, he doesn't mind. The rush of familiarity, the scent of spun sugar. This was his entire world for so long.

He should've stayed. Avoided the burden of the agency, never lost his humanity. Had the charmed life of a faerie and lived forever without ever knowing less than absolute devotion, magic, and freedom.

He tightens his embrace and Limerence rest her hands on his chest, plucking at his shirt as if it offends her with its existence.

"Perhaps I was wrong," she says. "Perhaps you are ready to learn the secrets of an open heart."

Jack brushes a strand of turquoise hair from her face, pausing to rest his hand against her cheek. The promise of both untold power and eternal love shine bright in her gray eyes. He's not sure which he wants more.

She leans into his palm. "I can give you what you want, my love. I can teach you to unlock your heart and the power that flows from it." Fluttering her eyelashes, she adds, "You know what I want in return."

He does. Through the haze of enchantment and

desire, he knows the underlying bargain.

I will teach you, but only if you stay and love me. Only if your opened heart is mine alone. Only if you never leave again.

The faerie brand, her claim on his life that he willingly gave, shoots electric sparks through his veins as she touches it again, underscoring the temptation. He shudders with a tormented breath.

She grins wickedly. "Isn't this better than whatever fleeting pleasure that half-breed whelp could ever give you?"

Cora.

Her name echoes quietly in a place where Limerence's magic can't reach. It clears Jack's mind with the swift force of a sniper round. She can read his memories but not the full depth of his heart. He inhales sharply, then presses his forehead to Limerence's to cover the wave of fresh resolve.

He has to move forward with his plan, even if it breaks his heart to do it.

Sweat pours down Cora's face and back as she exchanges blows with the Fae on her side of the field. He's toying with her, dancing in and out of her guard, never actually striking her, letting her parry blows that could've killed her instantly. All he's done is to wear her down and piss her off. Like a cat playing with a mouse before eating it.

She can hear Wex doing the same to the basilisk somewhere behind her. The dwarves, having failed to freeze the stupid thing, went to Plan B—

dismantling the production facilities on the north side—leaving the mage to dispatch the monster himself. It hisses angrily as he laughs at it.

This moron's gonna get himself killed. Finish the job and get over here and help me before we both get waxed.

Another clumsy blow to the Fae's midsection, another delicate leap out of the way.

And now he starts to taunt her. Great.

"Don't you know which side you're supposed to be on?" he grins.

She swings at his feet, a move he easily dodges. "What horseshit are you talking now?" she huffs as she regains her balance.

"Oh, come now, sweetling. Gray eyes, magic in your veins? Surely you don't think you're human."

He reaches in with his rapier and flicks one of the buttons off her suit jacket. She tries to parry, but the dwarf sword was too heavy to begin with; her weakening muscles make it difficult to swing without opening up her guard. The Fae giggles as she impotently spins herself around and waits for her to regain her footing.

"You're not going to use any of your damned faerie tricks on me," Cora growls. A heavy swing and a miss. "I know who I am."

Another dodge and laugh. "Oh, do you?"

It's a small but effective retort. Doubt creeps in. This wouldn't be the first time some supernatural asshole knew more about her than she did. The point of Cora's sword wavers, and the Fae smirks. He whips the rapier through the air, daring her to come forward.

You know what? Fuck this guy.

A surge of angry energy and good dose of fear guides her sore arms into a sudden, graceful arc that catches the smug faerie off guard, slicing him from collarbone to ribs. It's not a deep cut, but it's enough. The two stand in shocked surprise as he touches the bright green blood in disbelief as it beads up on his skin.

The moment passes. The Fae's playful facade burns away, replaced by a mask of hatred. He throws his head back and yells across the field.

"Braack! Get out here!"

Rumbling from the outbuildings snatches Sofi's attention from the scene of her team's victory. The ground vibrates with a steady pulse, like a heartbeat earthquake. She and her four companions turn to see a gray mound of moving stone burst from a wooden structure, splintering the door in its wake and swinging a club made from a single enormous tree. The troll stomps out into the center of the ergot field, smashing the crop underfoot, and bellows a war cry that Sofi's sure makes a few stars wink out.

Then the hulking monstrosity heads in Cora's direction.

Sofi doesn't stop to think. She darts into the field, frantically waving her arms and shouting, "Hey, ugly! Over here!" She picks up a largish stone and hucks it as hard as she can in the monster's direction.

That does the trick. The rock bounces off the troll's gelatinous belly, and a head the size of a Buick rotates on what passes for a neck, yellow piggy eyes refocusing on the bouncing human trying to get its attention. The creature swings itself around, striding to her side of the field, brandishing its club.

Sofi laughs and rolls out of the way easily as the troll tries to stomp on her, accompanied by the enthusiastic din of axes against shields. The warrior bear surfaces, roaring in battle frenzy, and she rushes the ten-foot-high monster while noting weak spots. A malicious grin spreads over her face, and she flexes her fingers like claws.

One more human thought before they collide: *Finally, a real challenge.*

Little has stuck with Jack from his college days. As Agent 97, he put a lot of effort into excoriating those vaults, but some memories survived.

This is one of those.

"If it's what I have to do to survive, how can it be evil?" Wex says through a cloud of exhaled cigarette smoke. He leans against the stone steps of the cathedral, eyes turned to the sky but focused elsewhere. "Why would any creator invent me and then tell me not to do it? Sounds like a fucking stupid god."

Jack sits beside him, long arms wrapped around knobby knees, trying to keep warm between the crisp spring air and the marble step. "Because you're literally sucking the life out of someone to fuel your own magic, that's why," he says. "Can't you see how screwed up that is? How is that not evil?"

They've been arguing for an hour. Daria and Bethany took off a while ago, bored out of their tiny air elemental minds by the philosophical debate. Whatever. They don't get it and don't have to. Besides, it's not the first time they've had this argument. They have it every time Wex has to "feed." It's never sat right with Jack.

Wex takes another drag. "Don't hurt, if that's what you're worried about. Feels fantastic from what I can tell."

"That's not the point."

"Then what is it, Jackie?" Wex demands. "What's got you so worried about mundanes that you'd argue your best friend out of his gods-given power—his own damn life—to rescue them?" He stubs out his cigarette on the step. "They're not like us. They're not special or interesting. They're an evolutionary cul-de-sac" He waves a hand to indicate the city. "They already act like livestock. Why shouldn't I treat them that way?"

Jack lowers his head as his ire rises. Standing up to Wex when he's pissed off is like trying to stop a freight train with a tripwire. No point.

In his mind's theatre, though, he's reliving the scene from last night: the desiccated corpse of a once-pretty girl held in Wex's loving embrace, his friend revitalized to near adolescence where he'd looked sixty that morning. The draw of power from one being to another, one ruined to revive another. It's both horrific and enticing to know it's possible.

Jack has had nightmares about it for his entire life. He's been dreaming about it, too.

Cora watches wide-eyed and dumb as the troll bursts into the field. It heads her way for the briefest of seconds before it's distracted by something on the other side. There's an angry curse from the High Fae that called up the beast when he realizes it's not coming, followed by the sound of sliced air and an explosion of pain.

The dwarven sword clatters into the gravel as Cora clutches her forearm. Bright moonlight blackens the crimson blood welling up between her fingers. She sucks in breath through her teeth to dull the pain, but the cut's deep. Her attacker grins at her, then purposefully shoves his rapier into the meat of her bicep. This time, she cries out.

Flashbulbs go off in her vision, and she imagines what it's going to feel like to be literally cut into ribbons. She takes a defensive step away and nearly flips backwards over a charred basilisk carcass. Between the gushing blood, the pain in her arm, and the sudden stop, Cora's trapped as her attacker closes the gap between them.

"You should've stood with your people, stupid girl," the Fae says.

He makes a complicated arc with his sword,

grinning to show ever more teeth in the moment of his triumph.

She's got one last desperate trick.

Cora reaches into her jacket with her good arm and wraps shaky fingers around the bottle of Greek fire. Cid intended for the ergot field, but she'll happily smash it on her attacker instead. Maybe if she's lucky, she can get both at once.

But before she can wind up for the throw, the world is on fire. The faerie in front of her, the ergot field—and Cora herself.

Endorphins from the sword wounds buffer the first wave of agony and keep her from screaming. There's a crystalline moment in which her elementary school training to stop, drop, and roll takes over. Blood-dampened grass douses the magical orange flame crawling up her ruined arm and into her clothes. The bottle of unquenchable fire rolls anticlimactically out of her hand as she comes to a stop on her back in a cool patch of ferns.

The Fae isn't as lucky. Screaming and flailing, he runs blindly into the burning field, his body adding fuel to the blaze and abruptly ending his agony.

There's another movement out there, too, rapidly getting more complex. A tall figure laughing. A moving mountain. But shock swirls Cora's vision, and she can't analyze what's happening. Too much trauma, too fast.

Her eyelids flutter. First aid taught her that she's got to stay awake, but it's so hard. Heat from the razed field and the scent of burning narcotics are speeding her into sleep. Parts of her are already offline; the signal to shut down is working its way up from her toes. A lone tear trickles down her temple and into her hair as her overloaded senses block out everything except the pain.

As Cora closes her eyes against the orange glow and black smoke, a silenced part of her heart cries out, flinging a lifeline into the ether like a magical SOS.

Jack. Where are you, Jack? I need you.

It can't be that hard. It's a basic transfer of energy. No more complicated than opening a door that isn't there. Jack's done it before, tapping another meta's power to fuel his own sidesteps. Although, never to this degree. Or for this kind of 'step. If it's possible.

But she's not mortal, he reassures himself. Losing the volume of power he'll need won't kill her. Probably. The likelihood is extremely low, at least. It's simple. Blameless.

He moves his hand from Limerence's cheek to tangle his fingers in her hair. It's soft and inviting, begging him to bury his face in it and forget. But he's committed. Under the surface, below the level where she can skim his mind, comic book lore and magical memory synthesize and spin, building momentum. His power crackles awake as he pools what magic he can under her spell.

To his surprise, she smiles up at him. She must feel his energy moving. But he can see in her eyes that, even this close and with his brand active, she has no idea what's coming. He shoves aside actively thinking about it; she can read him, and it's vital to avoid discovery. She has to be comfortable and willing for this to work.

He smiles back and leans in.

It's got to be precise. Teleporting without direction could be deadly. He needs to arrive at the banks of the Waterfall, six feet from the shore, beside the ash tree. A pinpoint on a map he remembers with vivid clarity.

The kiss begins with earnest desire. All the longing and anxiety built up since the moment he arrived in Faerie poured into a touch. She presses back, telegraphing how badly he broke her heart, how much she needs him, how deeply her love runs. He lets her wash over him. For long moments, they're bound together as if he'd never left. One being with one heart. Perfectly, eternally matched.

And then the tide shifts.

The seawall restraining Jack's will cracks, and he inhales with intention, tasting the sugar of Limerence's breath as he latches onto her energy. It takes half a second for her to understand what's happening. Her eyes widen in shock, and her aura bursts violently into life. But the crimson fades quickly to dull red, then pink, then disappears altogether as he siphons away her magic with his will. It crashes through his mind in ruby waves turned amethyst as her power mixes into his blue-tinted reserves. The influx is hungrily claimed, assimilated, and transformed into magical fuel, the pressure of which he can barely contain.

The faerie woman sags in his arms as helpless

tears stream down her cheeks. The betrayal in her eyes punches him in the gut, and he almost stops.

How can I? I have to escape. At what cost? Am I as deranged as Wex? What about duty? And Cora?

As if in response, a plaintive voice rings out across the glen.

"Jack. Where are you, Jack? I need you."

Her voice.

He looks down into Limerence's ashen face, torn between what he's done and why he's done it. He kneels and gently lays the faerie woman on the cool grass. She's breathing shallowly and covered in clammy sweat—alive, if barely. Tears of regret work their way down his cheeks. But it's too late. It's done.

He stands, spooling up the massive reserve of magic, forcing himself to focus on the jump. He steals one last glance at his former lover, his master, his victim lying prone at his feet. She raises the fingers of her right hand in a feeble attempt at begging him to stay. But he closes his eyes against it and turns his back to her.

There's a crack like lightning striking a copper rod as he releases the pent-up magic, followed by a blinding violet flash. And then he's gone.

A cool shadow passes in front of the broiling poisonous plants. There's lightness as Cora's lifted gently from the hard earth.

A soft, worried voice. Jack's voice.

"I'm here."

She exhales with relief, something between a sigh and a death rattle, and succumbs to the sweet darkness of sleep.

TWENTY-TWO

Cora stirs. Just a bit, but it's more than she's done in the last hour, and it puts Sofi on the alert. Cora's sweating and gritting her teeth in her sleep, eyelids fluttering madly with whatever pain's visiting her in unconsciousness. Sofi took basic EMT training as part of agency prep work, but nothing she knows is helping Cora's magical wounds. She presses a cold compress against the other woman's angry burns, then looks toward the treeline, anxious for the rest of their party to return.

Their retreat from the burning ergot crop had been a direct line to the river that runs through Faerie. Jack knew exactly where they were going. In the excitement, Sofi didn't question how he'd arrived at the field; all either of them could think about was getting Cora to safety. Once they reached the bank, he'd instructed the dwarves to tear long strips from their tunics to make bundles filled with a random plant he'd found and dunked in the icy water. Then he'd handed the sodden pile to Sofi and disappeared into the woods with the king's loaned guards—minus Krigg, the poor bastard—leaving her to handle the situation alone.

Cora moans and tries to shift, but Sofi gently presses her back. The rookie's entire left arm looks more like a barbecued pork roast than a limb. If she rolls over on it, it'll wake her up for sure, and she'll start screaming again.

Sofi uses her heightened senses to try to pluck early signs of Jack's return out of the air. It's not that she's resentful of being left behind to tend to the wounded. Well, okay, yeah, it's that. Like having boobs means she's automatically a caregiver. She can take care of Cora, and her momma bear instincts encourage her to do so, but she'd rather be scouting or whatever the menfolk decided was more important than their fallen comrade. Add misogyny to the rather long list of reasons she doesn't like Jack.

A sharp inhale jerks Sofi's attention back to her patient. Cora starts awake, half-raising, unable to support herself on the ruined arm.

"Shh, shh, you're okay, I got you," Sofi croons.

She shuffles around on her knees, then eases Cora's head and shoulders into her lap, smoothing her damp red hair back from her forehead. No need for a thermometer to tell her the girl's running a fever.

"Where's Jack?" The words are hardly audible except for Sofi's unnaturally good hearing.

"He'll be back soon."

The tension falls out of Cora's frame, and she gives more of her weight to Sofi. They sit quietly as the injured woman gets her bearings. Sofi's still listening for signs of their allies, but all she can hear is rushing water and Cora's labored breath.

"How did he find us?" Cora eventually says.

A laugh. "If you believe Jack, you summoned him."

"What?"

"Some magical hubajoo involving harmonics and quantum somethingorothers. Says he was in the middle of something, but you interrupted it and brought him to you."

Cora's brow furrows. "That shouldn't be possible."

Shrug. "That's what he said, too. But it happened, so there's that."

There's a crispy sound as Cora flexes her hand. Watching the movement of her blackened forearm and bicep makes Sofi want to barf. She turns her head to look at the treeline instead. What is taking them this long?

"So, uh, you want to tell me what happened to my arm?" Cora says.

"I'd love to, but I don't know. Was sort of busy climbing Mount Troll and popping its eyeballs with my bare hands. When I got to your side of the field, Jack was already there and everyone was running, so I ran, too. And now we're here."

Another moment of silent contemplation.

Then Cora's eyes widen and she tries to sit up again. "Where's Wex?" she says anxiously.

"He's gone," says Jack.

Both women snap their heads toward the voice, as Jack steps out of the foliage silent as a panther. How long was he standing there without Sofi noticing? Creepy motherfucker.

"He'd taken off by the time I arrived," he continues, coming over to join them. "I don't see any trace of him in the surrounding area."

Cora looks up at the tall, dark man outlined in the moonlight. He looks down at her. Something passes between them that gives Sofi a twinge of jealousy. She makes a mental note to ask Cora about it later, when she doesn't so closely resemble a bucket of fried chicken.

"Are you okay?" he asks Cora.

"I'll live."

"Are you sure?"

She winces. "Let's call it fifty-fifty."

Jack kneels beside Cora and inspects her arm. Sofi had to cut away everything but Cora's undershirt with a pocket knife. The sleeves of her jacket and shirt protected her skin like paper against a blowtorch, and the flesh under the cracked black parts are raw red. Sofi hands Jack the last cool compress, and he presses it onto the burn at Cora's shoulder. To her credit, Cora doesn't cry out, though she does stiffen and tears of pain squish out.

"Isn't the grass you put in there supposed to heal burns?" Sofi asks.

He nods, eyebrows drawn together in a mirror of her own confusion. "It's a common remedy here, but...," he trails off. Gingerly, he uses two fingers to lift Cora's arm for a better look at the charred underside, forearm, and fingers.

"But what?"

He lays her arm down gently, then turns to Sofi. Is that actual worry she sees? "But it doesn't heal magical wounds."

Cora shifts. "Wex's hands," she says through clenched teeth. "He was using mage fire." She looks up at Sofi. "I didn't get a chance to use the Greek fire Cid gave us, so I figured you were burning the field. It must've been him."

"Must've been."

Another wince. "Caught in the crossfire." She gives a feeble laugh.

Jack's face darkens. He stands and strides to the river bank alone. Sofi's been in the SCD long enough to follow the train of logic that must be running through his mind.

"Hey," she says, looking down at Cora's sweat-shiny face, "I'm going to get more cold water on these things. Will you be okay for five minutes by yourself?"

Cora smiles as best she can. Brave face, like always. "Sure. As long as there aren't any more fireballs. Not sure I can take another one of those."

"That's the spirit."

Sofi stands, gathering up the used compresses and moves to the riverbank next to Jack. She kneels and dips the packets in the water one at a time, rinsing away the dead skin and blood, waiting for him to say something. When he doesn't, she pipes up, taking care to keep her eyes on the river and her tone casual despite the pounding in her chest.

"How long?"

"Six hours until the midnight switch. Seven before her wounds turn septic."

Silence. There's only thing to do as far as Sofi can see, but she's not sure how well it'll go over with Mr. Officialpants. To her surprise, though, he brings it up before she can.

"We have to go back," he says.

She shakes the excess water off the last compress and stands.

The last time they stood face to face, it was nearly two years and three thousand miles away. All her hate for him frozen in time as they kept vigil over Zara's body. When she'd looked into his eyes, though, bare of his sunglasses, she'd seen part of herself there. It's haunted her since.

Now, as they lock eyes on the banks of the Faerie river, another woman she cares about in peril, Sofi sees they're more similar now. Instead of angry girl versus machine, they're united in purpose now: Two people intensely worried about someone they love. Part of her anger at him melts away.

"No argument here," she says. She points with her chin to where Cora's laying. "Lead the way, boss."

He raises an eyebrow but doesn't say anything, and they walk back together.

Sofi plops down cross-legged next to Cora and swaps out the old dressing as Jack outlines the situation.

"As it stands, we've completed our primary objective," he says, pacing in short steps. "The field and processing plant have been effectively neutralized. The secondary objective of issuing charges to Mab can be put off for the time being in light of the current situation. Aside from the gross changes in background magic we didn't account for, we've got an agent down and in need of immediate medical attention—"

Cora waves Sofi away as she pushes herself up with her good arm. "Hey, that's not fair. I'm hurt, but that's no reason not to finish the assignment. We can make it."

"You're obviously in large amounts of pain, Cora. Your usefulness in the field is next to zero." It comes out harsh, and she looks stung, but he presses on. "It's a long way to the Waterfall Court from here, and there's no telling what we'll find when we arrive. Eris' involvement makes the entire thing intrinsically chaotic. You can't adapt properly with one arm perpetually on fire." He stops pacing in front of Cora and looks down. He's doing a crap job of hiding his concern. "I'm not willing to risk your life for the sake of the assignment."

Cora's about to strike back when the sound of horses interrupts the argument. All three agents instinctively get low, heads on a swivel. Jack inches forward toward the treeline, and Sofi reaches for her gun.

"Och! Relax, ye twitchy mortals."

The leader of the dwarf contingency emerges from the trees with his hands above his head.

Everyone unclenches. The remaining six dwarves file out, accompanied by three black horses outfitted in full riding gear.

"Thought ye might need a bit of a boost to get where ye're goin'," the red-bearded leader says with what Sofi thinks is a grin. Hard to tell under all that facial hair.

Jack steps forward as the horses are brought to the river to drink. "A fine gesture, my friend. Should I ask how you procured them?"

"Only if you want to hear a hilarious story about beatin' up some drunk Fae on their way to the Hunt."

A hearty chortle from the band of miscreants. And Sofi.

Jack manages to keep a straight face. "While I appreciate the thought, perhaps stolen horses isn't the best way for us to approach the Court." Assorted chastised muttering. "But that's rather beside the point. We're heading back."

"Now, wait a goddamn minute," says Cora. She wobbles getting to her feet, and Sofi darts to help stabilize her. "Don't call this off on my account. I don't do white knight bullshit, remember? We've got a mission to finish, even if I 'm down to one arm."

"And no gun," Sofi reminds her.

A sour glare. "And no gun." She turns back to Jack. "With the horses, we can get to the Waterfall way faster. I can hold out if I get some bandages and a sling." She takes a step forward. "The field is burned, but that might not be the most important part of this expedition. If Mab can tell us about Eris' plans, that's worth more than my arm."

The determination in those gray eyes impresses the hell out of Sofi. Cora's injured, but whatever strength she has left could get her through if she's careful. As overprotective as Sofi knows she is, that little speech is moving her to finish the assignment, too. And she can't help being curious about the Eris thing.

Jack isn't sold, though. "And what happens if things go south? You can't fight, and you may not be able to gather enough energy to find a door for a quick escape on your own."

Cora sniffs and raises her chin. "I'm not worrying about 'ifs'. We need to see this assignment through. Besides," she says, casting a glance at Sofi, "I'm confident that between you and Mamma Bear here, you can handle any imminent violence that comes our way."

Tense silence between the two sidesteppers ripples the air as they stare at each other. Even the dwarves, notoriously slow on the emotional uptake, fidget uncomfortably. Sofi wonders if she should step in as comic relief, but blessedly, Jack breaks first.

A resigned sigh. "Fine. We'll go to the Court."

Cora grins and makes the universal gesture for "goal!," then hisses and clutches her scorched arm. Jack starts to go to her, then stops himself. Wouldn't be professional of him to comfort her. Not in front of strangers, anyway.

Sofi reaches out to steady her friend, then turns

her attention to fashioning a more durable wrapping for their trip. As she works, she can hear Jack discussing the rest of the situation with the dwarves.

"No ponies, I see. You're not going with us."

"Nay. Our end of the bargain's fulfilled and then some. We've been above ground too long and lost a brother. Time t' go home."

"I understand. Give Brolin my regards and apologies. Tell him I'll do my best to uphold the bargain he made with my agents, but if there's war on the horizon, it may come to nothing in the end."

"Understood. May the sky nae fall on yer heads."

"May the gold you find enrich your heart."

Sofi tightens the last knot on the makeshift sling around Cora's neck as Jack returns. The healing grass should keep Cora from feeling like she's on fire for a couple hours, and tying the arm to her torso should help avoid jarring it. Good enough for government work.

"Ready to go, tough girl?" she says.

Cora nods and takes a deep breath, testing the security of the dressing.

"Can you ride with one arm?" Jack asks.

"I've done it before. Broke the other one falling out of a tree when I was twelve and could steer okay in the cast."

"These aren't normal horses, Cora," he warns with an eye on the beasts at the riverbank. "There's no telling what they'll do."

She laughs. "You act like you've never ridden before."

"Of course I have. I just...don't trust horses."

Sofi gigglesnorts. "Oh my god, the biggest, baddest motherfucker in the history of SCD is afraid of horses? Holy shit, wait 'til I tell Cid."

"These aren't normal horses, Strella," Jack snaps back. "Fae animals are wilder and less sane. You can't trust them, even with a saddle and bridle."

Cora waves her good hand, failing to hide an amused grin. "Guys, we don't have time to argue. If you're that worried, Jack, ride with me. I'll promise to protect you from the dangerous beast of burden."

She walks over to the horses, clicking her tongue to get their attention. Three black heads swing around, and the horses lope obediently toward her. Sofi does note that they're different from the animals she's ridden on trips to the country with her dad. These have an unpredictable air to them, like they might bolt or bite at any minute. Suddenly, Jack's fears don't seem so silly.

But they like Cora fine. The faerie horses shuffle themselves until they're evenly spaced in a straight line in front of her like soldiers awaiting inspection. The petite woman circles the animals, making soothing noises and stroking their coats. When she comes to the horse on the right, she says "You're excused," and swats it on the rump, sending it running into the woods.

Turning her attention back to her companions, she says, "C'mon, guys. Gotta get a move on."

Sofi looks to Jack, his face a picture of ball-shriveling anxiety. "Ride 'em, cowboy," she says and slaps him on the back so hard he stumbles forward.

She steps up to her horse, then stops short of putting a foot in the stirrup.

Can't forget that.

It takes a quick second to run and grab the long stone from under the tree where she'd dumped it earlier. If she left this thing behind, she'd never forgive herself.

As she jogs back, Cora raises an eyebrow. "And that is...?"

Sofi grins. "What's the point in taking down a twelve-foot troll with your bare hands if you can't prove you did it?" She hefts the retrieved object, the monster's stony middle finger, fitted with a leather strap she begged off the dwarves. "Makes a pretty good club, don't you think?"

"God, you are so weird, Soph."

She laughs and slings the trophy across her back, then hoists herself up. It's been a long time since she's been in the saddle, but it's coming back fast. Like riding a thousand-pound bicycle that can kick your teeth in.

Jack sidles up to Cora's horse. The horse flares its nostrils at his diffidence and tries to retreat, but Cora coos in its ear and it relents. She's squirmed into the oversized saddle without help, and she offers her free hand to Jack. He takes a deep, resigned breath, and swings up awkwardly behind her. Sofi has to bite her lip to keep from laughing as he tangles his foot in the stirrup.

"See, that wasn't so bad," Cora says reassuringly.

He wraps his skinny arms around her waist, taking care to avoid her hurt arm. There's a brief blue glow as they touch.

Sofi rubs her eyes. Faerie is weird.

"Which way?" she asks out loud.

She's expecting Jack to answer, but it's Cora who points off to the west. "That way. We can find a spot to cross, then head northwest and follow the river upstream to the Waterfall. Easy."

Before Sofi can ask how she knows, they're are already galloping away over the low grass. She digs her heels into her own mount's flanks and tears off after them. Questions later, action now. Exactly the way she likes it.

TWENTY-THREE

The ride is shorter than Cora anticipated. She can't be sure exactly how long because of Faerie timey-wimey weirdness, but the river trail makes navigation simple. So does the disturbing sense of familiarity.

The closer they get to the Waterfall Court and the center of Faerie, the stronger the warm pulse in her chest grows. It's not her heartbeat or the throbbing pain of her burnt arm—she can identify those easily. It's something more. Deeper. The same odd déjà vu she had before realizing her year of nightmares actually took her to the underworld. They've stopped since she returned, but the memory lingers: She knows where they're going without ever having been here. And that's getting to her.

Cora's horse reacts to her distraction by slipping out of her control. It's drawing something from her, she can tell. Both fighting her and eager to please, tuned to her energy. She shunts aside the unsettling familiarity and concentrates on not dumping her and Jack onto the ground.

She hears the music before she sees the light. Lively jigs played on flutes and drums and stringed things set against the unmistakable sound of churning water. Coming gently downhill through the thinning forest, she can see the valley is illuminated by ceramic pots filled with glowing plants. They throw soft shadows on the ground and rocky banks that hug the smooth, wide river as it pours down from the dancing waterfall at the far end. Maybe two dozen High Fae, adorned with various scraps of cloth and greenery, dance and make merry in the fine mist. No one seems to notice the hoofbeats as they approach.

When they reach the last of the tree cover, Cora stops the horses. Jack swings down immediately, somewhat more graceful escaping from the horse than getting onto it.

"I'll handle this," he whispers. "Don't try to intervene, no matter what happens. In and out—quick."

She nods. While it chafes her pride not to be involved in the climax of the investigation, exhaustion is descending quickly, and she's admittedly not much use with one arm if things go south. She takes the hand Jack offers and dismounts with a wince.

The stolen Fae horses, now riderless and free, trot off into the forest, leaving the three humans standing awkwardly at the edge of the Faerie

Court's party. Cora can practically read the minds of her companions without magic. Sofi's itching for a fight, fretting about Cora's injury, and aching to go home. Jack's anxious too, but he's filtering it into the job and pretending not to care. Her own internal landscape is flattening by the minute, pain leveling her as she tries to keep it together long enough to finish the assignment. If they can last another half hour, they'll be home free.

"We're going to do this fast and by the book," Jack whispers. "Sofi, stay to my right. If there's trouble, get Cora to safety. There's too many of them for us to fight, so run if it comes to that. She can find a door and get you out. Understood?"

Nod.

"Cora, all I need you to do is focus on staying conscious. Can you handle that?"

Nod.

"Good." He takes a deep breath and exhales slowly, eyes closed. There's a long pause. When he opens his eyes again, they're darker somehow. "Let's go," he says, then turns on his heel and heads toward the sound of laughing faeries.

Cora and Sofi fall into step on either side of him. Every nerve in Cora's body clangs with pain and high alert. Her vision swims, and it takes her a moment to grasp the layout of the Faerie Court as they step into the pool of greeny-yellow of light. The river cuts a straight line from the waterfall's rocky basin, heading out into the countryside. A wide swath of trees has been cleared on either side to form a glade that could hold a minor festival. Long tables on the west bank of the dividing river hold dishes of fairycakes and large wine jugs, the east bank is populated by musicians, and faeries on both sides are dancing with abandon.

At the juncture where the waterfall's basin becomes the river sits a broad platform that stretches from bank to bank. It supports a modest throne of branches held together with living vines near the back edge, leaving plenty of clear space in front for audiences.

The woman seated there can only be Queen Mab. Her elegant, brocaded gown drapes across her fine frame in ribbons of gold, and her thick, crayon-red hair hangs loose around her shoulders, pinned back from her navy blue face with a simple silver circlet. She's talking quietly with a handmaiden, smiling and gesturing as she speaks.

As the three mortals approach the throne from the eastern side, the dancers and musicians carry on as if they don't notice them. Cora raises a questioning eyebrow at Jack, who shrugs. They proceed toward the riverbank, passing close enough to a pair of dancers that Cora sees the sweat glistening on their bare chests. Sofi accidentally knocks into a drummer, but no one stops their reveling or even glances at the intruders.

Until they reach the throne.

The instant Jack puts his foot down on the wide platform, everything stops. Dancers land and turn to stare. Music cuts off in a discordant screech of strings. No one's laughing anymore. Two dozen sets of eyes snap forward, burning with gray fire. The agents continue to mount the platform accompanied by the sound of rushing water and stand before the queen.

To Cora's surprise, Mab stands and holds out her arms in gracious welcome. "Finally," she says. "We've been waiting for you. Won't you join us?" Her voice is low, almost manly, and resonates peculiarly in Cora's mind.

Jack positions himself in front of the other agents and holds up his badge. Cora mentally rolls her eyes. How many times has the official route worked on this trip, exactly? But he's determined to do it by the book.

"Queen Mab, as the current ruler of Faerie, you are ultimately accountable for crimes committed in your realm. It is my duty to inform you of the following charges issued by the Supernatural Cases Division of the FBI on behalf of the people of Perat."

He pauses to let her reply. The queen's eyes rest on him for a moment, then she sits back in the throne without a word, crossing her legs and folding her hands, and waits for him to continue.

Jack doesn't miss a beat. He ticks off charges on his long fingers. "One: The production and distribution of the magical narcotic known as creed. Two: Assaulting an officer. Subcharge, obstruction of justice. Three: Suspicion of terrorism, including aiding and abetting a known enemy of Perat, namely the goddess Eris." He lowers his free hand but keeps the badge up. "While the ergot field and associated production machinery have been disabled, the gravity of the situation, particularly charge three, cannot be ignored, and as such, I am formally requesting you accompany me back to the SCD for further questioning."

The Faerie Queen bursts out laughing. And not polite or dismissive laughter, either. This is a full-body, holding her sides, tears leaking out sort. After a couple of seconds, the entire court erupts into laughter right along with her. Every faerie is doubled over, guffawing at the ridiculous mortal's demands.

Cora's ears redden, and she exchanges a worried glance with Sofi behind Jack's back. But the senior agent doesn't flinch. He waits for the laughter to die away, which takes an agonizingly long time, then takes another step forward, as if to underline the fact that he's serious.

"Your Majesty...," he begins.

Without warning, his upraised badge is ripped from his fingers by invisible strings and flies into Mab's waiting palm. The queen turns the worn leather square over to examine it, tracing the SCD shield with her fingertip. She smiles, then drops Jack's symbol of office unceremoniously into the river behind her.

Jack doesn't blink, but Cora knows this is bad. While the SCD doesn't have ultimate power in the Otherworld, numerous treaties and contracts with the real world give them authority here. If Mab's literally throwing that out, the effects of the belief imbalance run deeper than they suspected.

The queen stands, putting her hands on her hips

as if addressing a mischievous toddler. "You poor mortal," she tuts. "Do you truly believe your silly games have power here any longer? Or that I will deign to speak with someone of your filthy blood?" A haughty scoff. "If there's to be any discussion of the 'situation,' it will be between me and my kin."

There's a hot prickle on Cora's scalp that zooms down her spine, making her nerves shiver. She casts a glance around the glade behind her. Two dozen sets of unblinking faerie eyes bore into her skull.

She quickly turns back around. "Why are they staring at me?" she whispers to Jack.

He looks to Sofi, who shakes her head violently. "Nu-uh. I want to live. You tell her," she says.

"Tell me what?"

Jack swears under his breath, then turns and puts a hand on Cora's shoulder. The resulting tremor disrupts her delicate equilibrium of pain and attention. Blue sparks shoot through her vision, nausea blooms in her gut, and she lets out an involuntary groan. Between her magical injury, the bizarre déjà vu, and the pulse of energy from Jack's touch, she feels like a leaky dam about to burst.

"Cora," he says, voice low and urgent, "did Daniel ever tell you anything about where he came from?"

Her eyebrows beetle up as she tries to understand why he's asking personal questions about her father in the middle of a power struggle with magical beings suspected of trying to overthrow humanity. She starts to object, but her quiet common sense voice chimes in.

He never did—not once. He had a story for everything, but not for that. Not a single story about his childhood, his home country, his family, his background. He's always been about the present and future, never the past.

Jack must read the conflict on her face because he bows his head to whisper. "Nothing?" His closeness muddles her thoughts, and all she can do is shake her head.

He grimaces and curses in a language she doesn't understand, though she recognizes her father's name. Then: "Cora," he says, "you're Mab's granddaughter."

She laughs right in his face. "What? That's ridiculous. Sofi, tell him that's ridiculous." But Sofi's eyebrows are unhelpfully raised in the "well..." position.

Cora scoffs. "How could either of you possibly know that, even if it was true?" It comes out more certain than she feels. Something's niggling at the back of her mind.

"Sidestepping abilities are rare because they're gene-specific," Jack says, low and rushed, as if he's worried. "We don't know much, but we do know that no one's ever manifested them unless they were a grandchild of a full-blooded supernatural. Your father's been on record with the SCD as a permanent resident of Perat since he was twenty-one. Daniel Riley is Mab's son by a human father, which makes you her granddaughter."

For a moment, she feels nothing. Not disbelief, not shock. Then there's a sound inside her head like the chiming of a bell, followed by a tidal wave of understanding.

For thirty years, Cora's wondered where her strangeness comes from, all the knowing and easy acceptance of magic in the real world. She'd thought after discovering her sidestepping abilities that she'd found her answer. Now, hundreds of seemingly innocuous details point in one obvious direction, pieces of ignored information smoothly sliding together into a complete picture.

Every Fae has gray eyes like me. I have new powers here. The cold iron burned my hand. I led us to the Waterfall Court like I knew the way—because I did know the way.

Cora slowly turns to face the Faerie Queen. "Oh shit...," she whispers. "It's true."

Mab beams and opens her arms wide. The gesture's warm and inviting, without magic or malice, and the tug of it pulls Cora to her. Jack's hand slips from Cora's shoulder as she walks toward the queen; she hears Sofi shushing him as he tries to stop her.

The queen folds Cora into her embrace. They don't quite fit together. Mab's so tall and thin Cora that feels stumpy and huge by comparison to her grandmother. She tenses as she's drawn in, anticipating fireworks of pain when her burned arm is touched, but instead there's a soothing sensation that washes up her hand and over her entire body. Like aloe on a sunburn. The clammy sweat and tightness of her charred flesh fade away. She exhales with relief and relaxes in the queen's arms.

When Mab straightens to release her, the bandages fall from Cora's arm, revealing whole, pink flesh underneath. Cora flexes her fingers and rolls her shoulder experimentally. Nothing hurts. In fact, the arm might be better than it was before. She looks up at her grandmother, full of questions but not sure where to start.

"I.... Thank you," she says.

"You are so very welcome, dear one."

Mabs strokes Cora's hair lovingly, then sits down in the throne so they can look one another in the face. She examines Cora head to toe, to the point where Cora blushes and looks down at her shoes.

"You are the spitting image of my son, do you know it?" she says after long seconds.

Her father's face rises up in Cora's imagination, followed by a flare of indignation. He kept this from her—her powers and her heritage. For her entire life, he's taught her that the world is magical but never mentioned that she might be, too. How dare he? Her thoughts are tinged with red, but she lets them flow through and out of her with a quiet breath. There'll be plenty of time for angry phonecalls when she gets home.

She dips awkwardly at the queen's compliment, halfway between a bow and a curtsy. "Yes, Your Majesty. Thank you."

An amused laugh. "You don't need to be so formal, my darling. You are safe here. This is your home."

The gathered faeries raise a cheer at that, and Cora looks around, embarrassed but weirdly pleased. Warmth seeps into her bloodstream as she realizes she feels welcome. Not a sensation she's used to. Her small-town life was about forcing herself to blend in and not be noticed; here, she truly belongs. She's actually a goddamn faerie princess. She can't help laughing out loud at the thought, and the crowd cheers louder.

When the ruckus dies down, though, Mab's face gets serious, which has an automatic sobering effect on everyone, including Cora.

"Now," she says. "There is the important matter of this agent's accusations to consider. I sense that your goals are aligned with his, which saddens me." She reaches out and encloses Cora's hand in hers. "Tell me what is in your heart."

The abrupt change in subject jars Cora back into the moment. Between discovering her ancestry, having her arm magically healed, and this sense of being wanted, she'd forgotten why they were standing here in the first place. She risks a glance at Jack and Sofi standing at the far side of the throne's platform. Sofi makes a "go on" sign, but Jack is unreadable. Turning back to the queen, she lays it out as best she can, opting to stick with her SCD voice. Whatever she's feeling needs to take a backseat to the job.

"From what information we have, Your Majesty, it appears that you're working with Lady Eris in what we suspect is a plot to tear down the Gauntlet and take over the mortal world. Creed use has strengthened Faerie in particular, which violates the Otherworld treaty. That's the primary reason for our presence here. However, we're also here to determine if our suspicions about your alliance with a known terrorist are true."

Mab's lips curl into a catlike grin. "Your honesty is refreshing for an agent. You get that from your mother." She drawls the last word like a sneer. "As you have been honest with me, I shall be honest with you." There's a flash of gold in Mab's gray eyes, and a gust of wind fills the glade with the heavy scent of apples in fall. "We have chosen Eris' side in the war that is to come. There is no other alternative if we are to survive the destruction Perat is causing us."

"Good to know," Cora quips.

Her mind calculates all the ways this could go. If Faerie's aligned with Eris, the goddess herself could show up at any moment. The thought of having to stand up to her again makes Cora's gut flip.

But Mab assuages that fear immediately, although with a hint of venom. "Don't worry, sweetling. She cannot come here. She's far too busy overseeing the many other branches of the growing coalition. You are safe with me." Pause. "For now."

"What's that supposed to mean?" It comes out sassy. Even FBI training couldn't beat that habit out of her.

Mab doesn't care. "It means you must choose which side you will fight for now that you know who you truly are." She gestures at the Faerie Court. "These are your people. I am your elder. We have chosen to aide Eris in her efforts to save the population of the Otherworld."

"But...," Cora stammers, "you'll be sacrificing humanity. These people who believe in you and give you life would be slaves. If the Gauntlet comes down, there's no way mundanes can stand up to you. And mortals won't survive rule by magic. Supernals will use up humanity, then die off because no one's left to believe in them." She shakes her head. "We'll all die in the end—no one wins."

The Faerie Queen smiles. "Then my people will live that much longer. Better to grasp the potential for continued existence than to sit by in the semblance of honor and fade out of memory while humanity continues to believe solely in itself."

Cora's mouth works in an attempt at a comeback, but then she snaps it shut, her breathing short and hot like a bull about to charge. Resentment is a coal fire in her chest. She's tired of being asked to choose her fate every time she leaves the house. The fact that she uncovered her heritage three minutes ago and is already being asked to choose between races is pissing her right the fuck off. It's so cosmically unfair.

And so ludicrously dangerous. Is this backwards, selfish thinking why her dad left Faerie in the first place? Did he know the role she'd play in the days to come, that long ago? He did choose a mortal life rather than live forever with his people in Faerie, after all. That counts for something. Right?

Slowly, carefully, Cora steps backwards until she

reaches Jack and Sofi. He puts up a hand to steady her when she tromps on his shoe, and a jolt of their shared energy snaps against her skin like reassuring static.

"I can't let you do this, Mab," she says.

It's not like when she denied Eris. This time, there's no screaming, no violence, no gnashing of teeth. Just a quiet sigh. To Mab's credit, it sounds genuinely pained.

"So be it, changeling," she says. "I'd hoped you would join me in our glory, not stand against me in your defeat." Another a flash of gold in her eyes. "But you are mine, Cora Riley, and I will have you, one way or the other."

"It's the other," she says with a surge of confidence. "I can't watch you bring about the apocalypse for all our people. And I definitely can't be part of it myself." Cora lifts her chin. "I stand with humanity."

The queen nods, and there's a subtle ripple in the texture of the air. Cora carefully raises her sensor circle out of curiosity. Immediately, she notices an interworld door in the stone cliff that contains the waterfall, off to the right of the throne. The agents could escape through it if they bolted and made a spontaneous sidestep. Except that its signature is flickering dimly. Held closed by magic.

Mab is keeping them prisoner.

Before she can relay this information to the other agents, the queen stands and addresses the crowd. "The choice has been made. Now there is but one course by which to resolve this impasse.

There will be a duel of champions." A rousing cheer from the Court. "The mortals will choose who will fight for their freedom...."

She claps her hands twice, and there's a crack of fire-orange lightning that grounds itself next to the throne. It evaporates in a curl of smoke, leaving behind a familiar man in a white linen suit.

Cora gasps as Wex, grinning from ear to ear, moves to stand next to Mab.

"And I will fight for Faerie," he says.

PART III
VOICES OF THE PAST

TWENTY-FOUR

Fifteen years. That's how long it's been since I last looked Wex full in the face. Since the night I turned my back on his twisted ideas and joined the SCD. He's exactly the same as when we were students at Loyola together, stirring up magical trouble and coaxing pretty succubi into our beds. The longest-lived sourcerer in recorded history at over a hundred years old, and he undoubtedly gets carded at the liquor store.

He grins devilishly at me from his spot by the queen, triggering a rasping need to forgive him. I want to call him my brother again, to erase the darkness in his mind and start over. To have him fight at my side against the destruction of the shared worlds rather than standing against me.

But it'll never happen. I can see the soul-rot in his eyes. Being a serial killer does that to you.

After I left, there was nothing to keep him in check. He rampaged across the South, draining both mortals and supernaturals to slake his thirst for power, burning through his natural reserves chasing immortality. He murdered dozens, sucked dry of their life force, before we caught him the first time. But the Roosevelt can't hold him; magic tech hasn't caught up to his level yet. He escaped. Over and over and over. Mocking me with each fresh kill, knowing I could arrest him as many times as I wanted and never permanently stop him.

I hate him—who he's become, what he's done—as much as I love him.

My fists clench until the nails bite into the flesh of my palms. I search for something meaningful to say.

But Cora beats me to it.

"Hey, motherfucker, you blew me up!" she shouts.

I grab her elbow as she storms forward, tugging her back to my side with a covert shake of my head. She has no idea how much more damage he can do to her. She glares at me but stays put.

Wex laughs at her indignance and shrugs. "Collateral damage, cher."

What he says and what I know of him clash. I replay the scene I teleported into at the side of the ergot field, scanning for forensic details I missed in the initial chaos. The fire started at the eastern edge, inches from where Cora lay burnt, and spread directly into the field without touching surrounding foliage. Add in Wex's alliance with Mab and Eris, plus in his history of casual violence....

Hot ice trickles down my spine as I piece together the truth.

"This wasn't an accident," I snarl at him. "You were aiming for her."

Another nonchalant shrug. "I mostly missed." He throws a leer at Cora. "Maybe I couldn't bear to deprive the world of such a beautiful creature." Then he winks at me. "Or maybe I knew that mutilating your cow would bring you right to me."

My entire body itches with the need to attack, to make him pay. But the press of Cora's hand on my back reins me in. I inhale sharply, willing myself into a modicum of professional calm.

"What are you doing here, Nathaniel?" I say through clenched teeth.

"Oh, Jackie, why so formal? Aren't you glad to see me?"

"Not on this side of a prison cell."

"Well, it's certainly not for lack of trying." Wex turns to Cora. "Did you know he had me locked up five times? Can't believe I let him get away with it."

"You didn't," I remind him.

Wex breaks into a broad grin. "Oh, that's right. You and your soft, human-loving toadies can't hold onto me. How unprofessional."

"Don't worry. Agent 75 will be thrilled when I haul your ass in this time. He's got a brand-new cell prototype he's dying to test."

Wex is about to retort when Queen Mab waves them into silence. "As amusing as it is to listen to you trade barbs, I believe we should concentrate on the matter at hand."

"Yeah, girls, you're both pretty," Sofi chimes in. "Snark on your own time. That whole 'fate the world is in your hands' thing."

Mab claps twice, and the faeries on the west bank respond with a flurry of graceful motion. Some clear away the feasting tables, others pace out measured steps on the grass, others draw careful lines of magic along the ground and take up positions in four corners. Those not involved with the preparations mill about, forming a sizable audience at the edges of the squared circle.

Doubt churns my stomach. Wex regularly beat me bloody when we'd fight as impetuous boys, but that was before I had FBI training and lycan strength in my blood. Could the power I developed in growing up be a match for Wex's sourcery?

There's also the wildcard of Cora's presence to consider; the bizarre conjoining of our abilities since arriving in Faerie could be either a vital help or a dangerous drawback.

I swallow my warring thoughts and take a step forward, more to get my blood moving than indicate courage. I hope it does both.

"You're forgetting something, Mab. We haven't agreed to the terms or conditions of the duel. What do you expect to happen here?"

"Oh, yes, the terms. I apologize." She laughs like a schoolgirl flirting her way out of a failing grade. "Since you have refused to join our cause, and I naturally refuse to come with you to Perat for torture and imprisonment, we will break this impasse with a show of arms. The side favored by the Fates will prevail." The queen looks over my shoulder. "Granddaughter, do me the honor of explaining the ritual's details to our guests."

I half-turn and look to Cora. She shifts her weight uncomfortably and doesn't meet my gaze as she answers.

"There are two kinds of duels," she says. "In normal ones where Fae fight for honor, you win by drawing first blood or forcing your opponent to surrender. The loser's shamed, but everyone goes home afterward." A thoughtful pause. "The other kind's for outsiders trying to escape or break a deal." She chews her bottom lip. Then: "They practically never win. And if the loser doesn't die in the fight, they're bound to the land forever."

Warm longing radiates through me at the thought of being eternally bound to Faerie. A familiar tingle from my brand that urges me to stay, and I clench my teeth against it. Being stuck here myself is one thing; I might even enjoy it. But I can't subject Cora and Sofi to that hell. I have no right to make that choice for them.

And I'll be damned if I let Wex beat me one more time.

I take a deep breath, then square my shoulders and step forward. "I accept the terms. I will be humanity's champion."

"As do I, as champion of Faerie and of Lady Eris," grins Wex. I've never wanted to punch him in the teeth so badly in my life.

"And your choice of weapon, Mr. Alexander?"

the queen asks.

Options are limited. My swordsmanship is passable, though there doesn't appear to be any blades in the Court. I briefly consider my sidearm with its cold iron clip but reject it. Too risky—a mistimed or interrupted shot could hit one of my agents at the sidelines. That leaves me one choice.

"I decline a weapon," I say, flexing my fingers.

A susurrus of intrigued muttering from the onlookers tells me I've made, if not a stupid choice, then at least an interesting one.

The queen's eyebrows lift. "Very well," she says.

Rising to her feet, Mab makes a complicated gesture with her hands that ends with her drawing a glowing line through the air in front of her with one finger. Once the line is nearly as long as she is tall, there's a sucking sensation, followed by a dimensional split that opens into nowhere. She reaches through the opening, her arm disappearing to the elbow. When she pulls it back, she's holding a silver longsword in a plain leather sheath. She hefts it easily while magically stitching up the rift.

Taking the weapon in both hands, she tugs on the handle and pulls the blade free, giving it an experimental twirl as if it weighed nothing. It makes a sound like wet silk ripping.

She holds the sword out for the crowd to see. "And Mr. Wexford will be using this," she says.

Behind me, Cora gasps, but there's nothing notably dangerous about the sword that I can see. Perhaps she's concerned about me fighting barehanded against a blade?

"It's fine," I say to her with less certainty than I feel. "I've fought against worse odds before."

"It's not that," she says in a worried hush.

Queen Mab practically purrs. "Do you know what you are looking at, law-man? Have you ever beheld an artifact so commonly believed in yet so misunderstood?"

I search my mental files for a name. There are dozens of legendary swords, but only three have been authenticated by the SCD. And they're all secured in the Roosevelt's archives.

"It's Excalibur," whispers Cora from behind me.

"Well done, little one," chirps Mab. "That it is."

I peer at the blade more closely this time. The etching in the pommel does resemble the illuminated Arthurian texts I've studied, but I can't be sure. Between the faerie tendency for mind games, Mab's involvement with Eris, and the current volatile belief levels, I'm doubting my situational analysis.

I flick my eyes back to Cora. Sofi's holding one of her arms, but red marks on her pale skin show where she's fought to twist away. The more Mab talks, the less sure Cora seems of her choice to stand with humanity. I hope she's strong enough to keep resisting. It would be easy for Mab to Call through Cora's blood tie and force her into doing what she wants.

I, on the other hand, am not swayed.

"With all due respect, Your Majesty, that's bullshit." There's a snicker behind me. I instantly regret my language; I've let Sofi rub off on me. "Our records maintain that Excalibur was destroyed by humans during the eighteenth century. A peasant was caught with it during the witch trials, and it was melted down to slag, then thrown into the Atlantic Ocean off a fishing boat."

Rather than the explosion of magical anger I expect after such a brazen challenge, though, the queen laughs with delight. "How precious. You humans cling so desperately to your confidence that history and science are all that shapes reality." She waves a dismissive hand. "Why do you think there are so few magical arms left? Surely you don't believe that to be an accident."

Dread starts a slow burn as I do the supernatural math. It's conceivable that the centuries-old debate over Excalibur's existence generated sufficient belief to preserve it. The idea of a thing can withstand the object's destruction if it's powerful enough. If what she's suggesting is true, then Arthur's sword survived its mutilation and was able to feed on the essence of weaker magical weapons to strengthen itself with corrupted magic.

The same way Mab became queen—by consuming her competitors.

Cora moves up beside me, staring at the sword with unfocused eyes. The color has drained from her face. She presses against my shoulder, and I feel a ripple of faerie magic run through her skin. Perhaps the queen is Calling her after all. But she hasn't budged—she's resisting. I'm unexpectedly proud of her for it.

I shift my weight to steady her. "What do you

see?" I ask.

"It's all wrong," she mutters distantly.

"What is?"

"The sword. Can't you feel it?"

I turn my attention back to Mab. She obliges me by turning the blade at reflective angles to the glowing pots illuminating the glade. I squint hard, willing my enhanced senses to help me understand. Three seconds pass. Then, like a developing Polaroid, I start to see what Cora sees: The light collects at the edges of the blade, but rather than the buttery gold it should reflect, the sword is haloed in a bloody crimson aura that fades to black toward the hilt.

"What have you done, Mab?" I say.

Her lip curls, as if she's resentful at having to explain. I'm less happy about it than she is. I've spent my entire career at the SCD being the Man with All the Answers; I should have known about this. For me to discover the existence and perversion of history's most famous weapon by way of a Fae cannibal at the brink of impending doom reeks of conspiracy. On whose part, I couldn't say. But I'm going to find out.

When Mab does deign to speak, I wish she hadn't.

"It is simple, agent. Lady Eris rescued humanity's most storied weapon from annihilation and forged it into her own sacred blade: one that can cut any substance, mundane or supernatural." She spins the sword in an easy, graceful arc, admiring its form. "All it requires as payment for its service is the spirit of its victim."

Laying the flat of the blade on her arm, she offers the hilt to Wex, who takes it eagerly, if less adroitly than the queen.

"Excalibur no longer exists," she says triumphantly, turning back to me. "This is the Sword of Souls. And it is eager to consume you."

TWENTY-FIVE

The pool of silence following the pronouncement doesn't last, though I wish it would. The Faerie Court breaks up and moves to the dueling field, streaming around and past me without acknowledging my existence.

Information logjams my mental filters as I screen it for the truth. A blade that cuts any substance. Could it pierce the Gauntlet? If so, why hasn't she done so already? Why use it in a common duel if it's so powerful?

The sudden scent of apple blossoms assaults me as I process, derailing my train of thought. I start and see Queen Mab passing by me. Our eyes meet briefly. She winks. Then she's on the far bank, leaving a faint trail of golden glitter in her footprints. The attention-hungry data points that paralyzed me are abruptly silenced by a single, quiet fact as she takes her place in the audience.

Eris is in control here.

Mab believes she commands Faerie, but in allying herself with the goddess of chaos, she's relinquished her power. Eris owns her and everything she touches. While she may not be physically present, the creed distribution, Wex's arrival, and this duel are all part of Eris' grand design. I don't have concrete proof yet, but I'm learning to trust these leaps of logic; my instincts see her in every corner. The thought that she could be pulling my strings without my knowledge sends hot ice through my veins.

But I can't spend too long deliberating. There will be plenty of time for that when—if—we return home. Here and now, I must focus on the task ahead.

With the Court in place along the sidelines of the squared circle, I find myself momentarily alone on the throne's platform. I take advantage of the moment. I close my eyes, draw in as much air as I can hold, then exhale hard, expelling my fear with the breath. On the inhale, I summon my personal energy in broad cerulean ribbons, winding them together into a cool ball beneath my ribcage. It's less power than I'd like—the faerie brand's muting effect—but it detects the sealed interworld door nearby. Good to know. I direct what magic I can access into clearing my mind. Knowing that the outcome of this fight is crucial to humanity's survival is doing an effective job of focusing me already, though.

A hesitant but determined tug on my jacket breaks my concentration. But I know who it is. The scent of warm fur and pine needles gives her away.

"Yes, Agent 21?" I say.

"Don't worry, boss. These guys try any funny stuff, I'll take care of it."

"I have no doubt."

"And I'll take care of Cora if anything bad happens."

A twinge of guilt. That's my job. "See that you do."

She moves off toward the defender's side of the field—my side. Her steps over the platform are supernaturally light. It calls up memories of our first meeting. How she bested me on the road, how she crept through the woods, how she slipped away without a trace after it was over. How she was the first person to see me without Agent 97's protective shell. A fist clenches my lungs. Guilt is no excuse for how poorly I've treated her since Steeltown. She's one of the SCD's best agents, and she's on my side. She deserves better.

I open my eyes and call after her. "Sofi...." Her name, not her badge number.

She stops as she sets foot on the riverbank and turns with curiosity. "Yeah, boss?"

"Thank you."

The words hang for so long I'm unsure if I've done the right thing. Then she gives me small smile and a nod, and she's gone.

A moment passes. Then a small, rough hand slips into mine. I squeeze it gently and look down.

Cora's eyes shine up at me. Everything we want to say weighs down the air around us. There are too many questions and no time for any of them. Briefly, I wonder if I've made a grievous error by volunteering as champion. This is her land and her people; even facing a sourcerer wielding a tainted sword, she might be the stronger fighter here.

But it's too late for that now. I made the choice, and now everyone has to live with it. A dark voice from a buried part of me laughs humorlessly. Wex has shoved me right back into my rash, childish ways in less than ten minutes.

I want to say something to Cora. Anything to comfort her should this fight turn fatal. But I don't know what to say. The words aren't there.

She responds to my conflicted silence by squeezing my hand and pushing herself up on tiptoe. I have to dip my head to meet her lips as she brushes my cheek with a kiss.

"Be good. Don't die," she whispers.

Then she's across the river, joining Sofi as the sole supporters on my side of the field.

I'm alone on the platform again, the last person to cross the river. Everyone is waiting for me.

"What are you waiting for, Jackie?" Wex calls out from the challenger's side, the one crowded with High Fae. He's grinning like he can't stop. "Let's play."

I'm already moving, stripping off obstructive clothing as I go, arriving at the field barefoot and shirtless. Murmurs from the Fae as they notice Limerence's brand on my back. It seems that word's gotten around about my magical stunt. About what I did to her.

A nauseating tingle curls around my spine as I remember the horror in her eyes. I don't know what would've happened if Cora hadn't summoned me away. Another ripple of magic from the brand tells me she must be alive. Without her, the tattoo has no power. I shove aside the possibility that she'll appear during the duel, but part of my mind stays alert for her approach. The ramifications of that are too devastating to ignore.

I square my shoulders and step into the dueling space. Living white light zips around the boundary as I cross it, outlining the field and sealing the combatants inside. The metallic tang of burnt magic cuts the air. I file it away for later; they shouldn't be able create binding dimensional pockets without somatic or verbal components. Whatever twisted power Eris has gifted to them, it runs deeper than Mab implied.

On the other side of the squared circle, approximately ten yards away, Wex is dancing with anticipation. I get low, head down, feet solid under me, bracing for the first attack. Despite all my time here, I'm uncertain of the ritual's rules.

Another wave of nerves leads me to close my eyes and send up a short prayer. I'm not sure why— I haven't prayed with any seriousness since I was a small child, not since Madaar died. Never seemed to be any point after that. All my gods were gone.

Except one.

Lady Ishtar, watch over me, I think.

Always. Hot wind over a sand dune.

I smile as the word burns away my thoughts,

replacing them with pure battle instinct. Perhaps my accidental vow to her will bear fruit after all.

And then Wex is charging.

I dive to the ground to avoid the ham-fisted feint, rolling back up in a low crouch to wait as Wex recovers from his momentum. Calculations whizz through my mind, adjusting probabilities of attack. The key is getting inside his guard. It shouldn't be too hard; with all my supernatural "extras," I'm faster and wiser than the last time we had it out. I'm 71% sure he's had no swordsmanship training, but with his sourcery and longevity, who knows what he's learned over the years. Or absorbed from his victims.

Wex moves in again, the brutality of the first attack replaced with a calm, graceful swing. I dodge the blade, missing being gouged in the shoulder by inches, and responding with a fist to his gut as he follows through, knocking the wind out of him. I could hammer him twice more in that half-second, but I let him go. He grunts and stumbles as I dance out of range.

A disapproving hiss goes up from the watching Fae as Wex leans heavily on Excalibur's hilt to catch his breath. As he gulps air, there's an odd flicker of light across his entire body, turning him incorporeal for a millisecond. He doesn't seem to notice, but it trips a warning bell in my mind. It could be anything: readying a magical attack, faeries playing tricks, Mab augmenting him from the sidelines. Any of which could fatally tip the scales against me.

I incorporate those possibilities into my tactics matrix and refocus, waiting for Wex to make the next move. Mab knew what she was doing with this duel, I think grimly. She probably thinks it's a delightful game to have former friends maim one another. More than that, though, she knew I'd refuse to kill. Even as the hot-headed boy I was when I lived in Faerie, I'd sworn to never take a life. Not after the way Dad died. But now, in defense of humanity, she's forced my hand. It's kill or be killed; my world or theirs.

It doesn't mean I have to enjoy it, though. And it doesn't mean I can't try to convince my old friend to do the right thing.

I call out across the field. "It doesn't have to be like this, Wex. We'll find a way to stabilize your system. You don't have to keep living off fear and death. But we've got to work together. Killing each other isn't going to solve anything."

A low chuckle. "Still don't know which side you should be on, do you, Jackie boy?"

Wex straightens back into a fighting stance, then rushes to reengage. New confidence shines in his eyes as he acclimates to the sword's weight. He flashes the blade in a complicated arc with one hand. It's mostly flourish, but it effectively keeps me from ducking in and pummeling him again.

"I'm not the one siding with the goddess of chaos," I say, looking for an opening.

Wex feints hard, slicing the air horizontally and forcing me to hop back, my arms thrust out and stomach sucked in to avoid being disemboweled.

He grins horribly. "You're just jealous. Like always."

Red mist starts to cloud my vision. But before it blinds me completely, there's another flicker of light across his face, and it breaks the trance. I shove my anger down with a huge lungful of chilly riverside air. The instant I lose control, I've lost the fight. Then this ends, either in my stolen soul or Wex's crushed skull.

I dig my bare feet into the soft earth, grounding myself physically and magically, then raise my fists. Wex postures but doesn't dive in.

We stand locked that way, sizing each other up across a dozen feet of damp air. The fact that he hasn't aged tells me he hasn't tapped his internal magic pool for the fight. Yet. The cost for sourcery is high, but this is a logical place to pay for blinding speed, telekinesis, or mind control. If he hates me as much as I remember, I should already be dead. I wonder why he's holding back.

The surrounding faerie mob gets bored quickly, though. They came to see a fight, not a staring contest. A driving chant starts in the center of the audience and ripples around the ring, dying out as it reaches the lone pair of humans on my side.

Then: "Hit him so hard he forgets math!" Sofi's version of cheering.

A derisive laugh bubbles up, but Wex doesn't join in. His face darkens as his allies mock him; Fae aren't known for their loyalty or attention spans. I straighten my own smile, then flick my leading hand to beckon him forward.

To my dismay, rather than attacking, he stays put and grins with fresh cockiness. "Oh, this is precious," he says. He turns to the Fae at the perimeter. "He actually thinks he's going to win!" Another laugh from the fickle crowd, this one for him. He turns back to me. "I'm only putting on a good show for our lovely queen. It's good manners to be a diverting guest. Besides, what chance do you have here, now, against me, this sword, and all these Fae?"

And then the arrogant bastard does exactly what I'd hoped he'd do.

Wex spreads his arms wide in a grand gesture of defenselessness, sword in one hand. "Come on, Jackie. I'll give you one good shot before I tear your soul out through your miserable skin."

"That's all I need."

Coiled muscles in my thighs and calves, aching to spring during his grandstanding, thrust me across the intervening space and directly into Wex. There's a sickening crack that echoes across the suddenly hushed clearing as both of my fists slam into his chest. It happens in a fraction of a second, but I can hear the bones creak, then snap in slow motion. Sternum, four ribs, one clavicle. In the moment between breaths, I look up into Wex's eyes, blinded by shock and agony. Then he starts to scream, and I spin away.

But not quite far enough.

The flat of the sword slaps across the back of my knees as I turn, upsetting my equilibrium. I throw out my arms to counter what had to be a lucky flail, but I'm moving too fast. I smash face down into the dirt, crushing my right cheekbone against a stone.

Ignoring the pain, I roll over to spring back to my feet. But Wex is standing over me, leveling the point of the sword under my chin. He clutches his broken ribs with his free hand, which glows a soft orange. One of them must have punctured his lung; he's drawing on his magic, visibly ageing himself into light wrinkles as he drains his life force to heal.

I brace myself for the killing blow. But he doesn't strike.

"Why are you doing this, Jackie?" he wheezes, his voice deeper with the onset of ten years. "Why are you defending these insignificant sheep? They're meaningless to us."

There's a curious harmonic of uncertainty in his voice. Does he honestly believe he's doing the right thing? Or is he being controlled by Eris?

I inhale carefully to avoid nicking my Adam's apple. I'm not sure how grievous an injury I'd have to take for the sword to de-soul me, and I'm not anxious to find out.

"Because I'm human," I say. "It took me a long time to accept that, but now I'll fight for it until I die. You can strip away whatever power I have— under it all, I'm just a man." Cautiously, I get to my feet, mindful of the sword point that follows me up. "And so are you."

Wex growls. There's another flicker of light across his skin, this one longer and more pronounced. Up close now, I can see it's his entire being going to static. Two images struggling to occupy the same space. But he's unmoved by the shift. How can he not notice it's happening?

"I am not a man," he hisses. "I am infinitely more." His eyes light with non-metaphorical fire. "Lady Eris has promised to fulfill my wish: I serve her in this, she'll make me a god. Immortality, eternal youth, unlimited power without cost. Ain't no way I'll let mundanes kill me slowly over centuries because they can't accept true magic. It's them or us, Jackie. Every one of us has to pick a side." Then, he lowers Excalibur. The fire fades, replaced by a pleading look. "Which holocaust will you choose?" he asks, barely above a whisper.

The set of Wex's shoulders and the longing in his voice snatch at my heart, trying to capture it. I'm stung with nostalgia for the bond we once shared. Although I was the one who abandoned him, he left a gaping hole in my life I've never known how to fill.

What's worse is that he's logically right. The symbiotic relationship between worlds can't continue this way. Mortals have forgotten too much, crumbling the Otherworld to dust. Yet humanity can't survive rule by magic, which is why the Council created the Gauntlet in the first place. One side must give; the other must perish. The final outcome could come down to a handful of metahumans, beings caught between worlds and faced with a horrible choice. Beings like me.

Wex must read my hesitation, and he reaches out with his free hand, hope high in his eyes. "Join us, Jackie. It'll be like old times. You and me being who we really are, unapologetic, without worrying about the cattle and their petty lives."

My hand is a hair's breadth from closing with his before I realize what I'm doing and drop it. I take a long step back, then another. Rage rises fast in Wex's face. The endgame is nearing, but I won't choose against everything I believe to make him happy.

"No," I say. The syllable rings out strong across the field. "She's lying to you, Wex. There's no way Eris will ever give you what you want. I seriously doubt if she can. You do this, you'll have sold your soul for nothing."

The answering strike is clumsy and easily dodged. A blow of anger on top of the adrenaline of shattered bones. I dip sideways and sprint around Wex's left side, forcing him to make a cross-body strike. The awkward angle gives me the advantage, and I come around to stab into his exposed right armpit with three fingers in an attempt to disarm him, then finish the job.

But rather than dropping the sword, Wex tightens his grip, making it glow red around the edges. White hair peppers his scalp and face as he taps his lifeforce for the power he filters into the blade.

Then his entire body flickers dramatically, and he's suddenly invisible. I can't see or scent him. No trace at whatsoever.

As my mind grasps for an explanation, a detail from the original case file drops into place with ominous clarity. For all his talents, Wex can't move between worlds on his own; he must've had help to reach Faerie. And since Mab's too low-powered to pierce the Gauntlet herself, that leaves one avenue to get him here: creed. The crucial question now is if he's disappeared because his dose has expired or if he's hiding himself with magic.

Where did he—?

Wex reappears before I can finish the thought. He's running up from behind me at full speed, growling like an animal and swinging the sword hard in a wide arc that I'm too slow to avoid.

It catches me directly in the back.

The ethereal blade bites its tip between my shoulder blades, skates down the ridges of my spine, laying open the flesh and carving into the bone. Gleeful crimson sparks of corrupted magic set fire to nerve endings and brain cells. When the blade reaches my faerie brand, the green triskelion tattoo is sliced neatly in half. There's a sound like a snapping rope inside my head, followed by the feeling of a long-held breath exhaled.

But I'm not dead. And every sense says I'm in full possession of a soul. I try to process how, but white-hot pain sears my thoughts to ashes. Agony so intense I can't scream.

I hang for a moment, frozen outside time with shock and fear, as Wex stumbles away. Then gravity takes over. I hit my knees, cracking a kneecap, and fall forward into the cool, dewy grass.

The crowd cheering. Cora shrieking. Mab laughing.

A foot on my shoulder flips me onto my ruined

back. Now I do scream as grass and earth pack the wound, pressing against exposed nerves. Hot blood pools around me like a warm blanket. I shudder with fever chill and look up into Wex's triumphant face, a near constant wash of white light through his dark features as the creed leaves his system.

"You chose wrong, Jackie," he says with a touch of sadness.

He raises the sword for the final strike, then seems to notice his flickering body for the first time. Lowering the blade, he extends his free hand to admire the phenomenon.

It is beautiful, I think distantly. *Like falling stars.*

Then Wex grins wickedly, regripping the sword with both hands, and says, "It seems my time's nearly up, cher. Guess I get to be the one that says goodbye this time. But let's see how your luck is holding out, shall we?"

He hefts Excalibur high over his head. A sharp silhouette against the bright moon. No more ploys, no more tactics. There's nothing I can do except close my eyes and wait.

I sense the blade swing down, then there's a sucking sensation like a drop in altitude and a tinny pop followed by a rushing breeze, the heady scent of overripe apples, and a collective gasp from the crowd.

I crack open one eye to see empty black sky.

Wex is gone.

TWENTY-SIX

Someone snaps their fingers in the resulting silence.

With titanic effort, I roll my head to see I've landed at Queen Mab's feet. We're inches apart, separated by the fading light of the magical borders of the dueling field. She looms over me with a cruel smile as the Faerie Court dissolves into the forest behind her.

"It is done," she says.

Too many questions cram together in my mind. *Where is Wex? Why aren't the Fae attacking us? What has Eris done? Am I going to die? Where's Cora?* The pressure kaleidoscopes my vision, but one thought tumbles out.

"What have you done with the sword?"

Queen Mab chuckles without giving an answer. There's a shimmer in the air, and she begins to fade away, the haunting echo of her voice remaining after she's gone.

"You cannot stop Fate, mortals. Despite your valiant efforts, your ignorance and pride have merely furthered the supernal cause. The war has already begun, and you have chosen the wrong side."

The finality of her statement rings across the now-vacant field, against stone and in my head.

I stare at the sky, numb with pain, unable to do anything else. The solid earth is soaking up my life, and I'm overcome with the urge to sleep. To finally rest. The familiar buzz of my lycan healing factor frantically trying to stabilize me adds to the lullaby. I'm not sure it'll be fast enough.

Then Cora's there, running her hands across my face, through my hair. Her comforting scent of cotton and leather drowns out the reek of my own blood. A tear runs down her cheek when she sees the wreckage of my body, her eyes filled with horror. I want to brush away her tears, but my arms aren't responding. She pretends not to notice the gaping wound that is my back as she helps Sofi prop me up to sitting. She supports my limp shoulders with one arm as Sofi tries to staunch the bleeding with my discarded clothing.

I hiss through clenched teeth as the material stabs into my lacerated muscles. My vision goes gray, and I have to fight to stay conscious. Magic is literally all that's holding me together right now. Desperate to stay awake, I fix my eyes on Cora's face.

She gives me a brave smile. "You can't avoid getting stabbed when I'm around, can you?"

"You're worth it," I manage.

She laughs self-consciously. "At least I stayed to help this time."

"Uh, guys?"

Sofi's staring off to the right, eyes wide. Cora's head snaps up. Whatever she sees brings cold fury to her face. I try to look but can't. The lack of control over my own body is maddening.

Cora's stands to meet the intruder, letting Sofi support my full weight as Limerence appears.

She doesn't sweep. She doesn't have a guard or her white horse. Her hair is loose and bedraggled around her ashen blue face, her posture painfully stooped. She's alone, bereft, and drawn, but she's alive. And angry.

She storms up to Cora. They're inches apart, the faerie woman towering over her with unrestrained menace. Cora's not cowed. She lifts her chin to look directly up into Limerence's face and says nothing. They stare at one another for a long moment in a power struggle that has nothing to do with magic.

It's Limerence that blinks first, weak where Cora is strong, ceding the opening volley.

"What do you want?" Cora snarls.

The faerie woman extends a shaking arm to point at me. "I have come to claim what is rightfully mine," she says.

Cora blinks slowly and shifts her gaze. Our eyes meet. Most of my vision has gone dark, but I recognize the question she's asking. Even though I've never told her about my past in Faerie, somehow she knows. And despite how I've treated her these last five months, there's hope in her eyes. She's asking me to choose.

I can't speak. I mouth the word instead. *No.*

There's a twinkle in her gray eyes, then she turns back to Limerence with an impish grin. "You can't have him. He's mine," she says cheerfully. "Fuck off."

Limerence gasps as if Cora had slapped her. She lowers her arm, looking from Cora to me. I brace for a pull on my brand, preparing to be hauled away on my enchanted leash. But nothing happens; it's a mundane look we exchange. Her face speaks volumes that I cannot read through the haze of pain and drifting consciousness.

She swings back to Cora. "What have you done to him?" she hisses.

"This is terribly entertaining," Sofi interrupts, "but we need to go. What with Ninety-Seven bleeding out on the lawn and all."

Cora smirks and closes her eyes in a show of fearlessness. For a moment, I'm afraid Limerence will attack her out of fury, but she doesn't. Perhaps she's too weak. A tingle on my scalp tells me Cora's raising her sensor circle. She points to a crack in the stone side the waterfall near us. Mab must've unlocked the doorway when Wex escaped. Further evidence of grander plans.

Ignoring Limerence, Cora leans down and gingerly hooks an arm under mine, helping Sofi lift me to my feet. I don't fight it. I factually can't walk; trying to out of pride would be idiocy. The three of us move at a glacier's pace to the edge of the waterfall's basin.

"This isn't over, mortal," Limerence says behind us.

"I don't know. Sure feels over to me," Cora says.

"You have no idea what torment I will visit upon you, filthy changeling! When Lady Eris brings down the Gauntlet, I—"

"Hey, look, we're walking away!" Sofi exclaims. "It's been real, L. Let's not do it again, though. Your hospitality's so bad it kills people, and your food sucks."

Limerence sputters impotently as Cora traces the edges of the interworld door with her free hand. The outline glows faintly, then dissolves into a shimmering space large enough for us to pass through side by side.

We step through. I let myself go.

When I regain consciousness, my surroundings couldn't be more different. Enclosed, sterile, white—the med bay. The hum of electricity entices me back to sleep, but I shake my head against it and shift to get out of bed.

Two nearby voices shout for me to stop as fresh explosions of pain burst all over my body. I drop back the two inches I moved without argument. Whatever painkillers they gave me aren't working; the price for accelerated healing. My knitting muscles, nerves, bones, and sinews itch terribly. Sweat beads on my forehead and soaks the pillow.

"How long was I out?" I croak, trying to keep my

face stoic.

"About an hour," says Cora. She's perched at the edge of a metal folding chair against the far wall, smiling but visibly worried. "It's been about thirty-two since we left on assignment."

Two and a half days in Faerie to one day in real time. The exchange rate is accelerating. Perhaps another side effect of creed: Keep wanderers longer, multiply their belief level. Absently, I wonder how long Wex's dose lasted. And where he disappeared to.

The smiling face of Dr. Sandow appears at my bedside as I ponder this. He's flipping through paperwork with casual concern. Damien's cared for me through worse than this.

"If you clench your jaw any harder, Agent 97, your teeth are going to crack. And I'm an awful dentist." I grumble but relax as best I can. "The cut's deep, but your unique physiology is repairing the damage faster than I can bandage it, so we're leaving it open to heal. Stay on your side like that another three hours, tops, and you should be good to go. A nurse will be by to check on you for a final once-over and to drop off an incident report. Until then, try not to move."

"Understood."

He nods once and clicks his pen, then brightens. "Oh, and incidentally, your tattoo seems to be fading. We're not entirely sure why, but it should be gone shortly." He produces a black business card from an interior pocket and lays it on the bedside table next to my badge, sidearm, and wallet. "Call

Poppy if you want it redone. Losing ink like that'd be a damn shame, and she does fantastic work."

A stunned nod is all I can muster in response. He has no idea what that news means to me: The faerie brand is gone. The bond to a love and the life I both craved and despised is finally severed. My chest tightens with equal measures of gratitude and grief. I set it aside; there'll be time for that when I'm home again and not being observed.

After taking note of my waking vitals, Damien hangs up my clipboard and exits the room, leaving Cora and me alone. There's an awkward pause filled by the buzz of overhead lights. Neither of us is willing to break the silence. There's too much to say.

She works up the courage first.

"Well," she says, "you're all set up here. I should probably head to the debriefing. There's a shitload of paperwork on this one, not to mention getting the ball rolling for tracking down Wex and his freaky-ass sword." She stands and crosses the small infirmary, pulling a hand on the door. "Call me if you need anything, okay? I'm sure I'll be dying for a break in ten minutes."

I almost let her go without saying anything. But I call out as the door swings shut behind her.

"Cora, wait."

She pops her head back in. "Yeah?"

"Do you have a second now?"

She raises a skeptical eyebrow and comes back, crouching down to lean on the mattress. "What's up? she says.

The careful way she avoids looking at my back tells me it must be fairly gruesome. Perhaps fatal if I'd twitched a millimeter to one side. All the more reason to say something now.

"I...." My voice falters, but she doesn't look away, and the words tumble out. "I'm sorry for how distant I've been since you came to DC. I didn't know what else to do except give you space to get settled and figure out how you wanted to...handle things."

My face reddens as I speak, renewing the torrent of sweat, and I shift awkwardly, trying to pass off my anxiety as physical discomfort. It's not far from the truth. I look down at the floor, unable to meet her steady gaze. It's too open, too trusting.

There's a beat, then her pale hand lifts my chin. A slow, empathetic smile crawls over her face.

"You've never apologized for anything in your life, have you?" she says.

"Not that I can recall. But you deserve an apology. Especially after the way you summoned me at the field."

She brow creases. "What do you mean?"

"I was in the middle of...." I hesitate, not wanting to explain my actions with Limerence. "...attempting a 'step I essentially invented on the spot. I'd intended to land at the Waterfall Court, but I heard your voice one second and materialized at the ergot field the next."

She tilts her head to the side, and my hope sinks. She doesn't know anything more about it than I do. Though I do at least have a theory.

"I don't know how you did it precisely, but I suspect it involves our energy being bonded."

"How does that work?"

"I'm not sure. It's common with telepathics and empaths, though I've never heard of it happening with sidesteppers."

"How does it work with them?"

Strange excitement builds in my chest, tugging at strings I wasn't aware existed until this moment. My palms are sweating now, though I'm positive it isn't from my healing back this time.

Slowly, I explain what I've learned through hearsay and old texts. "Supernaturals who are tightly connected, in mind or heart or spirit, can become psychically bonded. They form a type of unit where they can influence or even use their partner's powers."

A blush creeps up to the tips of my ears as I struggle to keep my emotional momentum. I don't know when I'll have this chance, or this impulsive courage, again. I lay a hand over hers. A solitary blue spark ignites at the touch, drifts to the floor, then winks out. Understanding brightens her face, and she smiles, laying her free hand over mine, joining them together.

"I think it's time to visit the Lorekeeper," I say, sounding breathless and rushed in my own ears. "Between the teleportation, Arachne's tapestry, and the way Eris is using Excalibur, there's sufficient reason to see him. I'll put in the paperwork tomorrow, and we'll go. Together."

"Sounds like a plan."

"And maybe we can get a drink sometime."

It's said before I knew I'd wanted to say it. Panic. That's too far, too fast, too much.

I immediately backpedal. "I mean, if that's okay. If you—"

She laughs sweetly and squeezes my hand. "It's a date," she says, then leans over and kisses my cheek. "Heal up. I'll see you later. Right now, I'm dying to give Ninety-Nine a piece of my mind. He's going to shit his pants when I tell him Excalibur's gone dark."

I grin too broadly, high from several varieties endorphins, as she stands and heads out. She pushes through the door, waves to me through the square viewing window, then she's gone.

I take a deep breath, hold it as long as I can, and let it out slowly, draining away the many tensions of the visit. If I'd eaten anything in the last two days, I'd throw it up.

The force of the exhale makes my back twinge, which brings to mind the fading faerie brand. Curious, I check what I already suspect is true. Bundling up what energy I can spare, I run magical diagnostics. First through my spine, then out through my nervous system, then deep into the pits of my psyche.

But the hollow in my heart where my lovelorn master had entrenched herself is empty. Tears fill my eyes as I probe my soul's dark corners, looking for her in growing certainty. I find nothing.

I'm both relieved and bereft, unsure of how to resolve the conflicting emotions. Stronger than those, though, is the taste of freedom. First the machinery of Agent 97 was dismantled, now Limerence's ownership has been cut from my flesh. I'm free. Alone in my own mind at last.

You still have me, whispers Ishtar's sandy voice.

I sigh dejectedly. One voice is better than three, I suppose. But still. I was so close.

As I'm getting dressed to head home three hours later, an muffled voice outside my room catches my attention. I don't need to see the speaker to identify them: It's Cora. She must've come to check on me.

I pad to the door, my back hotly tender but whole, and peer out the small window into the hall. She's standing at the far end of the empty waiting room, phone pressed to her ear. The thick glass muddies her voice, but my sharp hearing picks out the words.

"Daddy? Hey, it's me. You'll never guess who I met today...."

EPILOGUE

Dora Boxer wakes without moving. He can see her through the magical walls of her cell, and it's better if he thinks she's asleep. The last round of "questioning" left her broken for a week. The bruises—both physical and mental—are nearly healed.

She listens to his shuffling walk across the concrete floor from the biometrically-locked outer door. Expensive shoes in a dirty flophouse. There's the tinkle of a chain and a light comes on behind the flimsy sheet that separates the two rooms. If she raised her head, she could see his shadow. But she doesn't—she's seen enough of Agent 99 for two lifetimes.

He walks past her to the oracle without a glance. He may not be getting what he wants from her, but she's learning a lot from him. He makes no effort to hide his conversations, disguise his voice, or even ask what she's heard. Funny how he writes her off because she doesn't have magic. She smiles to herself, proud of her fortitude and cleverness. It splits her chapped bottom lip.

As he speaks now, Dora listens.

A lilting, tenor voice with a touch of an Indian accent. "It is done, my lady. The champion has successfully transported the sword to this side of the Gauntlet."

A haughty, golden voice filtered through tinny speakers. "Excellent. All three relics are now within our grasp. We have but to reach out and take them. I trust you have informed our key allies?"

"I have. However, I must report that the sidesteppers successfully destroyed the drug supply lines, as well as survived their encounters in Faerie."

"No matter. It may be for our benefit that they live. They are known quantities to us, and they are both damaged and volatile. They may yet join us with the right amount of persuasion."

"How shall I proceed?"

"Continue to utilize them as the willing tools they have been. Perhaps to the exclusion of other servants. Either they will see the noble aim behind our goal to unify the worlds or they will die in a vain attempt to stop us. Both paths benefit our cause."

"Yes, my lady. What is our new direction now that the sword is ours?"

"The mirror has fallen into idle hands. You must retrieve it before it is broken or lost again. Without it, the ritual cannot be completed. Those who currently possess it do not understand its origins or power. The dead seek to destroy it, and they will succeed if we do not intervene."

"Yes, my lady. We have received numerous incident reports that point to the mirror's location. I will send the sidesteppers to investigate as soon as possible."

"And Samir...."

"Yes, my lady?"

"It will serve you well to mind your prisoner more intently. Her absence will not remain unnoticed for long. The others do not know her role as we do, but should they rescue her, it could mean the turning of the tide in their favor. This must not happen. We must possess her secret at all costs."

"I plan to move her soon. This location will not be secure for much longer, and she has revealed that the object has been sent to New York. We will search for it there."

"Excellent. You are an invaluable lieutenant, Samir. When the worlds are united under my rule, you shall be handsomely rewarded."

"It is my pleasure to serve, Lady Eris."

There's a crackle like static between channels, then the shuffling feet stop in front of Dora's cell. She pries open her heavy eyelids to peer at Patel. He stands with his arms crossed snidely, as if he's won some sort of contest.

When she doesn't address him, he says, "We'll find it, One Hundred—your precious box and what's hiding inside. You can't protect it forever." He gestures to the invisible wall that keeps her locked in. "Definitely not from here." Then he sneers and leaves.

She waits until the door seals behind him, then lets out her breath in one long stream of relief. He doesn't know. The memory alteration she paid so dearly for is holding under his repeated empathic assaults. How they can be this stupid, she'll never know. So many supernaturals have rallied to Eris' cause—none of them comprehend the apocalypse they're supporting.

With great effort of her failing muscles, she kneels at the side of her rickety cot and begins to pray.

"O Gray-Eyed Athena, protect that which I have hidden. Keep it secret until the darkest hour is upon us and it is most needed. Grant me the wisdom and cleverness to continue averting their eyes, until even my own death comes. Through your grace will the many worlds become whole. Though trouble will surely visit us, may it be resolved swiftly and without bloodshed, lest all we have done be in vain."

Hot tears course down her cheeks. Mnemosyne's charm keeps Dora from remembering what she's protecting, but it doesn't stop her heart from aching. And it won't stop the war from coming.

And so ends this episode of the *Forgotten Relics* series!

But there are so many
unanswered questions!

How are Cora and Jack linked?
Where did Wex go?
What ritual is Eris planning?
What is Dora Boxer hiding?

Stay tuned to find out!
The Mirror of Ashes – June 2015

Visit EllieDi.com
to keep in touch

ACKNOWLEDGEMENTS

Hooray! Yet another opportunity for me to slobber all over people who helped me get this book-baby born!

Thank you to my ever-intrepid beta readers, Katy Rose, Zack Eskins, and Dave La Rush. You're incredibly brave to subject yourselves to my hideously unpolished work over and over again. Thanks for making sure I don't embarrass myself too badly in public.

Thank you to Desiree Kern, my cover artist. Your work just keeps getting better and better. Let's continue annoying people with our giggly brainstorming sessions, shall we?

Thank you to Lino. This book was written during the most tumultuous time in our marriage since *Inkchanger*, but you've been unfailingly supportive of my harebrained schemes. Your love means the world to me.

A very special "thank you" to everyone on Team Patreon who contributes their hard-earned cash to keep this writing ball rolling. Dearest Nikki Colborn, Karen Coverett, Tori Deaux, Zachary Eskins, Megan Fair, Jo Gough, Jessica Lee, Shelby Olrich, Liz Patt, and Kyeli Smith: You make my work not only possible but fun. I'm so glad you're along on this adventure with me.

Thank you to Stephen Blackmoore, Karina Cooper, Eddy Webb, Julie Hutchings, Chuck Wendig, Delilah S. Dawson, and Jessica McHugh for their writerly ass-kickings, sage wisdom, sincere encouragement, and mutual adoration. You've become my inky mentors, for better or for worse.

And finally, should you not find your name explicitly mentioned here, know that I am thinking of you, dear reader, and I'm deeply grateful for your love and support. Thank you.

ABOUT THE AUTHOR

Ellie Di Julio is a nomadic writer currently living in Hamilton, Ontario with her Robert Downey, Jr. lookalike husband and their two cats. Between nerd activities like playing *Final Fantasy IX* or watching *Top Gear*, she enthusiastically destroys the kitchen and tries to figure out what it's all about, when you really get down to it. She also writes urban fantasy novels and short stories riddled with pop culture references, peculiar memories, and sexy secret agents.

Questions, comments, funny stories?
Reviews, interviews, guestposts?
Get in touch!
ellie.di.julio@gmail.com

Want to support this indie artist?
Join Team Patreon for as little as $1 per month!
www.patreon.com/elliedijulio

FORGOTTEN RELICS

Inkchanger
(Forgotten Relics #0)

Zara Carter has never fit in at in Runaway Heights, a secret community of teens hiding from their own personal hells. No one has been worth the risk of opening her heart. Things would've stayed that way had it not been for the inkpen, a device that pushes Zara's artistic talents into the realm of magic. The tattoos she creates come to life, and each design gives her a taste of her deepest desire: a heart filled with hope and love.

But power like that doesn't go unnoticed. Assigned to the classified Supernatural Cases Division, Agent 97's feelers are out, searching the decaying industrial town for a wild girl with a remarkable talent.

If only he could catch her.

FORGOTTEN RELICS

The Transmigration of Cora Riley (Forgotten Relics #1)

After thirty boring years, nothing about Cora Riley's life has measured up to her childhood dreams of being truly extraordinary. It's too bad that the night she decides to seek out her specialness she crashes on a rural highway.

Cora wakes in the clutches of the Mistress of the underworld who sets her a seemingly impossible quest. If she wants a second chance at life, Cora must find her way through the dozen heavens and return to the castle in three days.

With the help of an unusual guardian angel named Jack and a little boy named Xavier, Cora navigates the afterlife doorfield and quickly learns that gods and monsters are very real indeed. Terrifying and tempting obstacles litter her path; only the power of belief – in the Otherworld, in her companions, and in herself – will return her to the land of the living.